The Chicken Shak Spy

Simon Lucas

Published by Lulu 2011

Copyright © Simon Lucas 2010

First published as a Kindle eBook in 2010.

All characters appearing in this work are fictitious. Any resemblance to real persons, living or dead, is purely coincidental.

Cover illustration incorporates an image by markhillary@flickr.

ISBN 978-1-4467-6821-1

For Claire

Chapter 1

The door came crashing in, immediately followed by a crack team of armed police officers.

The four men sitting around the table were not entirely surprised. Indeed, this intrusion was almost inevitable, but that hadn't stopped them all hoping that it would not come to this. Quite how they were going to talk themselves out of this one remained to be seen.

"Guppy," muttered one of the men at the table.

"It was always going to be Guppy."

They had always had concerns about Paul Fish, known to them all as Guppy. If there was going to be a leak, it was bound to be Guppy.

"ARMED POLICE! GET DOWN ON THE FLOOR!"

Three of the men did as they were told. Johnson was rather enjoying his haddock and chips, so remained at the table, calmly eating as he observed the panic and fear of the others. Whilst the excitement of a police raid was something entirely new for the other members of the team, it was nothing unusual at all for him

"YOU! GET ON THE FLOOR!"

Johnson was amused to see that the police seemed to be getting rather riled.

"Look, I'm just finishing my supper," he told them, liberally dousing his chips with yet more vinegar. He steered clear of extra salt; his blood pressure was not what it should have been, and he did not want to cause it to rise further.

With that, the lead police officer stepped forward. There was not a sound from the other three men, all of whom were spread-eagled on the dirty floor of the near-derelict flat.

"Johnson, you ignorant oaf," the officer said, in a voice that approached something of a normal speaking volume – or the normal volume for Chief Inspector Ferguson, anyway. Ferguson, who headed up one of the Metropolitan Police's Anti Terror Units was not known for his timidity. He was known throughout the force, and further afield, by the uninspiring nickname of Foghorn Fergie. Uninspiring it may be, but it was certainly appropriate. It was felt by his colleagues that perhaps he had adopted this rather loud speaking voice to compensate for his diminutive height. He was also known as Runty Rich – but never to his face.

"Do you mind, Richard, you're disturbing our meal. And you've destroyed the door. You could have knocked, you know. Terribly impolite of you."

"Shut up with the cockish remarks, Arse Face," Ferguson boomed, grabbing a chip from Johnson's polystyrene tray. "I hope you realise what you've got yourself involved with this time."

"No? Do tell."

Ferguson finished his chip.

"You're the one who's going to be doing the explaining, Johnson. And just in case there's any confusion, you're nicked."

With one swift move, Ferguson grabbed his handcuffs from his utility belt, pulled Johnson's arms behind his back, and cuffed him.

"Get those reprobates into the back of the van," Ferguson ordered. "I want a quiet word with Johnson."

The police officers picked the other three men off the floor, and began cuffing them whilst Ferguson pulled up a chair and helped himself to a battered sausage.

"You've pulled some stunts in your time, Arse Wipe, but this one takes the biscuit."

Johnson remained calm, and looked at the dingy, blackened ceiling of the bedsit.

"I have no idea what you're talking about, Richard."

"Well, there's breaking and entering, for a start," Ferguson remarked as he cracked open one of the cans of beer on the table. "This your des res, is it?"

"I'm house-sitting, Richard."

"What, all four of you, in a poky little bed sit? Pull the other one, it's got balls on."

"No, just me. I had invited some chaps round for a game of Scrabble this evening. Anything wrong with that?"

"And it's pure coincidence that you're just round the block from Lambeth Palace, is it?"

"Funnily enough, it is. I don't tend to think about the presence of important ecclesiastical sites when I host my highly regarded Scrabble tournaments."

"Look, you tosser, I know exactly what you're up to, and Scrabble is not it. You saw this as a perfect opportunity to cause some trouble, didn't you? Why else would you be this side of town at the same time as the Pope is staying with the Archbishop of Canterbury? The pyrotechnics we found in the van outside are nothing to do with you either, I suppose?"

"They're for a charity Guy Fawkes' celebration I'm organising."

"A little early, no? It's September!"

"The middle of September. And I got a good deal."

"You're talking bollocks, Johnson, and I'm taking you in. Get up, get out, and get in the van."

Johnson reluctantly got out of the chair, just as the windows of the flat smashed and the missile burst inside. Milliseconds later and the whole flat became one enormous fireball, blazing in the cool, Lambeth night.

The chicken was going to be cold if he didn't move soon. There were three large family boxes of wings in the back of the car that were already half an hour late, and at this rate they were not going to get to their recipients this side of midnight, by which time they would be completely cold.

Graham stood up and kicked the wheel of his ageing Volvo 240. He simply could not get the wheel off. There was more chance of the monkey wrench snapping than the wheel nuts coming off. If he couldn't get the wheel off, he couldn't put the spare on. If he couldn't change the wheel he would not be going anywhere any time soon. Three families were going to be without their fried chicken tonight. And he was going to be in trouble again. Just for a change.

Traffic was speeding past him as he made his way to a nearby bus shelter and sat down. He put his head in his hands and pondered his next course of action. He had already notified the owners of the Chicken Shak – who also happened to be his parents – that he had a puncture, but that was forty-five minutes ago. He now had to face up to the fact that he was probably going to have to phone them and get them to come and rescue him.

Not for the first time, he wondered how his life had come to this. Decent grades throughout school, a first class honours degree from Cambridge, and yet here he was, in his early thirties, still working as a part-time delivery boy for his parents' fried chicken restaurant. It was those years between his graduation and the present day that were to blame. He had been an idiot. A complete and utter idiot. He had only himself to blame, but that didn't make it any easier for him to accept the position he now found himself in. To make matters worse, he still lived at home. A couple of years ago he had moved into what was in actual fact quite a nice attic room at the top of his parents' rather large house, but it was nevertheless a bedroom in the family home, and so could be considered something of a backward step.

From his present position in his early thirties, his twenties looked like such a waste. Not just a waste, but a decade of total idiocy. If only he had not run up such huge debts in his twenties. He had been a prolific gambler and drinker, and whilst he had been a very good drinker, the same could not be said of his gambling abilities. He had lost a small fortune, and had to be bailed out by his parents not once, not even twice, but three times. Or it could have been four. He couldn't recall.

That was before he had developed a passion for recreational drugs. It had seemed like an exciting thing to do at the time. He had begun with marijuana in Los Angeles, but had soon progressed far beyond soft drugs into the hard stuff.

He just had to face it; his life was seriously messed up.

And then there was his secret life. His alternative reality that he had not told anyone about. His parents and his friends had all just got used to him drifting off, sometimes for days on end, without explanation. Sometimes they feared that he had fallen back into his old ways, but they usually just put down his disappearances to his usual shambolic behaviour.

Graham stood up and started pacing. He always paced when he was angry, and he was certainly angry now. That stupid, bloody car. He pulled out his mobile phone and started pulling up the restaurant's phone number from his contacts.

Then he saw the Jaguar approaching. A dark silver Jaguar, brand new, with dark windows. He knew exactly what was going to happen. He considered running, but soon gave up that idea. They'd catch up with him in the end, and so he might as well give in to the inevitable. He didn't want to make life easy for them, though, so he climbed into the back of the Volvo and crouched down behind the passenger seat. You never know, he thought, they just might not notice me. Rather a dumb thought, it occurred to him, but then he seemed to be doing the rather dumb thing pretty well at the moment.

Sure enough, as predicted, the Jaguar indicated and pulled into the bus stop behind Graham's Volvo. Graham cautiously peered over the back seat of the car. There were two people in the Jaguar – a man and a woman. Both were immaculately turned out in power suits, in marked contrast to Graham's greasy red and white Chicken Shak uniform, which clashed horribly with his orange hair. Somehow, he thought, Jeremy had managed to find him. And he'd brought that bitch Helena.

Jeremy climbed out of the Jaguar's driving seat, and approached the Volvo. He opened the back door of the car and climbed in behind the driver's seat.

"What do you think you're doing?" he asked calmly, avoiding looking at the hunched – and smelly – form of his old school friend at his feet.

"I'm hiding," Graham whispered.

"Who are you hiding from?" That faintly irritating East Coast USA twang that Jeremy tried to hide was given away as he accented the word hiding. Those years in the CIA had clearly impacted Jeremy rather more than he might have liked to admit.

"From you."

There was a moment of silence.

"You're hiding from me. Graham, you're 'hiding' as you put it in a battered old red Volvo estate, emblazoned with the words 'Chicken Shak'. You might as well have fixed a large arrow on the roof of the car with the words, 'GRAHAM CHAPMAN IS HERE', you moron. And you know we've got your car chipped anyway." Jeremy had insisted on fitting Graham's car with a GPS tracking device after the first time he had tried to 'hide'. On that occasion he had been rather more successful, and it was several days before Jeremy had managed to find him. If he hadn't run out of money and fuel, he could have hidden for even longer.

"Look, this really isn't a good time for me. I've got three family boxes I need to deliver, and I've got a flat. Can't we do this some other time?"

"No we can't, you dope-head. Get in the Jag."

Graham huffed, but he knew there was little point in protesting. He extricated himself from his hiding place, and walked towards the Jaguar, hunching his shoulders like a teenager who had just been told off. He raised his head when he thought of an idea which might just save his bacon, at least as far as his parents were concerned.

"Can we deliver the chicken boxes en route?" he asked enthusiastically.

"Don't be a retard, you cock. Just get in the car."

"Let's dispense with the retard jibe, shall we?"

"All the time you try hiding from me in such a cretinous way, the retard jibe stays."

"Suit yourself."

"And all the time you insist on spelling Shak without a 'c', the retard jibe stays too."

"I told you – that's a trademark issue. We can't do anything about that."

"Like I give a shit. Just get in the car, retard."

Twenty minutes later and the Jaguar had left the decay of Croydon's concrete heart behind and arrived at 30 St. Mary Axe in the City of London, the location of the headquarters of the elite Hunter Group, an agency that specialised in carrying out the dirty work of the secret services. When Jeremy had been tasked with setting the unit up he wanted a discrete location to serve as base so, for reasons best known to himself, he had chosen one of London's most distinctive modern landmarks – the Gherkin. He reasoned that it was easiest to hide in an obvious location. Graham, for what it was worth, thought he might just be right. If he had based the unit in a grotty industrial estate in Wimbledon, say, people coming and going dressed in suits and driving Jaguars would attract attention. Here in the City, though, no one would even notice. They could just blend into the anonymity of fancy suits and posh cars. Life became slightly more complicated when they had to bring in someone against their will, but it was amazing what people turned a blind eye to in London.

Within half an hour of leaving his decrepit car in Croydon, Graham found himself in the rather more glamorous location of the group's glass-plated briefing room on the thirty-third floor of the Gherkin. He was not surprised to discover that Sally, Anthony and Tom were already present and were awaiting their return.

"Nice hat, Graham," Sally commented as Graham entered. "Nice of you to wear the fancy dress."

"This, as you know, is my Chicken Shak uniform," he responded.

"Yes, your Chicken Shak uniform. Of course it is. Because it's obvious that you should be moonlighting with a fast food restaurant whilst simultaneously working for a top secret security agency."

"Come on, team, let's get down to business." Jeremy called them to order as he entered the room, throwing out folders to each team member. "As you might have heard, we have a bit of a situation. You're aware that the Pope is in town this weekend. You'll also be aware that the security services have received various threats on his life over the past few months, all of which have been dealt with. Today, however, MI5 received an entirely new threat, which they believe is credible. A group calling themselves "The New Reformation" have indicated that they intend to take the Pope's life, and that they intend to do it tomorrow. This may or may not be connected with a call that came into the Met's anti-terrorism earlier today that a group calling themselves CARN, or the Campaign Against Religious Nutters, were planning on making a strike against the Pope tomorrow."

"CARN are a bunch of cranks, Jeremy," Graham responded, still annoyed at having been pulled in. "We all know that. They're hardly a terrorist group, and they're hardly likely to even to try to take out the Pope. They're more into 'countering religious propaganda' as they put it."

"Ordinarily I would agree with you, Graham, but the police followed a tip off earlier on this evening that CARN were holed up in some dreary council estate in Lambeth, just around the corner from the Archbishop of Canterbury's residence, and that they were sitting on a significant stockpile of explosives. When the police got to them, they found that they did indeed have the potential to cause a significant bang."

"Where are they now, this CARN group?" Tom asked.

"They themselves were taken out as the arrests were being made. Someone fired a missile into the flat they were hiding in, taking out the gang, the police squad, and making a mess of the flat. Almost no evidence remains."

There was silence around the table as this was taken in.

"So what are we saying? They were taken out by some militant Catholic congregation, or perhaps bumped off because they knew too much?"

"At this stage we know nothing at all. All we do know is that there is at least one heavily armed organisation out there that is capable and willing to kill. If they launch a similar attack on the Pope tomorrow, then he's dead."

"Is there any intelligence to suggest that such an attack is likely?" asked Helena, Jeremy's second-in-command, and a rather striking tall brunette who had caught Graham's eye on numerous occasions, despite the repeated barbed comments that she aimed at him.

"Until a couple of hours ago, I'd have said that there was nothing credible at all to suggest that an attack was likely. The warning from 'The New Reformation' came out of the blue, however. We have no idea who they are, and no idea where they've suddenly sprung from. No one's ever heard of them. I figured we could probably put the threat down to a crank, but tonight's attack on CARN was significant and unexpected. If that was NR, then they have firepower, they have secrecy and they have the potential to carry out their threat. We need, therefore, to investigate, and we need to move quickly. Your folders contain all that we know, which, at this stage, is very little. Anthony, I want you to search online and check for anything we can find out about NR. Sally, I want you to do the same for CARN. Tom, get over to the Met and see what we can find from them. Graham and Helena, get down to Lambeth and see what's going on at the explosion. I'll go over the Pope's schedule for tomorrow and see if I can identify any obvious weak spots in his security. We need to get to the bottom of this tonight, guys, so get to it!"

The team members made their way to the sliding door of the briefing room in silence. Just as Graham reached the door, Jeremy had an afterthought.

"Oh, and you two, Graham and Helena. Will you at least try to get on? We've got a serious incident developing, and I don't want any of your childish sniping tonight, please."

"But he stinks, Jeremy!"

"I smell better than you, you sour faced cow."

"That's exactly what I'm talking about," Jeremy said. "Just shut up and get to it. If you can't think of anything nice to say to each other, just stay silent. God, I feel like your mother..."

Chapter 2

Five minutes later, and Graham and Helena were in another Jaguar speeding towards the scene of the explosion in Lambeth. Graham was driving, whilst Helena, always concerned about her appearance, was beautifying herself. They had not uttered a word to each other since they had left the Gherkin.

Graham and Helena's relationship had always been somewhat tense. He viewed her as a stuck up bimbo with an overinflated sense of her abilities as an agent. She, meanwhile, viewed him as a joke, and a smelly one at that. Their backgrounds could not have been more different. Helena was a career spook with a distinguished career as a field agent behind her who had been head hunted by Jeremy specifically to join his team. Graham, on the other hand, had no discernable career behind him at all, certainly not one in the security services. As far as Helena was concerned, Graham should not have been on the team at all, and should have stuck to delivering fried chicken for his parents' restaurant. On that point, at least, they could agree. He was on the team, though, whether they liked it or not, and he should at least have made an effort. You could tell just by looking at him that he wasn't going to be any good. Anyone who went around in a fat-soaked fast food chain uniform was unlikely to convey a professional approach to his job.

Eventually, Helena broke the silence.

"We'll need to get Wiggy in for this. Give him a ring and tell him to meet us there."

"I'm driving, Helena. Why don't you do something rather than just sitting there filing your nails?"

"Would you like a stiletto in your testicles? Because that's where you're heading at the moment. Give me your bloody phone."

Graham fumbled in his pocket, trying to locate his mobile. As he did so, the car careered towards an oncoming taxi. The driver violently sounded his horn.

"Will you watch where you're going?" Helena shouted. "You'll get us both killed!"

"Well you're the one that asked me to find my phone! Why don't you just use your own?"

"Because I can't find it. It's in my handbag somewhere, but I can't see it."

Helena opened her enormous Prada handbag and rummaged through it.

"Ah, here it is!" she exclaimed as she pulled out her Blackberry. "Never mind Wiggy for the moment, though. Do you actually know where we're going? I'll swear we've driven past Waterloo Station at least three times now."

"It's round here somewhere," Graham responded, not entirely convincingly.

There was silence in the car for a moment. Helena was caressing her phone, keeping a watch on where Graham was driving. Once again,

Graham had shown himself to be completely incompetent.

"Look, Graham, you don't know where we're going." Helena was losing her patience. She was trying to hold back her anger, but unless she did something soon it was going to boil over. "If we don't get there soon, I'm going to scream. Pull over and I'll drive. You can call Wiggy."

Over the years that they had worked together, Graham had learnt that it was best not to argue with Helena, so not for the first time that evening he pulled the car over to the side of the road. Unlike last time, however, all four tyres of the car were intact, there was no audible rattling, and the engine was running smoothly. Brand new Jaguars, Graham found, were rather nicer than ancient Volvos.

They both got out of the car and changed places, with Helena now taking the driving seat. As she belted up she turned to Graham.

"You stink."

"Well I'm sorry, but I've been working at Chicken Shak all evening. Smelling of fried chicken is hardly unexpected in the circumstances!"

"You could have changed, though. You smell gross and you look like a clown. At least take that disgusting baseball cap off your head."

It was true. With his jeans and oversized red and white shirt, emblazoned with a chicken's head on the pocket, Graham did look a little like a clown. Or a baseball player. Or perhaps an escaped convict.

"I don't know why you persist in working at that place."

"I'm helping out my parents. And besides, it's good cover. No-one suspects I'm also an elite, international master spy." He grinned at Helena, trying desperately to lighten the atmosphere in the car.

Helena barely stifled her snigger as she put the car into gear and pulled off.

"That's what you are, is it? An elite international master spy," she said, tapping his thigh with her hand.

"You know I'm the brains behind this whole operation."

"Of course you are. You keep telling yourself that, won't you. Maybe one day the rest of us will believe it too."

Graham didn't respond to Helena's remark. It was easier to judge her feelings when she was angry, which seemed to be her default mood. When she was like this, Graham never knew if she was trying to be friendly in her own, special way, or if she was taking the mick. He decided to ignore her, and took his phone out to ring Wiggy.

Wiggy was something of a peripatetic member of the team; his day job was as a weapons developer for the military. He was also a complete genius. His specialism was weaponry, but his knowledge was truly encyclopaedic.

Whenever they needed someone to identify weapons, calculate where they were fired from, and even who fired them and from where they where sourced, there was no one in London to rival Wiggy. He was something of an elusive character, however. He turned up when you least expected him to, and didn't when you were expecting him. There were some in the team who thought he was a mythical character, since they had never actually met him. In their parlance, to "do a Wiggy" was to say something particularly insightful. Graham often "did a Wiggy."

Much to Graham's surprise, Wiggy answered the phone on the first ring. Graham had a quick conversation with him and hung up.

"He'll be at Lollard Street in twenty minutes."

"I'll believe it when I see it."

The two of them sat in silence as they entered the decaying remnants of the 1960s council estate. Whenever there was trouble, they ended up in similar environments. It was almost as if these sociological experiments in housing acted as breeding grounds for terror.

As they approached, their target became clear; the block was still blazing well, and was surrounded by blue flashing lights. It quickly became apparent that they weren't going to be able to get particularly close to the scene, so Helena parked the Jag up behind a battered old Escort that lacked any wheels and windows, and they walked down to the police line.

"Hey, it's the Chicken Shak guy!" exclaimed one of the officers patrolling the line as they approached. Graham's heart dropped. He had no idea who this offensive officer was, but he had met him on a couple of occasions, and he was, without exception, rude. He could really do without this right now.

"How's things, Shak Man?" the officer continued. "Did you bring us some food? I could do with a bucket right now!"

"Officer." Graham greeted the police officer as reluctantly as he could, looking around him as he did so. "What a mess. What on earth happened here?"

"Some kind of missile was fired into the building. We lost a bunch of crooks and five officers, including Chief Inspector Ferguson."

"Ferguson? Shit, I'm sorry," Helena said. "He was a damned good officer. What were they doing here?"

"Investigating a tip off that the crooks were planning an attempt on the Pope's life."

"This was CARN, right?" Graham said, staring directly at the block of flats as he spoke.

"Yeah. I think they'd got out of their depth this time, though."

"This doesn't ring true at all," Helena said. "CARN are more into public meetings, leafleting and publishing dubious websites than trying to kill religious leaders."

"If you say so, love. I can't claim to be an expert on the group myself, just saying what I've heard. They were found to have a van packed with explosives, though, which would suggest that they were upping the stakes this time."

"No, this isn't right," Helena replied. "Why would CARN have a van packed with explosives? It just doesn't fit at all. If you said they'd been found with a van of booze, maybe, but explosives? I can't believe it."

"Let's just take a look, shall we?" Graham suggested. "Where is the van?"

"Parked round the block. I really shouldn't do this, but I guess it won't do any harm. Come on, I'll show you."

The officer led Graham and Helena round to a large car parking area tucked behind another block of flats, to where a white Transit with "Green's Fruit 'n' Veg" painted on the side was parked.

"Nice to see a greengrocer who understands apostrophe usage," Graham said as they approached.

"Oh shut up, Graham," Helena said.

The officer walked them round to the back of the van, nodding to the single officer who was on guard. He opened one of the rear doors and shone a torch in.

"Shit."

As soon as the meeting had finished, Tom had headed for his own office across the corridor from the briefing room. Their outfit on the thirty-third floor of the Gherkin guaranteed that the Hunter Group had some of the best office facilities anywhere in London, certainly better than anything that Tom had worked out of as a police officer. Each of the six members of the team had their own dedicated office, which was not something that very many police officers were able to enjoy. Each of the offices was of a similar size, although Jeremy, as the boss, had secured himself a room that was slightly larger than the others. Anthony also had a room that was more generously sized. As the technical expert of the group, he needed plenty of space for his computer equipment.

In addition to their offices, the headquarters also included a large briefing room, in which the meeting had taken place. Kitted out with some of the most state of the art presentation equipment, it could have passed for the bridge of the Starship Enterprise. There was also a sitting area, which doubled as a reception area for the few visitors they entertained, a spacious shower room, and an interview suite including two individual interview rooms, and a cell block, right in the core of the building. They had provision for holding up to nine people, three to a cell, but it was rare for them to have more than one person locked up at any one time. If they apprehended a villain, they normally took him straight to police custody, usually to Charing Cross Police Station. Also scattered across their headquarters were two cloakrooms, a small kitchen, and several large storage rooms, all of which were tightly secured.

Security was, in fact, very tight across the whole floor. The only way into the compound was from the lift, which would only stop at the thirty-third floor if a Hunter Group security pass was swiped through the panel, or if called from within. Once onto the thirty-third floor it was impossible to pass beyond the reception area without using a security pass, a digital fingerprint and a retina scan. The offices were amongst the most secure in London.

When he reached his office, Tom sat on the corner of the desk, and picked up the half-drunk can of Fanta. He drank, and considered who the best person to contact would be. He picked up the phone and dialled the number for the Metropolitan's Police Counter Terrorism Command Unit - his old stomping ground. A civilian answered the phone, and Tom asked who the senior officer on duty was. Much to his delight, it was Chief Inspector Raymond, an old friend. He explained who he was and asked to be transferred.

"Matthew! How goes it?" he said.

"Tom! Hello! Things aren't too good here right now. You heard about Ferguson I take it?"

"No? What's Foghorn been up to?"

"He was killed this evening in that incident in Lambeth."

"Shit, Matthew, that's not good. I'm sorry to hear that. He was loud, abrupt and extremely rude, but he was a good copper, and deep down, a nice guy."

"Yes, he was, and he'll be sorely missed by us all. It's tragic, it really is. We lost several outstanding officers tonight, though, and are really feeling the pinch. Hopefully you guys are going to step in and take some of the pressure off us, aren't you?"

"We'll certainly try to, Matthew. We're working on this New Reformation thing at the moment, which may or may not be connected to tonight's incident."

"You mean this Papal death threat thing?"

"That's the one, Matthew. Just wondering if you've got anything you can give us to get us started. This New Reformation group's a new one on us. Rather worryingly, we don't know anything about them at all."

"I'm sorry to say, Tom, that we're staring at nothing here too. This group seems to have come out of nowhere, and we know precious little about them."

"You're treating the threat as credible, though, I take it?"

"I'm in two minds, personally. Prior to Lambeth, I'd have said it was a hoax. If they were responsible for what happened this evening, though, I find myself thinking that perhaps we should take this organisation seriously. If tonight is any indication of what they're capable of pulling off, we should be worried. The fact that they were able to pull off such a major incident without anyone having any knowledge of them scares, me, Tom, I'll be honest. I think we have to assume that the threat is credible, and so we're making enquiries."

"What line of enquiry are you looking at at the moment?"

"Tom, you know the routine. I can't comment on that."

"Oh, for goodness' sake, Matthew! You said you wanted us to take some of the pressure off you, and yet you won't tell me anything. How am I supposed to get anywhere unless we work together on this? I need anything you've got, and I need it now."

"Aren't you supposed to be an intelligence organisation?"

"We're a security service."

"That's a euphemism for an intelligence organisation, and you know it. I think, therefore, that you should get your own intelligence and stop wasting my time."

With that, Chief Inspector Raymond of the Metropolitan Police's Counter Terrorism Command Unit, Tom's old friend Matthew, hung up.

Chapter 3

They could not have chosen a worse day to make their threat. Jeremy was sat in his office, illuminated solely by his desk light. His computer monitor cast a blueish glow across the room. The last couple of months had been an extremely busy time for the Hunter Group, and he needed a break. He had spent the last couple of days trying to get on top of his paperwork, as well as updating the ridiculous risk assessments that he was made to complete every year. He had been keeping one eye on the Pope's visit, but had hoped that the mainstream security services would be able to handle this one without his involvement. Typically, though, they couldn't. To be fair, the Pope's visit was an unnecessary distraction as far as they were concerned. It was no exaggeration that they found themselves dealing with threats to UK security on a daily basis, and they could do without visits from controversial but nevertheless important world figures. They were coming to rely on the services of the Hunter Group with alarming regularity, and today was apparently no exception.

Jeremy should have been home at least an hour ago, but instead he was cooped up in his office studying the Pope's schedule, trying to establish where any threat against the Pope's life might be most likely. The highlight of the day was a Mass that was to be held in Hyde Park. They were expecting over 50,000 people, which made it something of a security nightmare. The more people who turned up, the harder it would be to scan every single person effectively as they entered, and, if someone had the inclination to do so, it would be fairly easy to smuggle a weapon of some description into the park. It would also be nigh on impossible to ensure that the entire perimeter was secure.

Originally, Jeremy's team were just instructed to act as consultants for visit security. Their initial role was simply to assist and advise in planning security for the events that were to take place whilst the Pope was in the UK. Jeremy knew just how hard it had been to put together a solid enough plan, particularly for maintaining security at the highest profile events, such as the Hyde Park Mass. The Hunter Group's involvement had ended once the plans had been drawn up, but now they found themselves back in the fray and taking a far more active part. They had been tasked with preserving the Pope's life. Jeremy had a good mind to simply recommend that the Mass should be cancelled. Not that anyone would listen to him, of course.

Whilst the Mass was the highlight of the day, it was not the only element. The Pope was due to spend that night at Lambeth Palace, the official residence of the Archbishop of Canterbury. The next day was to begin with breakfast at Lambeth Palace, where the Archbishop of Canterbury and the Pope were to have a private meeting. Jeremy was concerned that CARN had chosen Lambeth for their meeting earlier that evening. He couldn't believe that it was purely coincidence. As far as he knew, none of the leaders of CARN had any connection with Lambeth, and yet they had chosen to meet there. Lollard Street was just minutes away from Lambeth Palace. That surely couldn't be coincidence, could it? What if the attack was to be made at Lambeth Palace, rather than Hyde Park? It would be harder to penetrate security at the Palace, but if they had missiles of the calibre used at Lollard Street, they wouldn't need to get very close at all to cause serious damage, and potentially kill not only the Pope, but also the Archbishop.

Jeremy stood up and stretched. He poured himself a glass of whisky and walked over to the edge of the room. He could see across the whole of the City of London from here, and away over the south of the river.

He found it difficult to believe that CARN had anything to do with the threat; it was totally out of character for their group. It also did not explain why they had all been killed in a missile attack. Had they been recruited by a more powerful group to take action on their behalf? If so, why had the whole of CARN been taken out? And why were they taken out in such an unsubtle way? Any organisation that could secure weapons of the kind that had been used that evening could surely recruit a gunman to walk into the room and shoot them all. No, he thought. This was not meant to be a discrete attempt to wipe out CARN. This was intended as a show of strength. But by whom? Surely not whoever it was who had recruited CARN to do their dirty work – if anyone had done so. Presumably not a group who wanted the Pope dead, which would seem to rule out NR. It seemed logical to think that whoever had bombed Lambeth wanted to prevent the Pope from being killed. Surely no Catholic organisation could sanction such brutality, however? Innocent people, at home in their beds, had died this evening. That's hardly the action you would expect from a group of Christians, however seriously they took their views.

Something just did not add up about this case.

Maybe they were barking up the wrong tree completely. Maybe the missile attack and the death threat were totally unconnected. It could be the case. There didn't necessarily have to be a connection.

Whatever was going on, Jeremy's priority had to be to ensure that any plan to attack the Pope was foiled long before it had the chance to be carried out, and to ensure that whoever might be behind it was brought to justice. That might be easier said than done, however.

Jeremy was distracted from his thoughts by the phone. He sat back down at his desk and answered it.

"Yes?"

"Jeremy. It's Crispin." Crispin Fairweather was a senior member of staff at MI5. It had been his idea to recruit Jeremy to form his own little team, outside the parameters of the state's formal intelligence services. He had been the one who had convinced the Home Secretary that bringing in private companies to support the intelligence services with their work was in the best interests of the UK.

"Crispin. What's going on?"

"You've made a start on the death threat investigation, right?"

"Of course, we're already on it. We're particularly concerned about this New Reformation group. They seem to have come out of nowhere, and as such, it's very hard to assess the credibility of their threat. What do you have on them?"

"We have nothing on them. No names, nothing. And that's what's worrying us. Terrorist groups, which is what this group seems to be, don't just form overnight with no warning. I can't believe that they've managed to keep so low on the radar. Do you have anything on them at all?"

"Very little. I've been going back over what we do know, and it really is very little. As you know, the threat from NR was made via a website. Ordinarily we'd put it down to kids or Internet freaks having a bit of a joke, but if they're connected to the missile attack in Lambeth, which seems likely, we have to take them very seriously."

"Do you think there's a link between CARN and NR?" Crispin asked.

"We've had CARN on our radar for some time, and seen nothing at all to indicate that they might develop into a terrorist group. They've generally been pretty harmless in the past. I couldn't rule out a link between the two groups for the simple reason that we know almost nothing about NR, but if they are a hard line terrorist group, I would find it hard to believe that they had anything to do with CARN whatsoever."

"So who took CARN out in such a spectacular way, and why?"

"That is what we need to find out, Crispin. And we need to find it out sooner rather than later."

Anthony Healey had been Jeremy's computer whizz since the very beginning, from the day when the Hunter Group had been launched. Prior to joining the team he had made a killing through a number of rather dodgy deals and transactions, most of which were almost certainly highly illegal. Hacking had proven rather lucrative for Anthony. He still kept his hand in, but most of his life these days was spent working for Jeremy, either at the Gherkin office or in the flat that he shares with his widowed mother in Dulwich.

Anthony had needed a little persuasion - and a substantial financial incentive - to join the Hunter Group initially. He had believed that he would be joining a bog-standard security company, and fully expected to find himself dealing with alarm installations, possibly a bit of CCTV work, and maybe, if he was really lucky, a bit of computer programming. It quickly transpired, however, that he had misjudged the nature of the work undertaken by the Hunter Group. When they spoke about security, they meant the national kind, secret service, spying, that kind of thing. Suddenly, he had become very excited at the prospect of his new job. Although he knew that he had been recruited for his technical wizardry, and was likely to spend his days looking at a computer screen, he had secretly hoped that he might find himself out in the field, spying on baddies and perhaps even shooting one or two every so often. In his time with Hunter Group, though, he had barely left his office. The work was very interesting and exciting in its own way, but did not fulfil that dream that most small boys had of one day being a spy.

Anthony had spent most of the last hour scanning the Internet trying to discover anything at all about the group that referred to themselves as "The New Reformation." There was almost nothing out there. He had found one reference to them on Twitter, and that was all. At just after 2pm that day, someone calling themselves

@gupster365 had sent a message to another user, @infinitum_uk saying:

New Reformation for sure. As mentioned, Lollard Street c 1930 THIS EVENING.

This single tweet seemed to be the only reference to any modern day usage of the term New Reformation. Still, a single tweet could be the start of a whole trail of discovery. The tweet had not been geotagged, but had been posted from the iPhone Twitter client, so could have been sent from anywhere.

Anthony clicked through onto @gupster365's Twitter profile. It was almost entirely blank. There was, however, a website listed: gupster.co.uk. Anthony copied the URL, and trawled through @gupster365's tweets. There were only a dozen or so, most of them personal updates. The account owner spent quite a bit of time at Stratford, judging by the updates that had been made. Presumably whoever 'Gupster365' was, he lived or worked there.

Anthony pasted the URL of Gupster365's website into his browser. It was encrypted. This was no amateur encryption, either. Anthony would be able to get into the website, but it might take him a little while. He decided to return to that in a bit.

For now, he turned his attention to the other Twitter user - @infinitum_uk. This was even more of a dead end. This user had put no detail into their profile at all, had not sent a single tweet, and received only one – the message from @gupster365.

Anthony was about to run Google searches on gupster365 and infinitum_uk when his colleague Sally, the team's administrative officer, came bounding into the room.

"This CARN group are ridiculously lax on their privacy," she told Anthony as she approached. "Not only do they have their own website, but it's packed with information. Pretty much every leaflet they've ever published is online. Take a look – it's just carn.co.uk."

Sally pulled up a chair next to Anthony as he entered their URL. A rather poorly designed website, complete with the "under construction" animation that he had not seen since the late '90s, popped up onto his screen. Sure enough, what the site lacked in design, it more than made up for with content. There were links to a number of pamphlets, articles and publications dating back a good couple of years or so. Anthony clicked on the "About CARN" link.

CARN, he discovered, were campaigning against religion in the UK. They wanted to establish a secular society based entirely on reason. They campaigned against organised religion whenever they had the opportunity, leafleted churchgoers, and worked hard to counter religious propaganda. Religion, their site claimed, was responsible for many of the evils of the last couple of centuries, and should be consigned to the dustbin of history. The site suggested that CARN was a middle class, philosophical organisation rather than a terrorist group that might plan to assassinate the Pope. Interestingly, no updates had been made to the site for over six months.

"All very interesting, Sally, but there's nothing at all to suggest links to any terrorist organisations." Anthony took off his glasses and stroked his brow as he turned to her.

"There's plenty to be going on with though. We just need to get someone to wade through all their literature to see if there's something in there that will give us some kind of clue. To be honest, though, I don't think we're likely to find anything. CARN's no more of a terrorist group than we are."

Anthony nonchalantly scrolled up and down the website, immersed in thought as to what the next move should be. As he was doing so, he noticed a list of names of CARN's leaders. Most of the leadership committee seemed to have been appointed within the last few months. One name in particular jumped out at him.

"What's a guppy, Sally?"

"Some kind of fish, isn't it?"

"That's what I thought. Now, this might be a bit tenuous, but I think I might have found our link between CARN and NR. Look at this – I've got a tweet here from someone calling themselves

@gupster365 that references New Reformation. Then here, on the CARN website, their technical officer is named as Paul Fish. As I say, tenuous, very tenuous, but fish, Guppy, New Reformation? Might be worth pursuing?"

"Let's see that tweet again," Sally said, leaning over Anthony's monitor. "Look – he says 'Lollard Street, c 1930 this evening'. Well, Lollard Street is where the explosion was, and it occurred not long after 1930, probably around 1955."

"We need to find this Guppy character. Let's Google him."

Anthony punched gupster365 into the search engine, and had immediate success.

"Look at this bozo – he's on Foursquare under the same pseudonym."

"What's Foursquare?"

"It's like a GPS check-in game. People check-in whenever they go somewhere and get points or something. I don't really understand. I do know how to get into the site though so we can see where he last checked in."

Anthony called up Foursquare, logged in, and called up Gupster365's profile.

"This is too easy!" Anthony exclaimed. "Gupster365 is this character's username, but his identity is shown as Paul F! Paul Fish! We're making progress. What's more, I can see that he checked into the Railway Tavern at Liverpool Street an hour ago. Chances are he's still there."

"Let's get Graham to check it out."

Chapter 4

Wiggy hadn't shown when Graham got the call from Anthony, so he left Helena to deal with the situation at Lollard Street whilst he got a cab to Liverpool Street. Sat in the back of the taxi, he gave Jeremy a ring.

"Jeremy, it's Graham. I'm following up this lead from Anthony and am heading to Liverpool Street now. The situation at Lollard has taken a bizarre turn, however."

"Really? How so?"

"When the police got the tip off about CARN's plans, they were told that all the equipment they were going to use was in a van parked outside. When they arrived they checked, the van was where it was supposed to be, and was packed full of explosives – enough to destroy the whole of Lambeth apparently. When we arrived a couple of hours later, the van was still there, but it was empty."

"Empty? How could it be empty? Are you sure you were looking at the right van? It wouldn't be the first time you'd mistaken a vehicle, would it?"

Jeremy's comment was harsh but fair. On not one, but two occasions in the last few months, Graham had mixed up vehicles. On one occasion he followed a hassled mother all the way to Tesco, thinking that she was a drug baron. On another occasion, Graham had made the rather more serious mistake of ordering the wrong van to be blown up. Unfortunately, the van that Graham destroyed contained a priceless antique piano. Its owner was not amused. Nor was Jeremy, who had to compensate the irate pianist for Graham's rather silly error.

"It was definitely the correct van, Jeremy. Helena will vouch for that."

"Was it not under guard? How could it have been emptied?"

"It was supposed to be under guard, but there was a lot going on. No-one could explain how the contents were removed."

"And they're certain the van was filled with explosives?"

"Definitely. It makes me wonder if perhaps the vans were switched. It would certainly be easier to switch the vans rather than emptying out the contents unobtrusively, if it was as full as they say."

"Same van though?"

"The same white Transit, same markings, same registration number. If whoever did it had planned carefully, though, they could easily have an identical van standing by."

"Well if they did, then there's a Transit bomb somewhere in London as we speak."

"It looks like that might be the case," Graham confirmed. "The police have put out a stop and search for it just in case, and seem confident that it will turn up. But then again, if they failed to notice the switch I'm not confident of their ability to recover it again."

Graham and Jeremy pondered the prospect of a bomb on wheels being driven around the capital. It was not a pleasant thought.

"Events are moving fast, Graham. I have a really bad feeling about this. Why had we not heard about this before today? And the whole series of events does not make any sense to me at all."

"Well I'll be at Liverpool Street in a sec. Anthony has emailed me a picture of this Paul Fish guy. If he's there I'll have a quiet word in his shell."

"Keep me posted." With that, Jeremy hung up.

The cab was heading over London Bridge when Graham looked up. This evening had taken an unexpected turn, but then that often seemed to happen to him. Ever since Jeremy had rescued him from his drug binges and brought him into the Hunter Group, he had found that his days were deeply unpredictable. One moment he might be cleaning out the fryers at Chicken Shak, the next he might be involved in a high-speed car chase around London. One day he might be delivering boxes of fried chicken, the next he might he flying out to New York to follow up a lead on a global terror threat. In many ways it was exciting, but Graham always had difficulties explaining his erratic behaviour and frequent absences to his family and friends. If he could only tell them the truth, things would be so much easier.

Graham was roused from his thoughts by the ringing of his phone. The taxi was approaching Liverpool Street Station, and that meant that he would arrive at the pub imminently. He would have to do his best to succeed. He couldn't afford to make a fool of himself again.

He took his still ringing phone out of his pocket and looked at the screen. Chicken Shak. Oh dear. He was in trouble again.

"Hi," he said as he answered the phone.

"Where are you?" It was his mother.

"I'm in the city. I've bumped into a few friends and have been cajoled into going out with them."

"So you just abandoned the car in Croydon did you?" His mother was a nightmare when she was like this.

"I got a puncture."

"You didn't think of calling us?"

"Look, mum, I haven't got time for this. I'll ring you later."

He hung up, just as the cab pulled onto the forecourt of the station. He got out, paid the driver. His phone started ringing again, but he ignored it and made his way into the Railway Tavern.

The Tavern was a fairly large establishment with several bars. At this time on a Friday evening, it was heaving, and noisy. There was some kind of disco taking place, with a random punter singing along to Chesney Hawkes' classic, "I am the one and only."

Graham pushed his way through the throng of people and made his way through to the largest of the bars. There was no way he was going to be able to find Paul Fish unaided in this crowd.

When he got to the bar, he managed to attract the attention of a rather pretty young barmaid, who, it turned out, was Australian.

"How can I help you, mate?" she asked, twirling her blonde hair as she spoke.

"Pint of lager, please," Graham said, taking a tenner out of his pocket. She poured the pint, and Graham glanced around him. It was then that he noticed, at the other end of the bar, the man he was looking for; Paul Fish. He was deep in conversation with another man. Graham apologised to the bar maid, and forced his way along the crowded bar to where Fish and his companion were stood.

Half way down the bar, Graham bumped into a rather large man who was passing a pint to someone behind him. As he bumped into him, the glass dropped to the ground.

"Oi, what do you think you're doing?" the large man asked Graham.

Graham looked around the angry punter to where the two men were standing. They both looked up, their attention attracted by the disturbance. When they saw Graham, Fish said something to his companion, pointing at Graham, and they both began calmly making their way to the exit.

"Sorry mate, take this," Graham said and proffered the £10 note he had been going to use to pay for his drink.

"I don't want that, I want to know what you think you're playing at, barging into me like that?" He grabbed Graham by the throat.

"Look, I'm sorry, no harm intended," Graham said as he tried to watch where Fish was heading. "Now, if I could just get past please."

"Did you say you were sorry? I didn't hear you."

"I said I'm sorry! Now will you let me go?"

"Say it nicely, punk!"

"I truly am most dreadfully sorry."

"That's better!" The man released Graham, and went to brush down his shirt when he saw the grease stains and thought better of it. "Just watch it, okay? You do that again and you're dead meat."

The large man stepped out of the way, and Graham tried to follow Fish and his companion out of the pub. He eventually made his way out, and looked around to spot where the two men had gone. He spotted Fish high-tailing it into the station, but the other man was nowhere to be seen.

Graham sprinted after Fish as he ran down the escalator and across the station concourse, pushing the late commuters out of his way as he went. Fish turned left into the underground station, vaulted over the ticket barriers and headed down to the eastbound Central Line platform. Graham followed, struggling somewhat with the leap over the barriers. Whilst Fish was a similar age to him, he was much more athletic in build, whilst Graham would be the first to acknowledge that he was carrying rather too much excess weight.

Graham made it to the platform just as the doors of a train closed. The platform was deserted as the train pulled out of the station. He'd lost him.

Brian had managed to switch the vans with relative ease. He had expected it to be rather more difficult. He had arrived at the estate at about half seven, and carefully selected his location. He chose a spot where he could clearly see the other van, but where he was not immediately noticeable to anyone who happened to be hanging around outside the block of flats. He fumbled around in the glove compartment, found the binoculars he had brought with him, and peered down the road towards the other van. All was quiet. There was no one about. It was still light, but would begin to get dark fairly soon.

The quietness was shattered ten minutes later when the police had turned up on site. Several cars and a couple of vans arrived in quick succession, their blue lights flashing, but their sirens quiet. Clearly they were hoping for a certain element of surprise.

The officers had quickly tumbled out of their vehicles. Those from the van quickly tooled themselves up with their Heckler & Koch MP5 submachine guns, and headed straight up to the flat. Brian watched as they ran up the stairs and took up their position outside the door of the bedsit. No warning was given – they simply waited until they were ready, then kicked the door in. They immediately surged through the doorway and straight into the flat. Once they were in, Brian lost sight of them. He tried to see through the doorframe with his binoculars, but it was impossible to do so.

Whilst the armed officers were in the flat, the uniformed officers had begun taping off the scene, reeling out yards and yards of "Police Line" tape all around the block. There were about half a dozen of them, led by an officer who clearly liked the sound of his own voice. He was probably audible to everyone in Lambeth, and he had not even begun to shout.

As had been expected, the police had brought a dog team with them to locate the explosives. They had been told in their tip off earlier that evening that CARN had a white Transit full of explosives, and it took them no time at all to find it. There were a couple of white vans parked in the vicinity – three if you included Brian's - which, he hoped, was not immediately apparent. Before the dog handlers had even begun to consider which van to search, the dog, a rather charming little spaniel, had picked up the scent of the explosives with relative ease. Their handlers forced the back of the van open, and had discovered the arsenal inside. This was a not insignificant collection of explosives, either. Brian peered through his binoculars into the back of the van, and couldn't believe quite how packed it was. The dog handlers radioed through their discovery, shut the doors, and stood on guard. A couple of minutes later, a couple of other police officers relieved them, nonchalantly standing around next to the van to ensure that no one should steal it. A van packed with explosives could pose a real danger to London, and the last thing the police wanted it to do was to fall into the hands of others.

Just you try and stop me, Brian thought.

The missile was fired bang on 1955, as planned. A flash appeared in the window of a flat in the block opposite the meeting room, and almost instantaneously there was the sound of smashing glass as it burst through the window of the bedsit. Milliseconds later, there was a huge explosion which ripped the block's walls out, and smashed every window in the building.

Chaos broke out amongst the officers on the ground as they struggled to comprehend what was going on. This was not what they had expected. As the building exploded, they threw themselves onto the ground. Once the explosion itself had passed, they quickly jumped to their feet, as dozens of radios kicked into life.

The van's sentries were caught up in the shock just as much as the other officers. Once they had picked themselves up from the ground, they had run back to the officer who was presumably their boss. This was Brian's cue. He calmly drove his van up the road and parked it directly behind the other identical white Transit. He jumped out, removed the magnetic panels that obscured the sign painted directly onto the side of his van and positioned them on the other vehicle. To anyone looking at Brian's van, it now looked exactly the same as the first van had. Brian jumped into the explosive-filled van, and calmly drove off. The chaos was such that no one even noticed him leave.

That was earlier this evening. He had now arrived at the industrial unit at Elephant and Castle that had been agreed as the rendezvous. He was early, so he opened up the unit and turned the lights on, drove the van inside, and closed the doors behind him. He had about ten minutes yet, so he pulled out the day's paper to read whilst he waited.

Anatole had been recruited specifically for his prowess with RPGs. In his career with the Russian army, he had built up quite an affection for the rocket propelled grenade, and was rather adept at handling them. Since then, he had served as a "gun for hire," taking work wherever he could get it. He had travelled the world with his work, generally employed by terrorist organisations. He'd worked for them all over the years: the IRA, al Qaeda, Hezbollah, ETA, the lot. He wasn't driven by any guiding ideology, only where he could make the most money. In the beginning, he'd sent most of the money back to a young wife in Russia who was bringing up his two children, but then there was the revenge attack. Somehow the wife of an Israeli politician he had assassinated had found out who he was and where he lived, and had herself recruited a little firepower to go and blast his loved ones off the face of the earth. From that day, every job he took was personal. His work was all he had, and he immersed himself completely.

This particular job was one of the most bizarre he'd ever taken on. His employer on this occasion was also rather surprising. He'd been sworn to complete secrecy, but that really was not a problem for Anatole. Who would he tell? He had no family, no friends, and if truth be told, he hated people. He suspected that that was a prerequisite for anyone who was going to do his job – at least if they were going to do it well.

The RPG was one of his favourite weapons. He liked the bang it made, the damage it caused, and the message it sent out. Why take a target out quietly when you could make a spectacle of it? Of course, he would use other weapons if specifically asked to do so by his employers, but normally the weapon type was not discussed. He was known as one of the world's best handlers of the RPG, and it was normally because of that that he was recruited. No matter how many times he used the weapon, he always got a buzz out of firing them. And he was about to release his second of the day.

His earlier shooting had been undertaken from another block of flats, immediately opposite the block he had destroyed. The owners had needed a little bit of persuasion to let him in to their home, but nothing that a few bullets from his trusty revolver couldn't resolve. He considered taking them out with the RPG too, but thought that might be a little over the top. There were occasions when even Anatole resorted to using other weapons.

After he had gained entry to the flat, the job was easy and straightforward. He had made his way to the window, and then went through the procedure that he had done on many previous occasions. He took the propelling charge out of his rucksack and screwed it onto the end of the warhead. Next he took the artillery and loaded it into the front end of the launcher, lining it up with the trigger mechanism. Finally, at exactly 1955 according to his watch, he fired the missile into the bedsit opposite, exactly as he had been instructed to do.

As soon as the weapon had discharged, he ran back down the stairs to the car that was waiting for him. He didn't fancy being caught, and that was a real possibility when using this particular weapon. It tended to produce a whitish blue-grey smoke that clearly indicated from where it had been fired.

Additionally, on this particular occasion he had another duty to fulfil almost straight away.

He jumped into the back of the car, and his driver drove him out of the estate and around the corner to Elephant and Castle. This time, there would be no need to find a high location to shoot from, since the target was at ground level.

The driver pulled up a few metres down the street from a rather ordinary industrial unit, and they both sat waiting in the car. As expected, about five minutes later a white van pulled into view.

Anatole watched as the van pulled up outside the unit. He saw the driver get out, open the large double doors of the unit, and drive the van in. As the driver closed the doors behind him, Anatole got out of the car, and prepared himself to fire his second missile of the evening.

A few minutes passed and, having loaded the weapon, Anatole pointed the RPG in the direction of the industrial unit's double doors, aimed, and fired.

No more than five milliseconds later, the building erupted into flames with what was quite possibly one of the largest explosions he had ever heard. This time, Anatole couldn't help but stand back and admire his handiwork.

Not for too long, though. He still had one more task to undertake that night.

Chapter 5

"I can't believe you lost him, you complete moron," Helena practically shouted at Graham. "Why didn't you just shoot him?"

"Yes, cos that would have been a great idea in a tube station, wouldn't it? We've not been there before, have we?"

The team had reassembled in the briefing room in 30 St Mary Axe. It was 10pm, and darkness had fallen across the city. The rest of the building was pretty much empty, with only a handful of cleaners finishing up their duties, a bunch of overworked executives still at their desks, and a few more enjoying the bar at the top of the building. By this time, though, even on a Friday night, most city workers had fled the City, either to head home to wives and families, or to hit the West End for a meal or a drink.

Graham ignored Helena's comments. He was used to being the target of her not infrequent outbursts. In the early days they had undermined his confidence, but now he was able to just brush them aside. Helena seemed to spend a large portion of her day criticising Graham. In a strange way, he had grown to quite like it. She was quite stunning, if a little too vain. Sometimes Graham wondered if the offensive comments she directed at him were simply a cover for warmer feelings. This was neither the time nor the place to dwell on these thoughts, however.

Whilst Helena was quick to attack Graham, Jeremy was always similarly quick in coming to his defence. This was no exception.

"I don't think Graham really stood a chance, Helena, and I'm sure he did his best. It was a packed bar, and Fish took fright when he saw Graham coming."

Just as Graham had come to secretly enjoy Helena's outbursts, he had come to find Jeremy's interventions annoying. If anything, his constant defence of Graham had served only to undermine him, at least in Graham's mind. He was more than capable of fighting his own battles, especially as far as Helena was concerned.

"Why did he take fright, though?" asked Helena, adopting a more serious approach. "Have you met him before, Graham?"

Graham had hoped that his colleagues' attention would turn away from him. He needed a few minutes to get his head together. He had just about recovered from his earlier attempts at running, which was not something that he found easy. He had never enjoyed physical exertion, even when he was thin. Now he was, well, fat, and running was a real effort. Now he found himself facing the wrath of several his colleagues for losing Fish. To cap it all of, he found himself gazing longingly at Helena. She was simply stunning, he thought. Her long brown hair was beautiful, and he loved the way she flicked it out of her eyes.

"Graham?" asked Jeremy, dragging him out of his daydreaming. "Have you met Fish before?"

"Hmm? Oh, no, not as far as I know. No, I'm sure I've never seen him before."

"Maybe he thought you were going to try to give him some of your awful chicken," Sally suggested. "That would certainly make me run."

Fantastic, Graham thought. Now Sally's joining in.

"Oh, do shut up, Sally," Jeremy said, as he refilled his coffee cup from the jug on the table. "Let's just go through what we do know. Let's start with you, Helena."

"Well as we know, a missile was shot into a flat in Lollard Street in Lambeth. A group of men, who we believe to be CARN, were evidently meeting in the flat. They were all killed, as were the arresting officers. Wiggy had no difficulty in assessing the situation. He believes that the weapon was an RPG-7, a very common shoulder-launched, anti-tank rocket propelled grenade, fired from the block opposite. There's no way of knowing at this stage where it was sourced from, but Wiggy's going to do his best to try to find out."

"They're awfully common, those RPG-7s," Anthony commented, looking up from his laptop. "They're widely used, and very easy to buy on the black market. I could pull up dozens for sale online."

"We've had a second incident this evening, probably with the same weapon," Jeremy told the team. "A light industrial unit in Elephant and Castle, just down the road from Lollard Street, was destroyed shortly after the block of flats. We suspect that there is a clear connection, but at this stage we're not really aware what it is. What's the other news from Lollard Street, Helena?" Jeremy asked.

Helena explained the situation regarding the white van.

"Was it emptied or was it switched?" Tom asked.

"A good question," Jeremy said. "I think in view of the timings, it must have been switched, which presents us with another major problem. The police are clearly trying to locate the van, but I think we should focus on that too. Not only do we have a highly explosive vehicle driving around, but we should be able to glean some clues from the van. In fact, Sally, get straight on to that. Find me that van."

Sally was clearly miffed at leaving the briefing early, but nevertheless left the room to return to her own desk.

"Helena, you'd better go too. We need this van found, and we need it straight away. Get onto the police and get any CCTV footage that you can find."

"CCTV, Jeremy? You want me to check CCTV?" Helena did not look impressed.

"Yes, Helena, I do. Get on to it right away."

Helena looked like a sulky teenager as she left the room. Jeremy ignored her, and turned his attention to the remaining members of his team.

"Now, Anthony, I believe that you've had a bit of a breakthrough?"

"Quite possibly," Anthony replied. "We've pinpointed a connection between CARN and NR." He explained how he and Sally had managed to locate Paul Fish, and tracked him down to the bar at Liverpool Street. "We have masses of information from CARN, and none of it suggests that they are a terrorist organisation. Active and vocal yes, but terrorists definitely not. It's worth mentioning, though, that they do appear to have had a near total change of leadership over the last few months. Whether this has brought a change of direction is something that is perhaps worth considering. Certainly, though, there's nothing whatsoever to suggest that they have any violent tendencies. The situation with New Reformation is a little different. We know almost nothing about them at all. All we know is that Paul Fish mentioned them in a message on Twitter referencing Lollard Street and the precise time of the explosion."

"So do we think that Paul Fish knew what was going to happen?" Tom asked. "He was the only member of the CARN executive not at Lollard Street, and his tweet suggests that he did."

"Probably, but the only way we can be sure is if we can talk to him," Jeremy replied. "We need to bring him in, and fast. Is there any way we can track him down, Anthony?"

"Well, he clearly has an iPhone, because he has checked into Foursquare and Twitter using one. In theory, it is possible for me to hack into his phone, and activate the GPS to find his exact location."

"Get onto it straight away, please, Anthony."

"Sure thing." Anthony flipped his laptop shut and headed through to his office to begin the process.

"Now, you've been very quiet, Tom. What news from our friends at the Met?"

"Very little to be honest, Jeremy. I spoke to the Counter Terrorism Command Unit, and they were somewhat reluctant to even discuss the situation with me. They were even less helpful than normal."

"Have they got any leads at present?"

"I suspect that their unwillingness to talk is an indication of how much, or should I say how little, they know. I think that they have been taken completely off guard by this evening's developments and are ashamed to admit it. It sounds to me like we've got far more to go on than they have at the moment."

"Bloody typical," Jeremy responded. "Get out there and rattle some more cages at the Met. We need to work together on this or else we're heading towards a major disaster tomorrow."

Tom headed back to his office, leaving only Graham and Jeremy in the briefing room. The two men were very old friends, having known each other since the age of ten. Jeremy had the utmost respect for Graham, which was why he had handpicked him to join his team. He recognised Graham had had his own struggles in the past, and he knew that he generally looked a mess, but he recognised him as a man of great intellect, whose incisive mind could cut through all kinds of difficulties that bewildered the rest of the team. It was for this reason that, although Helena was Jeremy's second-in-command, he often chose to confide in Graham. Helena was not too happy about this situation, although she put up with it because she, in turn, had the utmost respect for Jeremy.

"I'm stuck, Graham," Jeremy conceded, moving to the chair next to him. "I can't work out who is behind this, and what their motivation is. All I know is that we've got someone supposedly after the Pope, and a maniac running around with an assault weapon blowing chunks out of London. I'm relying on you to work out what the hell is going on, and to let me know as soon as you've worked it out. First, however, I have a task for you."

"Go on?"

"We need to try and get to the Pope's security team to warn them what is going on, and to liaise over security. They are being very difficult, though, and are totally non-communicative. They believe that they have everything in hand, and don't trust us. I need you to meet with them, and if possible, the Pontiff himself, and discretely bring this matter to their attention without causing undue alarm. Can you do that?"

"Of course. The Pope's at Lambeth Palace tonight, isn't he?"

"It transpires that he isn't, no. That seems to be a cover story to divert attention away from where he is actually staying. His true location was very hard to find out, which I guess is a good thing. It's a closely guarded secret, but tonight he's staying at a small abbey in Surrey. He is staying with the Abbot, who he intends to make a Cardinal. I want you to head down to Surrey straight away. There's a car waiting for you in the garage to speed you to the Abbey as quickly as possible. Do, please, give serious thought to what is going on, though, and keep me informed, won't you?"

Charlwood Abbey in Surrey is a modern monastery, founded in 1925. Its extensive site is home to a community of forty Benedictine monks, as well as around nine hundred children educated at its boarding school. Tonight, it was also hosting a very special visitor; the Pope himself.

The Pope had arrived at around eight o' clock, and, after celebrating Mass with the monks of the abbey, had enjoyed a late supper with the monastic community. At half past nine, he met with the Abbot in his private study to discuss his appointment as a Cardinal. By ten thirty, the Pope, Abbot and the entire monastic community had retired to their cells for the night.

At precisely ten thirty, a black Mercedes-Benz Viano MPV came to a stop outside the gates of the abbey campus. It paused at the gates for a while, before pulling off into a tree-lined track on the other side of the road. The car drove along the track for a short way, until the dense woodland had completely hidden the car from view. Once the driver was happy that the car was out of sight of the road, he jumped out and began trudging through the mud back towards the road.

The driver was in his mid forties, tall, over six feet, and slim. He had short, dark black hair and a certain air about him. This was in no small part as a consequence of his appearance. He was wearing a smart, pinstriped suit that looked like it had been tailored specifically for him. Beneath the jacket he was wearing a crisp white shirt, and a navy tie with red diagonal stripes. A pair of very expensive, Italian black leather slip-on shoes completed the look. He looked like he should be sat at a desk in a posh office rather than scurrying around the muddy Surrey countryside late at night.

The man from the Mercedes crossed the street and headed back towards the abbey. He scraped the bottom of his shoes on the tarmac in an unsuccessful attempt to remove the mud.

When he reached the wrought iron gates, the man from the Mercedes inspected the buildings either side. On the left hand side of the gates, a large house proudly advertised that it was the Headmaster's Residence. He could see into the kitchen without any difficulty; the lights were on, and no curtains were pulled. He could see a man and a woman sat at the table drinking coffee.

The building on the other side described itself as the South Gatehouse. It was in complete darkness. He approached to take a closer look inside, but as he got closer, a dog began barking. He rapidly retreated into the darkness of the night.

His first concern was how he was going to get the van inside the abbey grounds without being seen. With people in at least one of the buildings, it would be impossible to simply drive in without being noticed. Perhaps, he thought, all it would take would be to drive in with confidence, looking as if he had every right to enter. He had been told that there were several teachers' residences on site. Surely if he just drove in, anyone watching would just think he was a teacher returning from the pub? Or perhaps a taxi? His vehicle, after all, could easily be confused for a taxi.

The problem, then, would be getting through the gates. He took a closer look. They were at least twelve feet tall, and made from wrought iron. The abbey crest was displayed prominently in the centre, and they were topped off with an artistic flourish. The gates were set into a stone wall. Engraved into the stone to the left of the gates were the words "Charlwood Abbey", and on the right, "Founded 1925." What concerned him was that, at first glance, there seemed to be no discernable way of getting through the gates.

Lining the driveway up to the gates were two neat hedgerows. Having examined the gates, the man from the Mercedes looked carefully through the hedges to see if there was a clue that could help him open the gates. Very quickly, he found exactly what he was looking for – a numeric panel on a metal pole. Clearly the gates were opened by entering a code.

He had no doubt that he would eventually be able to get through the gates. It wouldn't take him long to guess the code, and anyway, even if he couldn't, he could simply short the circuit, which would inevitably open the gates - a trick he had learnt in his misspent youth. He pondered what would be a likely code – something that the many people needing to gain entry would remember easily. Perhaps a well-known scripture reference? He began by trying the number engraved into the wall next to the gates – 1925. He was rather surprised, but the gates opened straight away.

Ridiculous, he thought. Never mind, that would make life slightly easier.

He decided to take a quick look around the site to get his bearings. As he walked up the drive, he could see most of the abbey buildings clearly. Right in front of him, at the head of the drive, was the original old country house that the monks had purchased in order to develop the monastery.

Dotted elsewhere around the site were several other buildings. There was one to his left that contained classrooms; he could see a teacher still working hard at his desk in one of the rooms. He could see a large, industrial looking building, which he suspected was the sports hall. There were several other buildings that were well lit for the time of night. These, he suspected, were dormitories. He wanted to try to stay clear of these; he didn't want his actions to impact on any of the children.

He knew that the Pope was staying in the monastery building, which was a modern addition at the rear of the old house. He would try and gain entry through the old building, he decided, since that would take him straight through to the monastery.

The man walked calmly up to the front of the old house. He was quite surprised that there seemed to be no security on the site at all – surprising for a boarding school, he thought, but particularly surprising considering who was visiting tonight. He assumed that because it was such a low-key visit, security had been kept to a minimum. Excellent, he thought; that would make his job easier.

Having reached the front door, he took out his Maglite torch and made an inspection of the security. There was another keypad, this one with just five numbers. He had seen this type of lock before, and knew that it required just three digits. This would be a piece of cake, he thought. He started working through combinations: 123, 234, 345, 135. Bingo – the handle turned. This was going to be so easy.

It was not time yet. He needed to wait a little longer, so he walked back to the car, turned the interior light on, and pulled out his paper. Soon, but not yet.

Chapter 6

The Jaguar was just turning onto the M23 when Graham, who was sprawled out on the back seat, was awoken by the ringing of his phone. Barely conscious, he fumbled for it in the pocket of his jeans, and pulled it out. It was Anthony.

"Graham, it's Anthony. Have you got your laptop with you?"

"Laptop? Of course I have."

"Well would you like to turn it on?"

Graham fumbled around by his feet and retrieved his laptop computer. There was a half-eaten Mars bar attached to the lid, which Graham must have dropped when he nodded off. He peeled it off and ate the remnants whilst he restarted the computer.

"Hold on, nearly there," he mumbled, his mouth still full of chocolate.

"Oh come on, Graham!" exclaimed Anthony. "In case you hadn't noticed, we're hot on the trail of a would-be Pope killer here."

"Yeah yeah. Just lay off me, okay? I've had a busy day." The laptop sprang back to life. "Okay, I'm in now."

"About time. Right - go to your web browser and type in 'guppy.co.uk'."

"Hold on." Graham opened a new tab in Chrome, and tapped in the URL. When the page loaded it was blank, apart from two data fields –

one headed User and the other Pass. "It's password protected, Anthony."

"Not for the first time, I'm ahead of you, Graham. Listen carefully. Into the user field type capital G, lowercase u, p, p, and then capital Y, followed by one, eight, capital Q, three, lowercase b, y, q, and finally one, three, four. Are you there?"

"Don't go so fast, Anthony. Hold on... Q, one, three, four... Yes, I'm there."

"Right, now for password enter 'password' then one, three, two, capital G, lower case e, capital T, Y, P, at symbol, exclamation mark, followed by seven, six, three. All done?"

"Seven, six, three. Yep, I'm in now."

"What do you see?"

"I see a page of links."

"Look closer at the links? See anything significant?" Graham scrolled down the page. For the first time that evening, his eyes lit up and he became genuinely excited about the case.

"My goodness. There's stacks of information here about both CARN and NR! So this Fish character. Do you think he was involved with both organisations, then?"

"I've had a quick look, and I suspect not. He was certainly gathering information about New Reformation though. Somehow he had secured access to dozens of files about the work of New Reformation. Information that even I couldn't find."

"So, who are New Reformation?"

"Brace yourself. They're a militant Catholic group."

"A militant Catholic group? But that makes no sense. Okay, on the one hand they seem to have bumped off a bunch of anti-religious idiots, but are they not also the group who have threatened to assassinate the Pope? Why would a group of Catholics want to kill their religious leader?"

"Wait, there's more. New Reformation is not just a Catholic organisation. The majority of New Reformation's members were either abused by Catholic priests when they were children, or have family who were. It seems they blame the current Pope for covering up their abuse. They believe that he could have taken action that could have stopped them being abused, or at least brought the culprits to justice so that other children would not have to suffer the same way that they did."

"So they're people who would still describe themselves as Catholics, but who want revenge for the way they, or their family, were treated when they were younger?"

"That seems to be the case. They want the Pope to pay for what they had to go through, and to replace him with someone that they think is more deserving of the title of Pope."

"That certainly puts an interesting spin on this whole affair. Do they have any thoughts as to who should replace the Pope if he is killed?"

"No. They think that God will choose the new Pope through the conclave system. You're familiar with the Papal conclave?"

"I can't say that I am, Anthony."

"Following the death of the Pope, all Cardinals of the Catholic Church are sealed into the Sistine Chapel, and are not released until they have appointed a new Pope. It's a very bizarre system, but what else would you expect from the Catholic Church?"

"But if they believe that God determines who is elected as Pope, do they not also believe that the current Pope was chosen by God? In which case, how do they reconcile that with their plan to kill him?"

"Graham, who knows how the minds of these religious people work? Anyway, there is a more significant reason for me telling you this. Amongst the files on NR that Fish has gathered is a membership list. It turns out that there's a member of the senior management team at Charlwood Abbey School who is showing up on NR's membership list – Adam Michaels. I've checked up on the school website, and he's listed as 'Director of Pastoral Care'. Now, I don't know if Michaels is on site tonight, and if he is, I have no idea if he knows the Pope is also on site. I don't know how much of a secret this has been amongst the abbey community. I thought you should know though, because potentially he could be a threat to the Pope."

"Well that's an interesting development. Presumably the Abbot is unaware that Michaels belonged to a militant group that wanted the Pope dead. Has anyone warned him about Michaels? And have we let the Pope's security know?"

"The Pope's security team want nothing to do with us. They feel that they have everything in hand, so we can't get through to them. I've tried calling the Abbot but he is asleep, and no one at the abbey is answering the phone. Even their emergency contact number is just going through to an answerphone."

"In that case, I'd better get down there pretty damn quick. I'll tell the driver to put his foot down. Keep me posted."

Helena and Sally had been trying to locate the white van for thirty minutes. They were finding the police to be surprisingly uncooperative, and very reluctant to hand over any CCTV footage that they might have. Having established that they were not going to get the footage through legitimate means, Helena sent Sally through to see Anthony, to establish whether he could hack into the camera computer systems to grab the footage that might give them a lead.

"I'll get onto it in a sec," Anthony told Sally. "I've got a couple of things I need to do before I can find your footage, though. I need to try to establish exactly who these groups at work tonight are, and how we can stop them. I also need to find Paul Fish so that we can bring him in. I can't help feeling that he is the key to this whole affair."

"Okay, well as soon as you can." Sally plonked herself down into a chair next to Anthony's.

"I could really do without staying up all night tonight. I'm exhausted. Andy's been going on at me about the amount of time I spend at work, and he's going to kill me if I don't get home at some point."

Andy was Sally's secondary school teacher boyfriend. They had been together for two years, and Sally was hoping that Andy would pop the question any day now. She had not had a great deal of success with men in the past, but Andy was different. He was a kind and gentle man, but was tall, dark and muscular, a combination that Sally found very attractive. Even her parents, who had disapproved of pretty much every boyfriend Sally had ever had, liked Andy. They figured that her taste had matured as her thirties had approached.

Sally hated deceiving Andy about her job. He still thought that she was a City lawyer. There was no way that she could ever tell him the truth, though. Jeremy had expressly forbidden it. There were times when Sally thought that this was just a further indication that Jeremy did not understand life in the real world. He was quite an enigmatic figure, but as far as she knew, there was no one special in his life, and she didn't think there had been at all in the time that she had known him.

"Well we're all working as hard as we can, Sally," Anthony responded. "With respect, I think there are bigger issues here than whether Andy is cross with you when you get home, though."

"I know, but it just seems like I spend far too much time in this glass box at the moment. Where's Graham, anyway? Everyone else is here slaving away, and he seems to have bunked off again."

"He's running an errand for Jeremy."

"An errand? You mean he's getting the coffees in?"

"No, he's on his way down to Charlwood Abbey to keep an eye out for this Michaels character," Anthony reported. "The pace altered when we discovered that NR had someone on site at Charlwood."

"I'm sure it will do a lot of good sending Graham down there," replied Sally. "He shouldn't be trusted to follow anyone. Don't you remember that time he was supposed to follow that terror suspect on Oxford Street? Somehow the suspect managed to get himself to Heathrow and on a plane to Los Angeles whilst Graham thought he had him under observation in Starbucks. It's just as well the suspect was not in fact a terrorist, otherwise he could have brought that plane down, and all of our necks would have been on the line."

"Don't you think you might be being just a little unfair on Graham, Sally? We've all made mistakes, and yes, so Graham might have made more than the rest of us, but he has more opportunity to mess up because he's out on the frontline so much more than we are."

"Well I don't know why Jeremy uses Graham so much. If he entrusted me with more front line work, I would show him that I am a significantly better officer than Graham is."

"And there's the nub of it. Is there just a little bit of jealousy there, Sally?"

"No, not at all. I just think Graham is a liability and shouldn't be trusted. In fact, I'm going to get myself down to Surrey straight away. I'm bored sat here waiting for CCTV footage. Helena can cope without me, I'm sure. Give her the footage as soon as you've found it, will you? Tell her I've had to pop out."

"Are you sure that's a good idea, Sally? Don't you think you should tell Jeremy what you're up to?"

"He won't mind. He'll appreciate that I've shown some initiative. Besides, it's about time that he realised that I'm far better in the field than Graham. I'll give him a ring on the way down. I'm not going to let Graham mess this one up."

Sally stormed out of the room, leaving Anthony alone in front of his computer. He had so much he needed to do, but he had been distracted by the contents of Paul Fish's website, which seemed to change the whole nature of the operation. Assuming Fish was correct, New Reformation suddenly had a motive to want to take out the Pope. The pieces were gradually falling into place. What still baffled him was the link between CARN and NR. Why had NR seemingly blasted CARN out of existence? Was it because CARN represented a threat to NR? Was it that New Reformation were just the kind of 'religious nutters' that the Campaign Against Religious Nutters wanted to deal with? At this stage, that was pure speculation, but it seemed possible.

Anthony needed to try once more to locate Paul Fish, but for the moment he was more interested in the Twitter conversation between Paul Fish and the Tweeter who used the name @infinitum_uk. Fish had sent @infinitum_uk a message that had referenced New Reformation, as well as both the location and time of the explosion. That could just be a coincidence, but the odds would seem to be stacked against that. The big question here was who was @infinitum_uk? Was he – or she – a member of CARN whom Fish had been warning? If that was the plan, it didn't work, since it appeared that all of CARN's leadership, with the exception of Fish, had been in the flat when it had been bombed. If they were, then the entire leadership had been killed. Was @infinitum_uk a member of New Reformation? Was Fish affirming that he believed that New Reformation were the way forward? That would make sense of the statement in the message 'New Reformation for sure'. Had Fish been a traitor within the leadership of CARN? Had he betrayed them? That would explain why he had not been present at the meeting.

Anthony's head was hurting. He wrote down some of the questions that were spiralling around in his head. He needed answers, but he was running out of ideas as to where to look.

He began by checking through the NR membership lists for any reference to Infinitum UK. It was clearly an alias, but maybe, just maybe, it would show up. Perhaps it was listed as an organisation, or maybe one of the members had used the term in an email address. He ran a search. It came back empty. Search term not found.

Anthony had previously tried running an internet search on Infinitum UK, but the search engine had returned 321,000 results. Time to be a little more specific, he thought, and opened Google in his browser. He refined his search using quotation marks to ensure that only instances of 'infinitum' and 'uk' appearing together would be returned. This returned a far more manageable 757 results. He had a quick browse through the listings but found nothing that seemed relevant. He further refined the result by introducing the word 'catholic', searching for '"infinitum uk" catholic'. Just 121 results. We're getting somewhere, he thought. He scanned through the results, and finally, on page eight, he thought he might have made a breakthrough of some kind. He clicked on a link that took him through to the archives of the *Page Chronicle*, the local newspaper of a small town in Arizona. There, he found a page entitled, "Catholic Group Fights Back." He read through the article:

A local congregation in Page has spoken out against what they see as the increasingly anti-Catholic sentiments of US society.

Worshippers at the Church of St. Mary Magdalene on Main Street, Page, believe that the Catholic Church in the US is suffering from an increasingly unfriendly image in the United States, and believe that it is time to speak out. They plan a series of demonstrations throughout the state of Arizona, in partnership with other local congregations, which seek to highlight the true beliefs of the Catholic faith.

Local Catholic, Michael T. Smith, told the Chronicle: "ordinary Catholics are fed up with being portrayed as sexist, bigoted paedophiles. We want to show the world what we really stand for."

Smith says that he was inspired to action by a chance visit from a tourist to his church one Sunday.

"We have taken our example from Philip Brown, a UK Catholic on holiday at Lake Powell. He visited our church and, over coffee explained how he led a movement in the UK call 'Infinitum' which sought to show the love of the Catholic Church to all people, and to speak out against the common allegations the Church encounters."

Smith will lead their first demonstration outside Wal-Mart this Saturday afternoon.

Bingo, Anthony thought. We're making progress. He immediately punched 'Philip Brown' and 'Infinitum' into Google. There, right at the top of the returned sites was philipbrown.co.uk. Anthony clicked through to the link and read through the site.

Philip Brown, it transpired, was a London-based human rights lawyer. He lived in Hampstead with his wife Tessa, and two daughters, Sophie and Flora. He was a committed Catholic and sought to portray the Church in a more positive light, and stand up against the allegations that were frequently made against the Church. He wanted to show that Catholics still wanted to demonstrate the love that Christ had for all people to the wider community, outside the Church. A few years back, he had written several blog posts on the topic, and even organised some events in public locations. It seemed that over the last few years work had taken up significantly more of Brown's time, however, and he was not able to commit so much to Infinitum UK. Since he had been the prime mover – the website suggested the only mover – behind the organisation, Infinitum UK had practically ceased to exist.

Anthony was ecstatic to have made such a breakthrough. It looked like he had found the tweeter known as infinitum_uk. He was still very confused, however. Why was Paul Fish, a member of an organisation that wanted to bring about the end of religion in the UK, involved with Philip Brown, who wanted to strengthen the Catholic faith in the UK? And why had he sent him a message about that evening's missile attack?

Anthony printed out the *Page Chronicle* article, and the relevant sections of Brown's website, and stuck them in a folder for future reference.

Eleven o' clock. Time to move.

The man in the Mercedes put down the paper, turned off the courtesy light and started the car. He drove up to the gates of the abbey. The headmaster and his wife had obviously retired for the night. The kitchen lights were now off in his house, and there was no sign of life.

He punched the code into the number pad hidden in the hedge, and the gates slowly swung open. He drove up to the large, old house that formed the central point of both the school and the monastery, parked in the car park at the front of the building, and got out of the car.

He looked around. There was nobody about. The front of the building and the driveway were both well lit, but beyond it was pitch black. There was no moon, and very little light out in the Surrey countryside. The nearby airport at Gatwick was the only source of light, giving off an orange glow in the distance.

The man from the Mercedes made his way to the large wooden front door, and punched the code into the keypad. He turned the handle, and the door opened. He walked through into the large, ornate hallway of the old house. To his right there was a reception area, unstaffed at this time of night. In front of him there was a small seating area, with the day's newspapers and various school publications on a small coffee table in the centre. The walls around him were bedecked with panels that recorded various feats, including the names of school captains, and those who had gained entry to Oxbridge – a rather small number of students, he noted. Clearly Charlwood was not known for its academic excellence.

From here, he had little idea where to progress. There were several doors leading off the hallway. He knew that the monastery lay behind the old building, on the right hand side, so he took the door on the right of the far wall. It took him through into a small, dark, wood panelled corridor. Photos of former headmasters lined the walls.

He could not believe that this was so easy. Surely the security for the Pope should be much tighter than this, he thought.

He continued along the corridor, and opened a door that took him into a large, very ornate room. In the centre was a long table with chairs around it. On one side of the room large windows overlooked the well-tended grounds, which rolled gently down to a pond below. The walls of the room were once again wood panelled, but what really grabbed his attention was the beautiful plaster ceiling. Every foot or so, a plaster feature extended below the ceiling, rather like a stalactite. In fact, the whole atmosphere of this room was akin to a beautiful cave.

No time to admire the interior design, he thought, however. Time to press on. He headed to the door on the far side of the room and walked through, into a room very similar to that which he had just left. He continued straight through and let himself through yet another door. This time it opened into a narrow corridor, with a row of doors on one side. He had reached the monastery and the monk's sleeping quarters.

Immediately he entered the corridor, he heard a shout.

"Stop right there!"

At the far end of the corridor, a man in his mid-thirties, dressed immaculately in a well-tailored Italian suit was pointing a gun at him.

Excellent, he thought. This must be it! I must be in the right place.

He did not want to use violence; it was not within his nature to do so. Under the circumstances, however, he felt he had no choice. This was for the greater good. He took a pistol out of his pocket, aimed it at the security officer, and shot him in the thigh. The officer immediately dropped to the ground. The ketamine should keep him out cold for a good thirty minutes or so.

He began walking down the corridor when another security officer appeared. He shot him in the thigh too, then a third, and then a fourth. Finally, stepping over their inanimate bodies, he reached the end of the corridor. He opened the only door on the left hand side and proceeded through into the central hallway beyond the door. There was a door on the left, and another on the right.

Outside the door on the right were two men, who had clearly been alerted by the noises from the corridor. They barred the door, and stood with pistols drawn.

"Stop right there or I'll shoot!" one of them said quietly.

Immediately, the man from the Mercedes shot both the guards and entered the room they had been guarding.

There, sat up in bed with a look of fear on his face, was an old man dressed in white pyjamas.

"Please..." the Pope said.

"Good evening, your grace. I'm sorry to disturb you in this ungodly way, but would you be so kind as to come with me?"

The Pope looked confused. This man, who had shot his guards and forced his way into his bedroom, was being polite to him. He put it down to the peculiar habits of the English that he had heard so much about.

The man went up to the bed, and scooped the Pope out. He put the Holy Father onto his back as if he was a small child, and made for the window.

Chapter 7

Anatole had been dropped off in a quiet country lane. This was going to be the trickiest part of his mission that night, and he decided a silent approach was what was required. He had toyed with the idea of simply driving up to the monastery and blasting it into oblivion. That would give him an enormous amount of satisfaction, and would also bring the matter to a swift conclusion. He had specific instructions, however, that the Pope was to be left unharmed. His employer had been quite insistent on that point. He could not risk using his favoured weapon, since any use of missiles would leave collateral damage that could result in the injury, or even death, of the Pope.

He still took his missile launcher with him, in addition to a machine gun, a couple of handguns and some smoke bombs. Those, he thought, always came in useful when a little confusion was needed.

If only his employer had kept a tighter control of the situation, this whole outing would not have been necessary.

It was almost pitch black out here in the countryside. In the distance, up a hill, he could see a few lights at the abbey. Beyond the hill the orange glow from Gatwick airport was visible. The grounds themselves were mostly in darkness but there were a few floodlights around the estate that illuminated key parts of the buildings. In particular, the abbey church was well floodlit, and looked like some bizarre spaceship against the Surrey woods. Anatole pulled his night sight down over his eyes, and began the hike up to the monastery.

Within a few metres of the road, Anatole came up against a fence. Ordinarily this would have posed no threat to a six-foot-eight body-builder like Anatole, but he was well laden with weaponry and ammunition. He managed to climb over the fence without too much difficulty, however, and began trudging up the footpath through the fields.

He checked his watch. He would have to increase his pace if he was going to get there in time.

Anatole walked on for about a mile, his mind completely empty as he focused on the sound of his breath in the silence. He came across a stream in his path. He looked up and down for a bridge, but could see none. He considered building a primitive crossing using whatever he could find, but decided that the stream was not big enough, nor deep enough, to worry about. He simply walked through it.

Having crossed the stream, Anatole entered a timber yard. Huge piles of lumber were stacked up, ready for collection and shipping. A tractor was parked up in the yard. He thought about hot-wiring it and using it to drive up to the abbey, but decided that that was a ridiculous idea; it would be lazy, and he would not get the silent approach that he wanted.

Leaving the timber yard behind him, Anatole entered an area of woodland, presumably where the lumber had been harvested from. It was extremely dark in the wood and Anatole found it a real strain to see ahead of him, even with the night sight mask. He could just about make out the footpath snaking up the hill in front of him, running alongside a wire fence, so he pressed on, using the fence to guide him as necessary.

Five minutes or so later, and Anatole moved out of the woodland. To his left was a garden, the centrepiece of which was a large pond. In front of him, a well-manicured lawn stretched ahead, rising up the hill to the building. He could see the monastery clearly now, just a few hundred yards in front of him, at the top of the lawn. On this side, the building was in darkness. He could see built onto the side of the old building a more recent addition, with a line of windows facing across the grounds. That, he knew, was the sleeping wing of the monastery. The windows were in the cells in which the monks slept. On the far right hand side of the sleeping wing were two larger windows. Outside these windows Anatole could just about make out a solitary figure. This confirmed in Anatole's mind that this was the room he was after. This was where the Pope was sleeping, and that solitary figure was a guard. Rather lax security, he thought. Then again, almost no one knew that the Pope was staying at the abbey, and so clearly his security team hoped to keep a low profile to avoid giving anything away.

Anatole dropped his bag and pulled out a bipod that he erected, and topped off with a rifle. He fastened an infrared sight onto the top of the rifle, and peered through at the guard. He could take him out with ease. He aimed directly at the guard's head, and began squeezing the trigger.

At the last moment, however, Anatole changed his mind. The rifle would be heard for miles on a night as still as this. Even a single rifle shot would arouse suspicion, and could have repercussions for the rest of his mission. He decided against it, and quickly packed the gun and bipod away into his bag. Bare hands would work nicely, he thought.

Anatole followed the edge of the trees, trying to get as far away from the guard as he could. At some point he would have to make a break for it and cross the lawn, and he wanted to make sure he did so as far away from the guard as possible. When he thought he'd reached a safe distance, he paused, made sure his bag was secure on his back, took a deep breath and ran as fast as he could up towards the monastery.

Twenty seconds later, and Anatole found himself up against a ha-ha, which separated the gardens in the immediate vicinity of the abbey from the rest of the grounds. He took off his bag, and quietly dropped it onto the lawn above his head. Next, he carefully pulled himself up, rolling flat against the grass when he reached the top.

He peered over towards the guard. He was still looking out across the lawn.

Anatole jumped up, shouldered his bag, and crept up to the wall of the old building. He peered in.

"Shit," he thought. There was someone moving around inside the room. The person inside gave the impression of not knowing where he was, and having not been in the room before. He recognised the man as his target. This was not good.

He had to get to the Pope's room before the man did.

Anatole carefully crawled along the wall of the building, until he was just metres from the guard. He dropped his bag. He had to move fast. He waited until he was sure that the guard was looking in the other direction. Then he moved. He leapt up. He put his left arm around the guard's neck, and covered his mouth with his right hand. Then he squeezed. The guard tried to shout out. Anatole tightened his grip. The guard began to struggle. Then, very suddenly, he went limp. Anatole released him. The guard jumped up and went for his weapon. Anatole had fallen for the oldest trick in the book. He jumped away, and raised his leg, catching the guard in the groin. The guard emitted a stifled scream, and dropped to his knees. Anatole approached him, and kicked his boot down hard on the guard's head. Once. The head smashed against the ground. Twice. He heard the bone shatter. Three times. A steady flow of blood started flowing. Job done.

Anatole kicked the body out of the way, and sat in the guard's chair. He peered through a gap in the curtains. He could see the Pope in his bed. He could see his target. He watched as his target picked the Pope up, and put him on his back. He began crossing the room to the window.

Excellent, thought Anatole. This was going to be easy.

The car pulled up to the abbey gates. When Graham had finished his phone call with Anthony, he had asked the driver to put his foot down, and he had done just that. They had driven down the M23 at about 110 miles per hour, and had reached Charlwood in record time.

Whilst the driver fumbled with the number pad at the gates, Graham went through the plan in his head. He could not afford to get this wrong.

Jeremy had dispatched him to the abbey to warn the Pope's security team of the threat to the Pontiff's life. The situation had changed somewhat with the revelation that a member of the school's senior staff was a member of New Reformation, the organisation that had threatened to kill the leader of the Catholic Church. Graham thought that, under the circumstances, it would be best if the Pope could be persuaded to leave the abbey, and to return to London. If necessary, he could spend the night at the Gherkin, where he would be safe under the protection of the Hunter Group. Trying to persuade the Pope and his team to leave would be rather difficult, however. Graham knew that the Pope refused to wear body armour, believing that if he were to be killed, it would be part of God's plan for his life. Whilst the Pope might be happy to be a martyr, that did not make life easy for those sworn to protect him. And if the Pope should be killed whilst he was with Graham, that would surely destroy Graham as effectively as the Pope.

This was going to be very tricky, Graham thought. He needed to get in, find the Pope's head of security, talk to him, get him, the Pope, and their team to leave, and to ensure that Adam Michaels, the school's Director of Pastoral Care and member of NR, came nowhere near any of them. This was not going to be fun.

The car pulled up in the car park at the front of the abbey's main building. There were quite a few cars parked up, several that were clearly hire cars, and a large, black Range Rover with blacked out windows. Also, sitting rather incongruously amongst the other cars was a large, black Mercedes people carrier.

Graham got out of the car, and opened the boot. Laid out before him was a selection of firearms, other weapons, and a range of armour. He put on a bulletproof vest, and pulled several weapons into a rucksack. He kept a revolver in his hand, just in case.

When Graham got to the front of the building, he was rather surprised to find the door wide open. Had a pupil or absent-minded monk left it open? Or had someone entered – or exited – in something of a hurry? Graham was uncertain, but he knew he had to be on his guard.

Graham walked through the reception area, through a couple of large, rather showy rooms, and entered the rooms at the rear of the old house, which he believed was the monastery. The first sight that confronted Graham shocked him to the core. There were three bodies sprawled out on the floor. He took a quick look at them. They were all young-ish men in suits. Each had a bullet hole in their right thigh. Graham decided that this had happened only minutes before, since there was surprisingly little blood.

"Bugger. I'm too late," Graham thought.

He ran down the corridor, opening all the doors as he went. Each had a single bed, generally with a rather elderly male occupant.

"Where's the Pope? Where's the Pope?" he yelled at each monk as he passed through. He got no response, the monks clearly too stunned by being roused from their sleep by a man carrying a gun. As he progressed down the corridor, the monks began to leave their rooms to see what the commotion was.

As he got closer to the end of the corridor, the lights came on, and a voice shocked him from behind.

"Stop right there! Who are you? What do you think you're doing?"

Graham looked behind him. A short, ageing man with grey hair, a rather bizarre moustache and wearing a tracksuit, had appeared in the doorway.

"Graham Chapman, security services. The Pope is at risk and I need to take action."

"Security services? What does that mean?" The short man began walking towards him. He had a whistle around his neck.

"I'm with the Hunter Group. We're a private firm working with MI5 and MI6. Who are you?"

"My name's Adam Michaels, and I'm the Director of Pastoral Care at Charlwood Abbey School. I'm going to have to ask you to leave, I'm afraid. You have no right to be here. Unless you leave immediately, I will have no option but to take action."

Michaels was still approaching Graham. As he spoke, he pulled a large kitchen knife out of his tracksuit pocket.

Shit shit shit, Graham thought. This is him! This is the NR guy come to kill the Pope! Had he shot these guards? No, he had not. He clearly didn't have a gun, which is why he had threatened him with a knife. He had obviously just arrived on the scene. The person responsible for shooting these guards was clearly ahead of him, probably with the Pope by now.

Shit shit shit. What do I do? A Pope killer in front of me, and a Pope killer behind me. I can't afford to get this call wrong. He thought of how the rest of the team had gone on about how incompetent he was throughout the day. His head was spinning.

I could take Michaels out with no difficulty at all, he thought. But the Pope could be under threat right now, and dealing with this strange man in a tracksuit could use up precious time.

"Drop the knife or I'll shoot you!" Graham shouted. "I have to get to the Pope right away!"

By now, the monks were swarming around the corridor. One of them, a tall, elderly man with thinning white hair tried to take charge of the situation.

"Both of you, in God's name, drop your weapons! We cannot have this behaviour in a monastery!"

"Shut up, you duffer!" Michaels shouted at the venerable monk.

Whilst Michaels and the monk exchanged words, Graham ran on, turning left at the end of the main corridor, stepping over several more bodies as he went.

He soon found an opened door with two more bodies slumped outside it. He hurried into the room just in time to see a man dashing towards the windows, with an elderly man on his back. The Pope!

He's alive! Graham thought. Alive, but in the process of being kidnapped.

"Stop right there or I'll shoot!" Graham shouted.

The man with the Pope on his back turned round, a look of fear on his face, but he didn't stop. He arrived at the window and threw it open. As he did so, shots entered the room through the now open window.

What the heck is going on? Graham thought. I was only supposed to come and warn them of a threat! Now it seems there are at least three separate people trying to bump off the Pope.

The escaping man dropped the Pope to the floor, and peered out of the window. As he did so, more shots were fired from outside the room, missing the kidnapper by millimetres.

Meanwhile, Michaels tore into the room, knife drawn, lunging for where the elderly Pontiff was laying sprawled out on the floor, groaning.

"What do I do?" the kidnapper said, looking imploringly at Graham for answers.

Graham ignored him. There were two threats that needed to be neutralised, and fast. He had to deal with Michaels first. He was the immediate threat to the Pope, albeit probably the most amateurish.

Graham jumped at Michaels, trying to avoid the knife. He wrestled him to the floor, whilst

Michaels continued to wave the kitchen knife. As he tried to wrestle the knife out of his hand, yet another man entered the room, this one a tall, younger man dressed in pyjamas.

"STOP THIS IMMEDIATELY!"

"Abbot, this man is trying to kill the Pope!" Michaels shouted.

Deranged, Graham thought.

Graham was on top of Michaels. He needed to move fast. He had other situations to deal with. He tried to get up, and as he did so, he stamped on Michaels' wrist. Michaels screamed out in pain and dropped the knife. As he did so, the gunman outside moved in front of the window and let out a burst of fire into the room. Graham dropped back to the ground, and tried to slide on his tummy to the relative safety of the bed. He made it underneath the bed and turned round.

Shit, shit, shit, he thought. I really should stick to delivering chicken.

Graham assessed the situation. A large man dressed all in black, holding a machine gun, was peering into the room. That has to be my priority, he thought. The Pope was still sprawled on the ground. Michaels was screaming his lungs out. The kidnapper was moving towards the Pope. The abbot had beaten a hasty retreat.

Graham grabbed his handgun and pointed it in the direction of the gunman. As he did so, he became aware of the Pope crawling out of the room. Good move, your grace, he thought.

He was surprised that the gunman didn't move to shoot him. He had other, more confusing priorities, it seemed.

Graham let a shot off in the direction of the gunman. He stooped, and the bullet missed him. The gunman climbed over the window frame and entered the room, moving towards Michaels.

Just watch, just watch, thought Graham. If some kind of rival gang warfare was about to break out, that could help him. At least attention turned away from the Pope. And from him.

The gunman was now standing directly over Michaels. He took aim with his machine gun, and shot Michaels between the eyes.

Shit, thought Graham. Still, one threat neutralised, just one left.

"You, under the bed!" shouted the gunman. He had an eastern European accent.

Threat number two coming my way, thought Graham. He aimed his revolver as high as he could, which, from his position under the bed, was not particularly high. He shot. He got the gunman in the stomach. The gunman shrieked, but still managed to let off a stream of bullets into the bed. Luckily, the mattress impeded their progress.

Graham pulled himself forward.

"Come out and play!" shouted the gunman, firing off another round.

Graham could now see the gunman's chest. He aimed, he fired. He got the gunman in the chest. He dropped the gun, and fell to the floor clutching his chest. Two down, Graham thought, as he pulled himself out from under the bed.

He stood up and looked around. Michaels, dead. Gunman, dead. Pope – shit. Nowhere to be seen. Kidnapper – shit. Nowhere to be seen.

Chapter 8

Helena was sick and tired of scrolling through CCTV footage of Lambeth council estates. She was still absolutely fuming that Sally had taken off to Surrey without even telling her. She was even more annoyed that Jeremy had simply told her to take care, and had not reprimanded her and called her back. She was his deputy, for goodness sake, and here she was doing the kind of task an assistant should be doing. An assistant like Sally.

It was at times like this that Helena despaired of the lack of glamour her job brought. It had been the promise of glamour that had initially attracted her to the secret services, although she'd seen precious little in the last few years. She'd hoped for posh frocks and champagne, guns tucked into suspenders and big furry Russian hats. She thought she'd be chasing baddies with tuxedo wearing hunks. Instead, she spent most of her time in jeans, and worked with smelly men in fast-food restaurant uniforms. She was hardly living the dream.

Helena had been in her final year of an English degree at Durham University when she had been invited to attend a careers meeting with the Foreign Office. Her grades throughout her time at Durham had been pretty impressive, although not as exceptional as she liked people to believe. She had not had the slightest idea what she might do when she graduated. She had toyed with the idea of continuing her studies with a Master's degree. Working in the City had quite appealed; she liked the idea of the power dresses, the heels, and the ambitious young men, all eager to impress with their wealth. A job in the Foreign Office had not really been on her radar, but she went along to the meeting, more out of boredom than anything else.

The first thing that had struck her was just how few people there were at the presentation – only about fifteen or so, which was a drop in the ocean of Durham's 16,000 students. The meeting had begun with a short video presentation explaining how the threat of terror attacks against the UK had never been greater. They had then had a short talk from a rather severe looking man in his sixties, who said something along the lines of how he hoped that everyone knew where they stood, and anyone who didn't like it could now leave. No one had left. He had then passed round copies of the Official Secrets Act, with instructions that they should be signed, reaffirming that if anyone was unhappy with doing so, they knew where the door was.

And so had begun Helena's promising career with MI5. Initially, there had been very little glamour; the first couple of years or so of her career were spent processing paper work. Just over two years into her job, though, she was transferred to active duty as a counter-terrorism agent working in the City of London, a job that she had thoroughly enjoyed. At last she had found some glamour; big, flash cars, high tech toys and gadgets, and running around the City with a gun chasing baddies.

After two fantastic years, she had eagerly accepted a two year secondment to "Six," as MI6 is generally known to those within the security services. She had been excited about spending time in Iraq or Afghanistan, or maybe even Russia, but she had been deeply disappointed to find herself stationed on a base in Germany. The secondment had been what her line manager had described as a "valuable learning experience," but Helena had been bored out of her mind the whole time.

Upon returning to the UK, she had been hoping to return to active duty, perhaps even on her old patch in the City of London. Instead, she had found herself head hunted by Jeremy Hunter, a former CIA officer who had been tasked with launching a private security company in the UK. Hunter wanted Helena to join his new elite outfit, the Hunter Group. The Group aimed to handle the more dubious tasks that governments could not be associated with, offering services to whichever intelligence organisation was happy to pay for them.

Helena was asked to join Hunter as his second-in-command. She had initially been reluctant to take the position, but had been told by her line manager that if she refused to do so, there would not be an opening for her at "Five," so she had very little choice in the matter.

The early days with Hunter had been exciting and fulfilling. She loved being able to carry out fieldwork around the world free from the limitations that she had experienced with Five and Six. As time went by, however, she got more and more exasperated with her colleagues, particularly Graham. Graham had no intelligence background. In fact, Helena would go further and say that he had no intelligence whatsoever. She believed that he had been recruited because Jeremy felt sorry for him, which she thought was a pretty ridiculous reason to appoint him. Whilst she generally had the utmost respect for Jeremy, she did doubt his decision in this instance.

As far as the rest of her colleagues went, Tom wasn't too bad. He had been in the police before joining Jeremy, she thought, but other than that she knew surprisingly little about him. Even though they had worked closely together on numerous operations, he was still something of an enigma. He chose to reveal little about his past or his life away from work, preferring to keep himself to himself. He was a competent enough officer, and it was a shame, Helena thought, that he was so reticent. Of all the team, Tom was the one that Helena would like to get to know better. He was tall, muscular, and just lovely.

Anthony was okay for a geek.

Then there was Sally. She was a nice enough girl, and was keen to get out of the office and see more action for herself. In fact, that was something of an understatement. When Jeremy had recruited her as a secretary, he had led her to believe that if she played her cards right she could become a field agent in due course. As a consequence, she was positively champing at the bit to get out. Unfortunately, this meant that she often made rather rash decisions and acted without thinking through her actions first. The more eager she became, the more she pissed Helena off. Tonight was a perfect example. Scrolling through hours of CCTV was exactly what Sally should be doing. Instead she was out doing God knows what, whilst Helena was stuck in the office.

No, thought Helen. The sooner I can get out of this tin pot operation the better. Give me proper spying any day.

With Anthony's help, Helena had eventually managed to find footage of Lollard Street, and seen the white van parked in the car park. In a second, she would scroll back through the earlier footage to try to establish who had parked it there. For the moment, though, her priority was not how it got there, but rather how, or more particularly who, had taken it away.

Graham, it pained her to admit, was correct, in that the van had not been emptied. That would have taken far too long, and someone would

103

surely have noticed. Instead, as Graham said, the van had been switched. She saw the police officers look in the back and discover the explosives. Then she saw the explosion in Lollard Street. The officers who had been guarding the van rushed over to the block, and as they did so, a fairly young man had driven another white van up in front of the first, switched the signage and number plates around, and then driven off in the van packed with explosives.

She had tracked the van to the edge of the estate, but from there, it was proving rather more difficult to monitor its progress. It had turned to the east, but she could not find any footage of it heading beyond the estate.

Reluctantly, Helena had broadened the search out to take in the wider area. She had begun with the easy-to-locate footage – outside rail and tube stations, bus stops and shopping precincts. No sign of the van. She had then scanned through whatever other footage she could get hold of.

She was beginning to lose hope. There were just too many white vans in London, and it would be so easy for the driver just to change the number plates again. Wearily, she began looking at footage from the front of a light industrial estate in Elephant and Castle.

She almost wasn't looking. Then she jumped back to full consciousness. She thought she'd found the van.

She checked the number plates against the ones on the van when it had left Lollard Street. She had a match. She focused in on the driver. It was the same person. Result!

She watched the van pull into shot. It pulled up to one of the units and the driver – definitely the same man who had picked their van up from Lollard Street – got out, and opened the doors of the unit. He drove the van inside, and closed the doors behind him. She tracked through the footage waiting to see what happened next – perhaps the driver leaving the building, perhaps someone else arriving. That was not what she saw, however. She saw an explosion. She paused the footage. Had someone detonated the van? Why detonate it there, in the middle of a deserted industrial estate?

Helena scrolled back through the last couple of minutes of footage and watched it again. Nothing. The building just exploded. She went back again, and took it through a frame at a time. Then she saw it. It was barely noticeable, it happened so fast, but she definitely saw a flash in front of the camera, just before the explosion. She watched again. It was a missile. Someone had fired a missile into the van. Just like at Lollard Street.

This could be a breakthrough, she thought.

Helena grabbed whatever footage she could find of the industrial estate, and began looking at the scene from different angles. If she could find who had launched the missile into the unit, she may well have found the person who took out CARN.

It did not take her long to find footage from a camera on the perimeter of the industrial estate monitoring the street. Then she saw it.

A black BMW X6 pulled up into the street. A few seconds later, a tall man got out of the back of the car. He was carrying a shoulder mounted missile launcher. He crouched down on the street, prepped the weapon, and let a missile off into the garage. He calmly got back into the car, and drove off.

This was completely crazy. Nothing was making any sense this evening. Why had the van been switched in Lollard Street? Did the person removing it realise that it was going to be blown up? Clearly not, she thought, otherwise the driver would not have stayed with the vehicle. If the van was used to set up CARN, had it been destroyed by the same people who had blown up the flat earlier that evening? It looked like it, but again, that made little sense.

There were so many unanswered questions, but Helena still thought that she was making progress. At the very least, they now knew that the van was no longer driving around central London, and so was not a threat. It should be easy enough to identify the driver of the van. It should also be possible to identify the person who had not only taken out the van, but presumably, unless there were several people using missile launchers in London that evening, which was unlikely although not impossible, also blown up the flat in Lollard Street.

Was this their New Reformation man? Was this the man who intended to kill the Pope? It was eminently possible.

Jeremy had not initially been very happy when Sally had announced that she was en route to Surrey. He soon decided, however, that perhaps his administrative assistant should be given the opportunity to break out of the office for a while, and to spend some time in the field. She couldn't come to much harm, after all. Graham was only meeting with the Pope's security team and advising them to move the Holy Father away from the Abbey. He had heard from Anthony that there was a member of NR on the staff at the school, but he had every confidence that, should any threat to the Pope arise, Graham would be able to neutralise it before it became too much of an issue.

So it was, therefore, that Sally found herself speeding down the M23 towards Charlwood. She had not dared to take one of the group's fleet of Jaguars, and so was in her own nearly new Volkswagen Golf.

In no time at all, she found herself at the exit for Gatwick Airport. She turned off and headed towards Charlwood. She crossed a couple of roundabouts, and then followed the signs for the abbey.

A few minutes after the interchange, Sally came to a turn off on the right that was signposted to Charlwood Abbey. She took the turning, and then pulled over on to the grass verge. She was out in a remote woodland, and there was very little around. In the distance she could see lights, which she guessed would be up at the abbey. She decided that she would try to contact Graham and find out what he was up to. She checked the time – quarter past eleven – and took out her phone.

Graham did not answer. It went straight to voicemail. Very strange, she thought. She tried again. Still no response.

What was Graham playing at?

Sally decided to call Jeremy again, to see if he had heard any news from Graham since he had arrived in Surrey.

"Sally?" Jeremy said when he picked up the phone.

"Any news from Graham?"

"Not since he arrived in Surrey. Why do you ask?"

"He's not answering his phone."

"He's probably with the Pope. I'll try and give him a call and get back to you. Where are you now?"

"I've pulled over just down the road from the abbey."

"Okay, proceed with care. Be careful, Sally. Don't put yourself into any unnecessary danger."

With that warning, he hung up.

Sally was beginning to think that things were not as they seemed. She was concerned that Graham had messed up once again. She really didn't want to have to fix Graham's mess.

There was nothing for it but to head to the abbey. Sally started her Golf, and pulled forward. Just as she did so, she saw car headlights driving away from the abbey towards her. She turned her lights off. She couldn't be sure, but she was fairly confident that this vehicle had just left the abbey.

The vehicle had its headlights on full beam, so Sally could see nothing other than the lights until it had passed. Then she was able to see what it was. Some kind of black Mercedes MPV thing. As the car slowed down to take the junction, she was able to write down its registration number.

The Mercedes turned back onto the road leading to the M23, and disappeared in the distance. Sally turned her own lights back on, and started driving, slowly and cautiously, towards the abbey.

No more than thirty seconds later, and Sally found herself at the large, wrought iron gates of the abbey. She parked her car, and jumped out to see how she could gain entry. As she did so, she saw another car driving away from the main building, extremely fast. The floodlights showed exactly what the car was. It was a Hunter Group Jaguar. Graham's car.

As the car approached the gates, they opened automatically. Sally flagged the car down, and it came to a stop. Graham was seated in the front seat next to the driver, and wound down the window. He was holding a machine gun.

"What are you doing here?" he asked.

"Checking up on you."

"Never mind that. Did you see a car leave a minute or so ago?"

"Yes, a black Mercedes just drove past me, heading for the motorway."

"The Pope's been kidnapped and is in that car. Get in your car and follow it. Catch it up and don't let it out of your sight. It's probably heading back towards London."

"You idiot!" Sally exclaimed. "I knew this was going to happen!"

She wasn't going to argue about this, however. This was her opportunity to demonstrate to Jeremy just how competent she could be out in the field. She jumped into her Golf, manoeuvred back on to the road, and drove off as fast as she could.

Chapter 9

Graham watched as Sally disappeared into the distance. He hoped that she would be able to find the kidnapper, but he doubted that she would. The kidnapper had a couple of minutes head start, and that extra time would be critical. They didn't know for sure where he was heading. He might drive back to London, but might just as easily head to Brighton. Or to Gatwick Airport. Or to anywhere else in the UK for that matter.

He got back into the Jaguar and thought. He had really been caught off guard by recent developments. He had thought he might encounter Michaels, but he really had not anticipated the kidnapper, nor the gunman. Presumably neither had Michaels.

Graham played back the events in his head. The kidnapper had arrived on site only moments before he had himself. He had left the black Mercedes in the car park, and had followed the same route as he had through the building, to the Pope's bedroom, shooting the guards as he passed through. He had clearly been prepared to kill, but had not wanted to kill the Pope. Presumably he would seek a ransom; why else would he have tried the almost impossible task of kidnapping the Pope rather than just shooting him? He was the first into the Pope's bedroom, and could quite easily have executed him in his bed. Who was the kidnapper? Whoever he was, they needed to find him and quickly. That would not be easy. He hoped that Sally would have the good sense to phone through to Jeremy. They could study the cameras on the motorway and track the car. They could mobilise helicopters to follow it. He was confident that Sally would do so. She might not have much experience in the field, but she was a smart and efficient girl.

Michaels was easier to explain. He was an opportunist. Presumably, he had only recently discovered that the Pope was on site, otherwise he would surely have concocted a more elaborate plan. Walking into the Pope's bedroom armed only with a kitchen knife was not a plan that was going to succeed. They now knew that Michaels was a member of New Reformation. Had they given him the task of killing the Pope? Was he acting on their behalf? If he was, presumably the kidnapper would not have been there – neither would the gunman for that matter. Graham thought that NR would have had a rather better plan. Perhaps, though, they had only just discovered that the Pope was there; after all, it was an unscheduled visit. Perhaps they were being opportunistic, recognising that it would be significantly easier to gain entry to a monastery in Surrey than Lambeth Palace. That might go someway to explaining the disastrous actions of Michaels.

The gunman was another matter entirely. Whilst Michaels was an amateur, this guy was a professional. He was dressed appropriately. He had a complete arsenal, including some pretty impressive weapons. He had made a far better approach to the Pope's bedroom than either Michaels or the kidnapper. He too was clearly unaware of the presence of the others. He had been about to shoot the Pope when it had all kicked off in the bedroom, resulting in a melee that he clearly had not anticipated. The gunman was no opportunist. He had known that the Pope would be at the abbey, and knew exactly where he would be spending the night. How had he known this? Who had tipped him off? Where had he come from? How had he got to the abbey?

This, Graham decided, was the lead that he needed to follow initially. Michaels was irrelevant. The kidnapper was clearly significant, but presumably he would contact the authorities with a list of demands soon. They might even be able to locate him. No, Graham thought, I need to find out who this gunman was.

Graham asked the driver to turn the car round and head back to the building. As they drove, he thought about what he could remember of the gunman. He had been tall. He had been of eastern European, possibly Russian, extraction, he was a professional. That was all he could establish in his mind at that moment.

First things first, though, he needed to fill Jeremy in. He dialled Jeremy's number and told him exactly what had happened over the last hour.

Jeremy was not particularly impressed, especially with Graham's decision to delegate chasing the kidnapper to Sally. He conceded that it was too late to change, however, and instructed Graham to speak to the abbot and to try, if he could, to establish the identity of the mystery gunman.

By the time he had put the phone down the car was back at the front of the main building. Graham noticed that the abbot, who he had encountered earlier in the evening in his pyjamas, was in the process of leaving. Now, he was dressed in his black cassock and was heading for a car. Graham needed to intervene before the abbot left the site. He jumped out of the Jaguar and called over to him.

"Excuse me!" Graham shouted. The abbot turned to Graham.

"Excuse me?" the abbot responded. Graham noticed again the Australian tinge to the tall, holy man's accent. "But who are you? You've just caused a scene of carnage in my monastery, and aided the kidnapping of the Pope! Why are you back here?"

"I can assure you that I had nothing to do with the kidnapping of the Holy Father," Graham assured the abbot. "My name is Graham Chapman, and I'm with the Hunter Group, a private security contractor working with MI5 and MI6. I came to your abbey to warn you of an attempt to kill the Pope, and that a member of the organisation who had made the threat worked at your school."

The abbot looked confused. He clearly did not know whether to believe Graham or not. Eventually, he decided that perhaps he should at least listen to what this peculiar man in the bizarre clothes had to say for himself.

"You'd better come through to my office."

The abbot led Graham back into the main building, through to the monastery at the back, and into a large, modern office with windows overlooking the grounds. The abbot indicated a seat to Graham, and he himself sat down behind the heavy oak desk.

"I'm Abbot Timothy, Graham. I think we'd better have a chat. Now, you say you work for an organisation called The Hunter Group. Who are they?"

"We're a private contractor that works with MI5 and MI6. We helped to arrange the security for the Pope's visit, and have been brought in to investigate a death threat against the Pope that was received this afternoon."

"I see. And do you have any identification?"

Graham passed over his Hunter Group photo ID card.

"That seems to verify who you are. I suppose I'll have to take what you've said on trust, even though I haven't heard of the organisation before."

"With respect, abbot, we have a serious situation here, so I think it might be a good idea for us to cooperate with each other," Graham said.

"Of course. I was getting to that," the abbot said. "As you know, the Holy Father was entrusted to my care tonight, for one night only, and I feel we have failed him significantly. If you are who you say you are, you must locate the Pope as quickly as you can. I feel that it is my duty to give you any assistance that I can to bring about a positive ending to this situation. Tell me what you know."

Graham explained how the death threat had been received from an organisation calling themselves New Reformation, and about the explosion at Lollard Street. He told the abbot that they had established that Adam Michaels was a member of NR, and how Michaels had entered the monastery armed with a kitchen knife to kill the Pope. He explained how Michaels had not been the only person who had tried to kill the Pope, and told him about the mystery gunman, and how an as-yet unknown person had successfully kidnapped the Pontiff.

"So what are you doing now?" the abbot asked.

"One of our agents is trying to locate the vehicle in which the Pope was driven away from the abbey with the aim of recovering him as quickly as possible. We have a team in London checking intelligence to identify any further threats to the Pope. I'm about to investigate the scene in the hope of establishing the identity of the gunman."

"In that case, I must help you. There's a path through the woods that leads up to the monastery. I regularly walk it myself. It leads to a narrow road at the edge of the site. I think we should take a look down there. If the gunman arrived by car, it may still be parked up there."

"Let's go," Graham said. "We'll take my car."

Two minutes later, and the abbot and Graham were sat in the back of the Jaguar. The abbot was explaining his remorse.

"I do feel that I was responsible for this whole situation, Graham. You have to understand that the Pope was here at my request. It's true that he had very generously approached me about becoming a cardinal, but that had nothing to do with his visit. He had privately indicated that, by this stage of his visit to the UK, he would be rather tired. He has already met the Queen, preached in Scotland and Birmingham, and had several private audiences. Tomorrow, of course, is his big day, when he will address what will inevitably be his largest congregation in Hyde Park. All this for a man in his eighties. He wanted the opportunity to simply relax, and to escape from the burdens of a state visit momentarily. I was only too happy to open our monastery to him. You've seen for yourself how well situated it is. It's close enough to London and Gatwick, and just off the M23, but when you're in our grounds you could be a million miles away from the capital. Usually it's so quiet. Barely anyone knows we're here."

"That's an interesting point, actually, abbot. Just how many people were aware that the Pope was visiting?"

"Hardly any. All of the monks were aware, of course, since he joined us for supper and mass this evening. The headmaster knew, other than that, I think we'd managed to keep the visit secret. The Pope came here for peace and quiet, and we could only ensure that he got that by not telling anyone of his presence. Hence the need for a low key security operation, as you no doubt noticed."

"I did, and I'll return to that point in a minute, if I may," Graham said. "I'm intrigued that the Headmaster was aware of the Pope's visit. Why was it felt necessary to bring him into the loop?"

"I always ensure that the Head is aware of comings and goings on site. He, after all, lives next to the entrance, and I also have to consider the safety and welfare of all of the pupils of our school. This is best ensured if I share these things with the Headmaster."

"Would he have mentioned the visit to anyone? The senior management team of the school, for example?"

"I know what you're getting at here, Graham. You want to know how Adam Michaels was aware of our visitor."

"I do. I need to know if he found out internally, perhaps from the Headmaster, or from someone who is not connected to the abbey."

"The only way to ascertain that fact is to ask the Head. I will of course look into that as soon as I have the opportunity to do so. I am deeply shocked to know that there was someone amongst us who wished the Pope ill. I, of course, had no idea about Adam's feelings, otherwise I would have reconsidered inviting the Holy Father to be amongst us, and would probably have suggested that Adam consider employment at another school. I must say, however, that Adam was something of an unfortunate character. He did not find life very easy. I fear that the previous Headmaster, who was a very close friend, had promoted him beyond his abilities. He had something of a hard time fulfilling his role. I do not like to speak ill of the dead, but I do suspect that Adam was somewhat limited intellectually. He had immense difficulties handling the niceties and indeed normalities of every day life, and consequently had become something of a loner in recent years. He was married and had children, but I think relations were stretched to breaking point there. His family live in the village, but Adam often used to stay over on site. Each of the boarding houses has a bed for a supervising member of staff, and Adam often used to choose to stay. He said that he felt it was his duty as Director of Pastoral Care – that's Master in Charge of Boarding to you and me – but I suspect that there were other reasons. Most of our school staff would rather sleep anywhere than in the boarding houses. I'm obviously sorry that he felt it necessary to try to kill the Holy Father, but I suspect that there were deeper issues lurking beneath the surface. I'm also greatly saddened that he had to die in such an unpleasant way."

"You're a good man, abbot, and you clearly have a great love for your staff. Leaving Michaels aside for a moment, I'd like to know what the reasoning behind the limited security was. I would have thought, as someone who works in the security services, that the presence of the Pope would have required a significant security presence. Yet I saw very little to suggest that was the case on site this evening. I managed to drive up to the abbey and enter the main building with no trouble at all. It seems that our kidnapper did too. And our gunman managed to get to within a few feet of the Pope's bed. How was that allowed to happen?"

"As I said, his Holiness wanted to escape here for a little while. The public story was that he was staying in London with the Archbishop of Canterbury. Most of the Holy Father's security team remained at Lambeth Palace tonight. It was felt that leaving the security there would act as a decoy. If the entire team were relocated to the abbey, it would have been obvious to anyone who cared to look that the Holy Father was staying with us. His Holiness finds the whole security operation a great strain. He is followed around every day of his life by a large team of men, and has almost no privacy whatsoever. He had hoped that coming to Surrey would allow him to snatch just a few hours of quiet to himself. Had people known that he was here he would have been inundated with visitors – fellow believers, of course, but also the press, the general public, those who were merely curious, and potentially those who wished him ill. It would be very hard indeed to provide a secure cordon around our premises here, simply because of the geography of the area. Even with the full security team present, the Pope would have been considerably less safe that he would be in London. So for all those reasons, security was kept to a minimum tonight."

"I suppose that makes sense, but it still seems like an awfully big risk to me," Graham replied. "Perhaps it's just because I'm paranoid. Had it been me, I would have insisted he stayed in London. It would have been significantly easier to keep the Pope safe."

"Sorry to interrupt, gents."

For the first time during the short journey, the driver spoke.

"I think you should see this."

121

The car pulled to a stop. They had reached the country lane at the rear of the abbey's site. In front of them, a car was ablaze. A man stood by watching. When he saw the Jaguar, he began running into the woods, heading in the opposite direction to the abbey.

Giuseppe Campanaro was well aware of all that had happened at his school that night. He liked to think that not a lot got past him, although he was ashamed to admit that his staff might have a different take on that point.

Campanaro was a large man. He hadn't always been so rotund, but in recent years he had put on a great deal of weight. He was slightly embarrassed at just how huge he had allowed himself to become, and had intended to lose some weight, but had never quite managed to do it. He enjoyed his food too much.

Whilst his name sounded Italian, he did not. Both of his parents had hailed from Italy, but they had moved to England before he was born. Campanaro had spent his childhood in London, and, if he had an accent at all, it was a slight east end twang. He had worked hard over the years to eliminate it, feeling that it wasn't in keeping with his role of teacher, and latterly headmaster, in posh, independent schools, but there was always that slight edge that gave him away, particularly when he was tired.

Campanaro had previously been the Headmaster of a large school in Kent, but had felt rather out of his depth. He was therefore thrilled when he had been appointed to the Headship of Charlwood Abbey School two years earlier. The school was considerably smaller than his previous school, and he had hoped that he would find it easier to manage. If anything, though, Charlwood had proven even more of a handful. It was small, but it was currently going through a very difficult period. There was no money to invest, and the governors had racked up considerable debt over the last few years simply trying to bring the buildings up to a reasonable standard. School fees were high by necessity, yet there was very little to show for the investment made by the parents; no Astroturf, no swimming pool, no language lab. None of the features that other fee-paying schools liked to boast about.

Then there were the staff. It had proven very difficult to attract teachers to what was clearly a struggling school in the middle of nowhere. Those who could not see beyond the beautiful setting when they first visited quickly realised that perhaps they should not have been quite so keen to accept a job at Charlwood; the image it gave of a calm, restful institution were very far from the experiences of most people. Staff illness was high, and a number of teachers were off on long-term sick as a consequence of stress. Several had simply "disappeared" over the last couple of years, never to be seen or heard from again.

The monastic community were a crippling nightmare as far as he was concerned. Most, if not all of the monks felt that they should have a role in the running of the school. Every decision that Campanaro took was overruled by the monks. He regularly found monks wandering around the site, sticking their oars in where they were not welcome. All in all, they proved to be an undermining influence that meant that Campanaro simply could not run the school how he wished. It drove him absolutely mad.

As for the abbot, well, he was a complete nightmare. Campanaro had never managed to adjust to having someone effectively as his day-to-day boss. As the head of the Charlwood community, the abbot could overrule the school's headmaster on pretty much anything he chose, and he frequently did. Campanaro often felt that he was little more than the abbot's puppet. As time had progressed, he had become more and more concerned about his relationship with the abbot. There was just something about the abbot that made Campanaro unable to avoid doing exactly as he was told. Normally he was a tough character who could stand up to anyone, but he found it impossible to argue with the abbot. The abbot's controlling influence was beginning to stretch beyond just his work, and was beginning to impact on other areas of his life. He had even listened to him when he wanted to buy a new car. He had wanted to replace his Range Rover with a newer model, but somehow the abbot had convinced him that there was no need to invest so much money in a flashy car, and had persuaded him to buy a Mondeo instead.

His unhappiness with the school was not only impacting on his work, but it was also destroying his family life. He found himself arguing with his wife who was worried about the impact that the abbot seemed to have on her husband's life, and he saw his children far less that he would like. At idle moments, he dreamt about killing the abbot in a cruel and vindictive manner. Perhaps then he would be able to escape his control and run the school how he wanted to.

Campanaro had put this idea behind him, however, realising that it was just an idiotic dream.

Then he found out that the Pope was coming to visit. In his daydreams he thought about punishing the abbot by bumping off the Pope. That would show him who was boss. What better way of punishing the Catholic Church for making his life a misery than killing its head? That idea, though, was even more idiotic than killing the abbot and he had put the idea firmly behind him. Until one of his friends had introduced him to someone he referred to only as 'an acquaintance'. This 'acquaintance', he was told was the representative of a group who wanted the Pope dead. He had offered Campanaro a very large sum of money if he poisoned the Pope. Campanaro had paused very briefly to reflect on the proposition, but had quickly decided that he would go through with the plan. Not only would it irritate the abbot, but it would make Campanaro a very wealthy man.

Campanaro had been somewhat surprised when Adam Michaels, a member of his senior management team, had told him that he was a member of an organisation that wanted to kill the Pope during his visit to the UK. Campanaro did not think for one minute that Michaels would be able to pull off the murder of the Pope. He thought that Michaels was a complete idiot – most people at the school did – but he had seen an opportunity develop. Maybe he could use Michaels to bump off the Pope, whilst he claimed the cash.

Michaels plan had been primitive at best. He had hoped to secure a gun and shoot the Holy Father in cold blood. Campanaro knew that there was no chance of this plan succeeding; it was just one more example of Michaels' moronic tendencies. Campanaro had suggested that poison might be more effective, and also far harder to trace the murderer. The two men had spent several hours discussing the best options, and had eventually agreed on a plan. Michaels would try to strike the Pope whilst he slept. If he survived the night, Campanaro would poison him at breakfast the next morning.

That night, Campanaro had intended to head to his office around eleven. He had persuaded the governors to install CCTV around the site, and this had been accomplished, very surreptitiously. The feed led into Campanaro's office in the main building. From his desk, he could see pretty much every part of the site – including throughout the monastery. He had hoped, therefore, that he would be able to watch Michaels attempts to dispatch the Pope from his desk.

Before he headed up to his office, he had become aware of unusual activity around the site. From his house he had watched as a Mercedes MPV pulled up to the gates, then disappeared into the woodland opposite. A while later, the same car had driven up to the gates a second time. This time, the driver had entered the code and driven up to the main building. A short while later, a Jaguar had also pulled up to the gates and headed up to the main building. Highly suspicious activity, which left Campanaro assuming that something was afoot.

He gave the Jaguar a few minutes head start, and then walked up to his office, where he had booted up his computer and watched the action play out on the CCTV screens. He watched as a man entered the Pope's bedroom and then attempted to carry the Holy Father out through the bedroom window. He watched as Michaels intercepted the second man, before heading to the bedroom. He saw the gunman start shooting into the bedroom. And he saw the skirmish that followed, that resulted in Michaels being shot, the gunman being shot, and the kidnapper rushing through the main building to his car with the Pope on his back.

Campanaro had known that Michaels would fail, and realised that he would there was every possibility that he would be killed in the process. Never mind, one less moron on the planet. Few would weep for Michaels. He had not foreseen the extraordinary events that had unfolded before his eyes.

Campanaro had no idea if the kidnapper would attempt to kill the Pope, but that was immaterial. Having decided on his crackpot plan to kill the Pope, he would go through with it and kill the Pontiff himself. He had no intention of backtracking, not when there was so much cash on offer. His plan would have to change slightly, but he had the poison ready, and he would be able to pinpoint the Pope to within a few metres.

Campanaro waited for the one remaining intruder to head back to his car, then walked back down to his house.

Chapter 10

Jeremy put down the phone. He could feel himself shaking. He was shocked and horrified at the news from Charlwood. What should have been a simple visit had turned into something of a nightmare.

The biggest issue was that they had lost the Pope. Despite all the carefully laid plans, despite everything that had been done, the Pope had been kidnapped.

Jeremy did not know how the Hunter Group would survive this one. There were many within the intelligence community who despised the Hunter Group and all that it stood for. To Jeremy and his supporters, the group was invaluable. It was able to carry out so-called dark operations that the mainstream intelligence agencies would never be able to get away with in these politically-correct, human rights obsessed times. Any dark operation carried out by his team would be deniable by the likes of MI5 or MI6, even if they had ordered it. The Hunter Group also represented exceptional value for money. In recent years, particularly since the economic crash of the late noughties, the intelligence services had found their budgets hacked back to nothing. They simply could not afford to station active agents everywhere they wanted to these days, and the mobility of their agents was not as guaranteed as it once was. The Hunter Group provided highly trained agents, however, capable of working in any field of operations at short notice, which cost very little. It was hardly surprising, then, that more and more intelligence work was being farmed out to small, low cost, private outfits like the Hunter Group.

That would all stop if they messed up tonight. Jeremy had spent several years building up the credibility of his group. It had not been easy, but through hard graft, and being extremely good at what they did, they had survived the course, and were now regarded as one of the finest private intelligence contractors in the world. They were regarded as better even than Westhaven Military Intelligence, a highly regarded contractor in the United States that Jeremy had led after climbing the ranks of the CIA.

To their detractors, though, the Hunter Group was regarded as an ill-disciplined, illegal group of mercenaries who would do anything for money. Some viewed them as a bunch of rank amateurs who should not be trusted, despite all the evidence to the contrary. Losing the Pope, though, would enable their opponents to claim that they had been correct all along, that the Hunter Group were a waste of space. In fact, a high profile failure like this could threaten the whole system of private intelligence contracting. Jeremy had spent most of his working life in the field, and he was loath to be responsible for its downfall. He was also regarded as one of the leading proponents of the concept of private intelligence. If his organisation messed up, there was every possibility that he would never work in the field again. He had devoted too much of his life to the world of private intelligence for it to fail now.

Jeremy's life had taken a rather bizarre trajectory. He had completed his BA in War Studies at Kings College London in just two years, before serving as a Royal Marines Commando for two years. He had then returned to Kings to study for a Masters degree in international diplomacy, before completing a PhD in international espionage at the George Washington University in Washington DC in a further two years. Whilst in Washington he had attracted the attention of the CIA, and had worked with the agency for four years before being recruited by Westhaven Military Intelligence as one of their youngest ever security directors. After just two years in the post, he had been headhunted by MI5 to establish a private outfit along the lines of Westhaven Military Intelligence in the UK. So it was that the Hunter Group was formed. In comparative terms it was tiny, yet it had a reputation within the intelligence community as a world-class operator.

All that would be sacrificed if they messed up tonight. Jeremy simply could not allow the Pope to disappear – or worse still, be murdered – on his watch. Graham was his friend, but he had messed up this evening. There was no way that he should have left Sally to chase the kidnapper's vehicle. That was a gross misjudgement. Graham was correct that they needed to establish the identity of the mystery gunman, but not at the expense of losing the Pope. Graham was a highly trained and, contrary to what the other members of the team might think, a highly effective field agent. Sally was a secretary. If they did lose the Pope, then Graham would have to accept responsibility. He always maintained that he had never wanted to work for Jeremy, and tonight it was looking as if he might get his wish. Friend or not, Graham would have to be dismissed unless he made serious amends for his stupid actions.

Jeremy poured himself a glass of mineral water. He needed something significantly stronger, but he needed to keep a clear head. He dropped some ice cubes into his glass and swirled them around, producing that relaxing clanking sound that always accompanied a nice glass of whisky. It didn't seem nearly so effective at easing his nerves without the whisky.

He would need to get the rest of the team together. They needed to really up the ante in the coming hour if tonight was not to end in failure. They needed to start finding names and pulling people in. They had to get to the bottom of New Reformation and CARN, and quickly. They needed to find Paul Fish. At the moment, his was the only name they had. He seemed to know more than anyone else about what was going on.

He was the only one who could explain what was happening. How hard was it to hunt him down and pull him in? Graham should have grabbed him at Liverpool Street – yet another of his failures. Never mind that now though. They needed to locate him and bring him in, kicking and screaming if necessary.

Jeremy looked at the time. It was almost midnight. He should get the others in and check on progress. Perhaps someone had made a breakthrough. Maybe something had turned up in the CCTV. Maybe Anthony had found another lead. There had to be a loose end somewhere they could tug at. Perhaps by the time they had finished their meeting there would be good news from Sally or Graham. If Sally had located the Pope, perhaps things would look better. He realised that was unlikely, but he had to hope. Maybe Graham would discover who the gunman was. There was more chance of that. The question was whether it would do them any good at all.

Jeremy picked up the phone and dialled Anthony's number. Let's get them in, he thought.

The car was well ablaze. Graham knew that they were going to get little intelligence from the burn out wreck, but the driver – well, that was different. He had to get him.

"Stay here, both of you!" Graham shouted at the abbot and the driver as he jumped out of the

Jaguar. "Move the Jag well back before the fuel tank blows!"

He could feel the heat from the wreck of the burning car as he took off into the woods. The fire was crackling away well, and it was only a matter of time before the fuel tank went up in what would be a not insignificant explosion.

Not another chase, he thought. I'm not cut out for this. I need to lose some weight and take more exercise. I'm a chicken delivery boy, for goodness' sake, not a secret agent!

Luckily, whilst Paul Fish had been significantly fitter than Graham, the driver of the BMW was much older, and about as rotund as Graham himself was. Things should be more even this time, Graham hoped.

The driver was moving at a surprisingly reasonable pace, despite that. He was heading deeper and deeper into the woods following what seemed to be a well-established footpath.

It was getting darker and darker as they got further and further into the woods. Neither of the men could see very much at all. As it got harder to make out what was in front of him, the driver began to slow, not significantly, but a little.

Soon he paused momentarily. Graham tried to up his pace, but he was going as fast as he could. He could barely breathe now. If he ran any faster he would collapse with exhaustion and he would never catch the driver.

The driver looked around him, and shot off to the left. He had clearly found a crossroads. Graham followed, pleased that he had made some headway against the driver.

Seconds later, and the driver again changed direction, this time heading off to the right. When Graham reached the same spot, he noticed that the driver was heading off the beaten track. Risky, he thought.

The driver slowed down further as he carefully navigated around plants and debris on the woodland floor.

Graham had no wish to injure himself, so slowed down more significantly than the driver. The he remembered he had a handgun in his pocket.

He tried to take it out of his pocket as he ran, and, after slowing a little, managed to retrieve it. He aimed it towards the driver. If he was going to get a clear shot, he would have to stop. If he stopped, the driver would manage to retreat into the darkness and be able to hide.

Graham could not risk losing another witness.

He continued to run, but decided to let off a shot to warn the driver that he was armed. He aimed low and pulled the trigger. The gun emitted a loud 'crack' the echoed around the woodland.

The driver picked up speed.

Excellent, Graham thought. Not what I wanted to happen.

Graham put the gun away, and tried to up his pace. Graham was puffing away as hard as he could, and, although he was not catching the driver up, he was not losing ground to him.

This was going to be a race of stamina.

Or it would have been had he not lost the driver.

One second he was directly in front of him, no more than a few metres away. The next he'd disappeared.

Shit, Graham thought. He slowed down. There was almost no light out here in the depths of the wood, but his eyes were beginning to adjust to the darkness.

He had to be around here somewhere. He must have dived for shelter.

Graham picked up a large stick and began beating the undergrowth, hoping that he would find the driver somewhere.

Come on, come on, he thought. I cannot lose you.

Suddenly he heard the crack of a gun behind him. He felt a bullet whiz past his left ear, only millimetres away from his head. He threw himself to the ground and turned to where he thought the shot had come from. He couldn't see anything.

A minute or so went by, and then the driver let off another shot. It flew over Graham's head. The driver clearly only had a rough idea where Graham was. He was firing blind and hoping for the best. Graham decided to join in. He pulled out his gun again and let off a shot in the direction he thought the driver was. The sound echoed around the thick woodland, but there was no scream or any other sound to suggest that the bullet had made contact with anything living.

A couple of seconds later, the driver replied with another shot. His guess as to where Graham was sitting was better this time. The shot was at the level of his head, but a good four feet off to the left. One more shot and there was every chance he could hit. Graham had to get him.

If only I'd brought a machine gun, Graham thought.

In the distance, there was a blinding flash and an enormous explosion ripped through the silence of the night. The fuel tank had gone up.

Some of the light from the blazing fire percolated through the trees into the woodland. It looked as if they had run in a loop, since the car was only a few hundred yards off to their left.

Graham tried to take advantage of the light, aware that the driver would be too. He scanned the woods in front of him. Then he saw it. A blackberry bush directly in front of him was shaking. There was someone, or something, hiding in it. Painful, Graham thought. But not as painful as this.

Graham let off three rounds into the blackberry bush. He heard a groan and waited to see if the driver returned fire. One minute. Two minutes. Three minutes. Nothing.

Aware that he could be heading into an ambush, Graham very carefully walked over to the bush. There, hidden in the centre amongst the brambles was the body of the driver. Graham grabbed his arms and pulled him out of the bush. He checked for breathing and a pulse. Nothing.

He was dead.

The second lead they had found, and he was dead.

Jeremy was not going to be impressed.

Sally had driven after the Mercedes at breakneck speed. Having been so critical of Graham over the years, she knew that she had to make a breakthrough. She also knew that the chances of tracking down a high-speed car that had a five-minute head start on her were going to be next to impossible.

Within seconds of leaving the abbey, she hit the M23. She had to take a chance on the direction that the car had taken. The Mercedes could have turned south towards Brighton or north towards London. She figured that the odds were about seventy thirty in favour of London, so she joined the M23 heading north.

When she joined the motorway she pushed her car up to 110 mph and began to curse not having picked up a pool car that would have given her more speed. Still, she figured that her car was probably capable of going faster than the kidnapper's MPV.

She practically flew along the motorway, and was heading for the M25 interchange. She hadn't seen any sign of the Merc. Assuming that he had headed north, she had to catch up with the kidnapper before he reached the M25, otherwise he'd be as good as lost. At that point he could continue heading north, or could turn off onto the London orbital heading in either direction. One of three directions. The chances of Sally catching him then would be significantly reduced.

Just as Sally was about to give up, she saw the tail lights of what looked like a fast moving MPV about half a mile in front of her. It was approaching the M25 interchange. Sally's foot was already flat on the floor, and she couldn't squeeze anything else out of her poor little car. 116 mph. It would give her no more. She was gaining, slowly, on the car. As she got closer, it certainly looked like an MPV. She hoped it was the right one.

The MPV was approaching the M25 interchange. It was positioning itself to come off. Which direction would it head in? Sally couldn't tell. She overtook a slow moving lorry stuck firmly in the middle lane. She lost sight of the MPV as she did.

Shit.

She pulled in front of the truck and saw the car in front of her once again. It was definitely the right MPV. It was turning off, heading for the clockwise direction towards Heathrow. Sally was still slowly gaining. She signalled to turn off, also lining up for Heathrow. The MPV was no more than a couple of hundred yards in front of her now. She could do this.

At the last moment the MPV changed its mind, and turned onto the slip road for the anti-clockwise direction. Sally had sufficient distance between her car and the MPV to change direction too.

The slip road followed a very sharp trajectory to join the M25. The signs indicated that the safe speed to take the bend was 55 mph. Sally slowed down. The MPV didn't. It took the racing line down the middle of the carriageway, and finally began to slow down. It was now going slower than Sally.

As the MPV hit the bend, there were just a few yards between the two cars. Then, unexpectedly, the MPV driver pulled on the handbrake, and the car span through 360 degrees. It didn't stop there. It went through another 180 degrees. Sally was still travelling at over 80 miles an hour. She swerved to avoid the spinning MPV and passed it without making contact. As she went round the tight bend, she lost sight of the kidnapper's car, which was now travelling back down the slip road. She took her eyes off the road in front, and peered over her shoulder.

Shit.

She'd lost the car.

Just as she turned round, she saw a large motorway sign a matter of yards in front of her. She couldn't stop. She was going too fast. She knew what was going to happen.

Sally's car hit the sign at 70 miles per hour. The sign entered the car's engine compartment.

Chapter 11

Jeremy had gathered Anthony, Tom and Helena in his office to fill them in on the events in Charlwood, and in the hope that one of them might have made a breakthrough. He was not optimistic.

"Things are worse than we thought," he told his team. "It looks like we've got more than one organisation trying to take the Pope out. The best case scenario is that we have one shambolic organisation behind the threats, but that really doesn't pan out when we consider what else has gone on tonight."

"Do I take it that Graham has not managed to persuade the Pope to return to London?" asked Helena.

"I'm afraid it's far worse than that. When Graham arrived at the abbey, he found the corridor to the Pope's bedroom littered with the bodies of Papal security guards. Before he could get through to the Pope himself, he was accosted by Adam Michaels, the NR member on the school staff. He lunged for Graham with a knife, before being distracted by the monks. When Graham reached the Pope's bedroom, he found him in the process of being kidnapped by an as-yet unknown intruder. Whilst the kidnap was in progress, a gunman appeared at the bedroom window and started taking pot shots at the Pope, as well as the others in the room."

There was a moment of shocked silence as the team attempted to get their heads round what had happened.

"Christ," muttered Anthony under his breath.

"So...?" asked Helena.

"Whilst Graham was dealing with Michaels and the gunman, the kidnapper was able to make his way out of the bedroom. Unfortunately he had the Pope with him. Both Michaels and the gunman were killed."

"So do we know where the Pope is now?" asked Helena.

"Not as yet. Sally witnessed the kidnapper's car being driven away. She is trying to locate the car. Anthony, we have a registration number and description of the car. I'd be grateful if you could follow that one up, see if we can establish who the kidnapper is."

"Will do. What about the gunman? Do we know who he was?"

"At this stage we have no idea. Graham is trying to retrace his steps to see if he can establish any leads on that front."

"Can we just replay this?" asked Helena. "We know that Michaels was a member of New Reformation. They were the group that issued the threat against the Pope, so we can assume that they, as an organisation, and their members individually, want the Pope dead. Do we think that Michaels was acting on their behalf, or was he just some random nutter?"

"I don't think there's any doubt that he was, as you put it, some random nutter. He clearly had not thought through his attempt to kill the Pope, and had just decided on the spur of the moment that it would be a good idea. He was armed with a kitchen knife, which suggests that he had not undertaken any planning at all. Had the guards not already been taken out, then there is no way that he would have been able to get through to the Pope's bedroom. I think we can put him down as an irritant that happened to be in the wrong place at the wrong time. The gunman, however, gives the impression of being a pro. I think if we can discover his identity we will have a useful lead."

"You say Graham's retracing the gunman's steps, but do we know anything at all about him at this stage?" Helena asked.

"We know that he was of Russian or eastern European origin. We also know that he was equipped with a whole arsenal of state of the art equipment. I've just heard from Graham's driver who tells me that Graham has established that the gunman was driven to the back of the abbey and made his way up to the building on foot. Graham has found the car, and spotted his accomplice. Unfortunately, the accomplice seems to have found out that the gunman was killed and took fright. He torched the car, and was last seen legging it into the woods. I don't think we'll be able to get much information from the car, unfortunately, although, once again, Anthony, we have the details so if you could run a trace that would be helpful."

A thought stirred through Helena's mind at the news of the discovery of the car.

"Tell me more about the car, Jeremy."

"It was a brand new BMW X6. What's sparked your interest?"

"A bloody ridiculous car," Anthony offered.

"I think I know who the gunman is."

"Really? Spill the beans then!"

"Well, when I say I know who he is, I can't give you a name at this stage, but I hope to be able to very soon. I've seen that car before this evening though."

"Where?"

"Hold on, and I'll fill you in," Helena said. "I've been trawling through CCTV footage trying to find our white van. I'm happy to tell you that our white van is no more, and is no longer a risk. It was driven to an industrial unit in Elephant and Castle, where it was blown up. After the white van had parked up inside one of the units, a black BMW X6 pulled up outside. A man got out, and fired a large missile into the unit, destroying it and the van. Now, this is pure speculation, but it makes sense to me that the man who blew up the van was the same person who blew up our flat earlier this evening. The weapon used in Lollard Street, according to Wiggy, was a shoulder mounted missile launcher, and it looks to me like this is exactly the same weapon that was used in Elephant and Castle."

"Get some screenshots of this over to Wiggy as soon as we've finished here and see if he can verify that it's the same weapon that was used at Lollard Street. Then compare the registration numbers with Anthony to see if the BMW is the same one that has just been incinerated in Surrey. This is excellent, Helena, well done. I feel like we're making progress here."

"All we need to do now is to establish the identity of the kidnapper. Right – back to work, team."

Helena and Tom stood up to leave.

"Before we all head off, I have some updates myself," Anthony said, rather miffed at being overlooked.

"So sorry, Anthony," Jeremy said as the others sat back down. "What's new?"

"I think I've tracked down the reference to Infinitum UK in Paul Fish's tweet. It seems to be an organisation led by a human rights lawyer by the name of Philip Brown. The organisation has been rather quiet, but it is a Catholic organisation that wants to demonstrate what the church really stands for to the wider world."

"Not another militant Catholic group, please?" exclaimed Helena. "I'm getting a little sick of their squabbles."

"No, in this case Infinitum is a peaceful organisation that wants to re-establish the Catholic Church as a force for good."

"So how are they linked to this mess, then?" asked Jeremy.

"I need to do some more work on that front. What it looks like at this stage is that Paul Fish had identified New Reformation and was aware of the threat that they posed. He was affirming the existence of New Reformation in a message to Philip Brown. He also seems to have told Brown about NR's plan to take out CARN, but I can't be sure about that."

"I'm getting a little sick of this Fish character," Jeremy commented. "He seems to hold the key to this whole situation. I now want to make locating him a priority. Helena, you get out there and find him, wherever he may be. Do whatever is necessary to bring him in for questioning. Anthony, I want you to get an address for this Brown character. When you've done that, check the details of the gunman's BMW and the kidnapper's Mercedes, and then see if you can get an ID of the gunman from Helena's CCTV. Tom, once Anthony has tracked Brown down, I want you to get him in here. Let's start wrapping this up."

So much intelligence work in the twenty-first century is carried out electronically that Anthony found himself increasingly busy at the Hunter

Group. It seemed that no case would be solved, no terrorist intercepted, and no villain apprehended without his involvement. Anthony got an enormous kick out of this, and enjoyed being a central cog in the machine that was the team. He also had the greatest admiration for all of his colleagues. He practically worshipped the ground that Jeremy walked on. He was so grateful to him for recruiting him and for trusting him so implicitly with the tasks that he carried out. Tom was a smart guy who he had a lot of time for, even if he did know very little about him. Helena, meanwhile, seemed to be almost superhuman as far as he was concerned. Graham was a character, and, although he considered him to be rather bizarre, he recognised his superior intellect. Sally could be a little brusque, but was okay really. Of all the team, he probably spent the most time with Sally, since they were the two most routinely left behind whilst the others were out saving the world. He enjoyed chatting to her, though, and was sure that her time in the field would come.

Tonight was proving to be a particularly busy night for Anthony. Some of the only breakthroughs that had been made so far were a direct consequence of Anthony's work. Now he had a list of tasks as long as his arm to carry out. He recognised the importance of each, though, so as soon as he returned to his office, be began working through the tasks. He could have done with some food, but would only stop once he had completed his tasks satisfactorily.

His first task was to find Paul Fish. He was getting increasingly irritated with Fish. He seemed to be the central character of so much of this investigation. Anthony recognised the importance of finding him and bringing him in, since he seemed to know most of the answers that the team was searching for,

Anthony began by checking Fish's Foursquare account. Funnily enough, he had not made the same mistake he had made earlier on, and had not checked into the geolocation game since he had been at the Railway Tavern. His status now read "Off the grid." That would make it slightly trickier to locate him, but Anthony was confident he could find him relatively easily nonetheless.

His first step was to check whether Fish had a MobileMe account. Some iPhone users had registered for an account of online tools from Apple, one of which, the 'Find My Phone' tool, enabled someone who had lost their phone to track it simply by clicking a button on the website. Anthony hacked into Apple's database with ease, and ran a search for 'Paul Fish'. Quite a number were listed. Most could be ruled out since their billing addresses were in the USA. Three showed up in the UK, but none were listed in London. Fish activated the Find My Phone tool for each user. One was in Cornwall, one in Hertfordshire, and one in Newcastle. The Hertfordshire user could theoretically be Fish, although it was unlikely. Anthony made a note of the details anyway.

Anthony next hacked into the networks of the mobile phone operators to see if any of them had an iPhone user called Paul Fish. He found quite a number, but ruled out most simply by checking their billing addresses. There were several in the south of England. Anthony bookmarked the relevant pages, and then brought up an online tool created by a fellow hacker he knew that enabled anyone who could access the site to hack into the GPS chipset of an iPhone. Anthony entered his login details, and began checking the location of every Paul Fish in southern England. He found one that looked like a distinct possibility; the user was currently in Stratford. The web tool had a "breadcrumbs" feature that traced the movements of an iPhone over the last week. Anthony tracked through the last few hours of movement shown for the Stratford handset, and bingo - just a few hours ago this particular Paul Fish had been in Liverpool Street. Anthony checked the address for Fish's current whereabouts, and sent an email through to Helena to let her know. He bookmarked the page on the tracking site for Fish's phone. He would now be able to see exactly where Fish was at any given time, unless he turned his phone off.

Having found Fish, Anthony next turned his attention to tracking down Philip Brown's address. This, he thought, should be much easier.

He flicked back through his notes to establish what they already knew about Brown. He found the print he had made of the article from the *Page Chronicle*. Brown was a Catholic who led (past tense? Anthony thought) a movement called Infinitum. There was very little information about the movement in existence. It did not appear to have been a great success.

Anthony logged onto Brown's website once more – philipbrown.co.uk. Brown was a London-based human rights lawyer, who lived in Hampstead with his wife, Tessa, and daughters Sophie and Flora. Brown's website was unsurprisingly not any more specific as to Brown's address, but there were ways and means of locating him.

I should have done this before, Anthony thought, but he had been rushed off his feet all night, and Brown had not been his highest priority.

Anthony always started any search with the most obvious tool. If he wanted to find out something about an individual, seventy per cent of the time Google would give him the answers he wanted. If he needed an address or a phone number, BT's online phonebook was often surprisingly helpful. People were starting to wise up as to how simple it was to track them down, however, and so it was becoming more common than it once was to be ex-directory. BT was also just one phone service provider amongst many these days, and often these other companies did not share their data quite as generously as BT.

Anthony pulled up the BT website, and after he had navigated through all the guff about BT's broadband being the fastest in the UK (speeds of up to 20 Mbps. Yeah right, Anthony thought. 'Up to', as in nowhere near), he eventually found a small link that took him through to directory enquiries.

He entered "Brown" into the name field, and "N6" for the location field and clicked 'Search'. Eight results were returned, but only one that could possibly be Philip Brown, a P. R. Brown at 10, Hampstead Lane, London N6. Bingo. Just to double check, and just because it gave him a great deal of satisfaction just to be able to do it, Anthony also hacked into the Bar Council's database. They showed a Philip Brown at the same address. It must be the one. Anthony composed a short email to Tom with the address and sent it off.

Anthony next sent stills of the CCTV footage of the missile used at Elephant and Castle to Wiggy, with a request to confirm whether this was fired using the same weapon used at Lollard Street. He asked for confirmation as soon as possible, and, just to be on the safe side, also sent

Wiggy a text message telling him to check his email ASAP.

Next, Anthony logged onto the Police National Computer to check out the number plates of the vehicles used that night. Anthony always used to get a huge buzz accessing the PNC, but these days he had been granted permission to access it, and had even been given his own username and password. The excitement was not the same.

Anthony started with a search for the gunman's BMW X6. Its registered keeper was, as Anthony had suspected, a hire company, specifically Heathrow Car Rentals Group Ltd. Anthony knew that this was a large company that operated most of the big-name franchises at Heathrow Airport. A quick search through their database showed that the X6 had been hired out to a Russian citizen, Dmitri Nagragov. Anthony made a note so that he could trace the name shortly.

Next up was the Mercedes used to kidnap the Pope. This also turned out to be a hire car, the registered keeper listed as Avis Car Hire (UK) Ltd. Anthony brought up their database and ran a search. He could not believe the result that was returned. He exited the system and tried again, just to be sure.

This did not make sense. How could this be?

The Mercedes had been hired earlier that night from St. Pancras Train Station by one Philip Brown of 10, Hampstead Lane, London.

The same Philip Brown who led Infinitum, and had met with Paul Fish that evening.

Chapter 12

Tom had been hoping for a rather less busy night. He had been seeing a girl for a few weeks now, and things were going very well. They had planned a quiet date tonight – a nice meal in a tiny little Afghan restaurant he knew in Islington, and then onto the cinema to see a romcom. Tom hated romcoms, but Julia, somewhat unexpectedly, loved them. For a hardnosed member of the Met's Flying Squad, she had a surprisingly soft side. Tom thought that it was probably the juxtaposition of hard-as-nails and soft-as-Kleenex that he found himself attracted to. They had first met some time ago whilst Tom was still in the Met himself, but had only started dating once he had moved on to join the Hunter Group. She was his first serious girlfriend since the death of his wife nearly four years previously, and he wanted to keep hold of this one.

Tom was proud of his police background, and it had proved very useful on numerous occasions since he had joined Jeremy's little outfit. He had previously worked for the Metropolitan Police's Anti-Terrorist Branch, usually known as SO13, which had been subsumed into Counter Terrorism Command with its merger with Special Branch in 2006. He was quickly promoted through the ranks, reaching the post of Superintendent within a handful of years of graduating with a degree in chemistry from

Imperial College in London. He was unique amongst the Hunter Group in that he was not employed by Jeremy; he remained employed by the Met, but was on long-term secondment to the team. He had initially been recruited as a liaison officer. His primary function was to liaise with the police, but the role included liaison with other security services both within the UK and around the world. Consequently he had built up a number of important contacts that had proven invaluable for the Hunter Group. He had also proven invaluable as a field agent, however, especially in times of crisis.

Tom was also unique amongst the Hunter Group in that you could tell just by looking at him that he was a hard nut. Whilst most of the others in the team looked like accountants working in the city – with the exception of Graham who looked, well, like a chicken delivery boy – Tom was built like a brick house. At six feet six tall, he was eighteen stone of pure muscle, and certainly not someone you would want to antagonise.

Luckily for those who knew him, Tom was very hard to antagonise. He might be big, but he was extremely calm and placid. Whilst at work, he kept himself to himself, and his fellow team members knew very little about him. They knew vaguely that he had been in the police, but he could have spent his entire career as a beat PC in the West End and they would have been none the wiser.

Having lost his evening with Julia, Tom had hoped to see some action tonight. At least if he had an exciting night at work it might make up for missing his date. Unfortunately, most of his evening had been spent trying to extract information from the police about what they knew regarding the threat to the Pope. For some reason, they were keeping very quiet indeed. Either that, or they really did know very little. Tom was pleased, therefore, to have finally got out of the office and to be out and about. He doubted that tonight's trip to Hampstead to find Philip Brown's family would be particularly exciting. You could never tell what might happen when working with the Hunter Group, though.

He had taken one of the pool Jaguars from the underground car park, driven out of the City, and was now belting up the A1 at high speed. He pulled off the A1 at Upper Holloway and turned onto Highgate Hill. This was an area he knew reasonably well, since he had an aunt who lived nearby, and he was always amazed at how the feel of the area changed remarkably after passing the Whittington Hospital. Holloway was by no means the worst part of London, but it was not particularly pleasant either. Highgate, on the other hand, was full of charm. By driving just a few hundred yards up the road, one left behind the urban grime of inner city London, and passed into a rather more tranquil spot that could have passed for a rural community somewhere out in the sticks. Tom could see why lawyers like Brown chose to live here. It was only lawyers and other people with very well paid jobs who could afford to live here.

Tom pulled over outside a pub called the Gatehouse. Although it was late, there was still evidence of activity within. He thought he could hear strains of a live band inside. He turned the courtesy light on inside the car and checked his iPhone. The address Anthony had given him was on Hampstead Lane, just a few minutes up the road. He turned the light off, and continued on.

The houses in this part of London were simply stunning - enormous great piles that reflected the affluence of those who lived there. Just a few minutes ago Tom had been passing grim, 1960s tower blocks. Now he was passing large, gated properties that could best be described as mansions. The diversity of housing in London was just incredible.

When he arrived at Brown's house it was, like most of the properties in the road, huge. It nestled behind a tall brick wall topped with iron railings. Large double, wrought iron gates secured the property from the road. In the drive were parked three cars - a black Range Rover Sport, a Mercedes saloon, and a rather less extravagant Nissan Micra. The house itself had a large central porch, each side of which were two enormous wings, a gable end topping each off. The property ran to three floors, four if you included what looked like a substantial basement beneath the house.

What attracted Tom's attention most, however, was not the size or opulence of the property, but the fact that it was on fire.

The downstairs of the property was already well ablaze. The kitchen windows had recently blown out, and flames were soaring through the empty holes.

Tom considered what he should do. Leave the emergency call to someone else, he thought. Someone would spot the fire soon enough. There were people in the house who were clearly unaware of the fire, and he needed to get them out.

Tom climbed over the wrought iron gates, and dropped down to the driveway the other side. He ran up to the front door and felt it. It was hot. The black paint had absorbed the heat and was now peeling. Too risky, he thought.

The fire seemed to be contained within the left wing of the property at this stage. Tom peered through the large windows facing the driveway of the property. A large full-length sitting room. The door to the hallway was closed, and there was no evidence of fire within the room yet.

Tom considered smashing the windows, but noticed that there were French doors on the other side of the room that opened into the garden. That's my best option, he thought. He sprinted round the side of the house, into the vast garden at the rear of the property. He was mistaken. The French doors opened into a vast conservatory.

Tom dashed to the doors of the conservatory and tried the handle. They were securely locked. He stepped back, kicked the door hard, and the lock gave way. Surprisingly easy, he thought. He let himself into the sitting room, and felt the door at the other end. It was hot. There was nothing for it. If he was going to get the occupants out, he would have to gain access to the stairs, which were in the hallway.

Once again, Tom stepped back from the door as far as he could, and tried to press himself into the wall. Once he was in what he thought would be a reasonably safe position, he kicked the door open. As it opened, a huge blast of fire entered the sitting room, consuming the new oxygen, before retreating back slightly.

Tom dropped to his knees, and crawled to the door. The heat was incredible, like nothing he had experienced before. It was almost unbearable. The crackling of the flames as they consumed the fixtures and fittings of the house was painfully loud. It was quite remarkable that the fire couldn't be heard outside the property.

Tom crawled forward and crossed the threshold into the blazing hallway. As he did so, he heard a woman screaming at the top of the stairs. Must get to her, he thought.

He crawled as fast as he could, keeping himself low where there was still a little oxygen. The flames were blazing all around him, consuming anything in his path. The heat by now was unbearable, but he pressed on.

Tom got to the stairs, and decided there was nothing for it but to make a dash for it. The fire was confined mainly to the ground floor at the moment anyway. He leapt to his feet, and dashed up the stairs. The screaming woman was fixed to the spot at the top of the stairs, and was now hysterical. Tom bundled her through an open door, which he shut behind him. The woman was still screaming and he tried to calm her down.

"Tessa? Sssh, sssh! It'll be all right! Calm down!"

He sat her down on a large, super king size in the middle of the room, and stroked her forehead. She was an attractive woman in her early forties, rather petite, with shoulder length brown hair streaked with blonde.

"It's okay, we'll get you out of here! Trust me! Is there anyone else in the house?"

"Flora and Sophie, my girls," she said between sobs. "They're in their rooms. I need to get to them, I need to get to them."

"Calm down, Tessa. I'll get them," Tom reassured her. "Other than Flora and Sophie, is there anyone else in the house?"

"Eva, the nanny. Upstairs. Philip. My Philip. He's upstairs too!"

New screaming was now audible, coming from further down the landing.

"Listen to me, it's going to be okay. Trust me. I'm going to go and get your daughters, and then I'm going to come back here. Just don't panic. Wait here and don't move, okay?"

"Okay," she said. Tessa had calmed down considerably, no doubt comforted by Tom's presence, and was now gently sobbing.

Tom crossed back to the door and put his ear against it. It sounded like the fire had yet to reach the landing to any great extent, and the door was nowhere near as hot as the sitting room door had been. He let himself out of the room and closed the door behind him.

Further down the landing was a thin blonde girl of about thirteen. She appeared to have frozen in terror, since she was not moving at all. She was screaming as loudly as she could. Tom rushed down to her, passing the stairwell as he went. Any minute now the fire was going to reach the first floor landing, so he had to move fast.

He approached the girl and tried to calm her down. If anything, the presence of a strange giant of a man in her home made her even more afraid, and there was no indication that she was going to stop screaming any time soon. Tom made an attempt to grab her to take her into her mother's bedroom, but she tried to beat him off. Her tiny fists just bounced off Tom's enormous chest.

"Get off me, get off me, get off me! Get away from me, you perv!" she shouted. As she did so, Tom noticed as a door further down the corridor opened a crack, and then shut once more. The other daughter. He made a mental note of the room she was in.

Tom managed to grab the blonde girl and throw her over his shoulder, and he began to make his way back to Tessa's bedroom. He went steadily, being careful not to drop the girl when he became aware of someone kicking his legs from behind. He looked round and saw a short young woman of about twenty, also with long blonde hair. As he turned round, she began shouting at him.

"Get off her, get off her!" She spoke with a thick French accent. Must be Eva, the nanny, he thought.

Tom ignored the woman, and upped the pace as he went back to Tessa's bedroom. He let himself in, and dropped the girl onto the bed.

"Oh, Sophie, thank goodness!" the mother said, as she began kissing her daughter and running her fingers through her hair. "Thank goodness you're okay!"

"Is zis man a rescuer?" the young woman who had been kicking Tom asked as she walked into the room, her accent giving her a rather cosmopolitan image.

"Yes, yes, he's saved my Sophie!" Tessa exclaimed. "Get Flora, get Flora!" she shouted at Tom.

For the second time, Tom crossed onto the landing. This was not going to be so easy. By

163

now, the fire had climbed the stairwell, and was beginning to travel fast along the thick, heavy piled carpet of the landing. Small holes were beginning to appear in the floor where the fire from above had met the fire burning through from below. Things were moving fast. Tom had to act quickly if he was going to find Flora.

Tom edged along the landing, trying desperately to avoid the rapidly expanding patches of fire. He pressed himself against the wall, hoping that there would be a strong joist beneath that would take his weight if the floor began to give way.

Soon he arrived at the door he had seen Flora open. He opened it, and saw a small girl of about eight hiding beneath her bed. She had piled her duvet and sheets up against the bottom of the door. Smart girl, he thought.

"Flora, come here!" Tom called. "I'm going to take you to your mummy and make sure that you're safe."

"I'm safe here," said the girl, completely devoid of any emotion.

"Please, Flora, come here. I'm going to take you to mummy and Sophie."

Reluctantly, Flora pulled herself out from under the bed and approached Tom. He took her hand.

"You're a very brave girl, aren't you, Flora!" Tom complimented her. "Right, listen carefully. We're going to walk to mummy's room, but we're going to do it quickly, and we're going to keep against the wall, okay? We'll be safe then."

Tom led Flora out of the bedroom onto the landing, which was well ablaze by now. When Flora saw the fire, she began crying.

"Our house, our house!" she cried.

"Don't worry about the house, Flora, let's just make sure that you're all safe."

Tom led Flora back down the landing, and soon had her safe in her mother's bedroom. Tessa threw herself at Anthony.

"Thank you, thank you, you kind man! Who are you? Are you a fireman?"

"I'm a police officer," Tom replied, avoiding explaining the complications of his secondment. "Now don't worry, Tessa, everything will be okay. I'm going to go and check on your husband. You think he's upstairs?"

Tessa took a sharp intake of breath.

"Philip! Philip! He's in his office!"

"I didn't see him," said the French girl.

"He's upstairs!" Tessa insisted. "He's working on an important case in his office."

"Okay, I'll go and check," Tom reassured her. "Listen carefully, though. I'm going to shut the door behind me, and you need to pile wet towels up at the bottom of the door. The Fire Brigade will be here soon. When they appear, you must attract their attention so that they know where you are. Do you understand?"

"Yes, yes, just please find my husband!"

Tom let himself out onto the burning landing once more. The fire had spread extensively, and it was going to be very hard to get to the second floor office now. He had the feeling that he was wasting his time. Surely if Philip Brown had been in the house, he would have shown himself by now? The fire and the screaming of his family were enough to rouse anyone, even if they had been sleeping.

Tom made it to the bottom of the stairs to the second floor, and shouted up.

"Mr. Brown, are you up there? Mr. Brown?"

No reply. Tom could hear the sound of sirens approaching the house.

"Philip?"

Tom made a dash up to the second floor. There were five doors leading off the upper landing. He opened them all. One led into a small flat with a sitting room with a kitchenette area, a bedroom and a shower room. Presumably the nanny's residence. Two opened into bedrooms. One opened into a bathroom. The other opened into a large office. There was no one in it, but Tom's attention was immediately grabbed by a large map of London and the south east of England, which covered the whole of one wall, stretching from floor to ceiling. On it were marked Lambeth Palace, Buckingham Palace, Westminster Abbey, Westminster Cathedral and Hyde Park. Red cotton marked out all the possible routes between the locations. In the centre of the map was a large photograph of the Pope in a Popemobile.

Brown, what on earth were you up to, Tom thought. He took out his iPhone and took snaps of the maps before looking at what else he could find.

On Brown's desk was a list of contact numbers of key figures in the Pope's party and people he would be visiting. The Archbishop of Westminster was there, likewise Canterbury. Prince Charles' private secretary was on the list, as was the Prime Minister's. Tom took another snap.

Tom heard the fire crew smash through the gates and pull onto the gravel drive. Help was at hand, he thought.

Next to the list of phone numbers was a small photograph showing a well-dressed handsome man in his forties shaking hands with the Pope. Presumably Brown, Tom thought. He's met the Pope?

There were more papers on the chair, which looked like they'd been dropped in a hurry as Brown rushed out. Amongst them was a page with full contact details for Paul Fish, and a time and place – the Station Tavern, Liverpool Street, 9.30pm. That was where Graham had tracked down Fish earlier on. Had he been meeting Brown? Why? Tom pocketed the sheet, and continued shuffling through the papers.

Another paper was headed Charlwood Abbey. It showed a map of the site, details of the Abbot, and details of Adam Michaels. Michaels' name had been heavily underlined in red. Tom stuffed the paper in his pocket. There was firm evidence that Brown knew that the Pope was going to be staying in Charlwood that night, but how could he possibly have known that? There were very few people in the entire world who were aware of the Pope's visit to Surrey that night.

At that moment, a very loud creaking noise was audible over the racket from the burglar alarm and the flames. That can't be good, Tom thought. He quickly took multiple photos of the rest of Brown's office, not really looking where he was shooting, but thinking that, if he made it out of the house alive, Anthony could analyse the shots later.

Tom dashed out of the office. The fire had well and truly reached the second floor now. The first floor must have been well ablaze – Tom could feel the heat radiating through the thin floor below. He took his jacket off and put it over his head, and made his way gingerly towards the first floor. The whole landing was blazing, and most of the floor had disappeared. He quickly picked his way over the joists and back into Tessa's bedroom. He was just in time to see Tessa being led down a ladder by a fire fighter. He dashed to the window and climbed onto the ladder himself. Just as he stepped onto the ladder, there was another ear splitting crack. Tom watched as the floor of the bedroom fell out, disappearing into the fire below.

Chapter 13

Graham had arrived back at the Hunter Group's offices feeling both ashamed and embarrassed. Jeremy had been angry when he had told him that he had delegated pursuing the Pope's kidnapper to Sally. Now he had to admit that he had stupendously failed in his mission to establish the identity of the mystery gunman. Not only were they not going to be able to retrieve any hints from his car, but Graham had accidentally shot his driver. He was the only firm lead that they had had, and Graham had killed him. He was aware of how bad this would look, and knew that his colleagues were going to rip him apart over this for years to come. They were right. He was an appalling secret agent. But then, he'd never wanted to be a secret agent. He had made that clear to Jeremy on multiple occasions. He just wasn't cut out for this sort of work. Yet for some reason, Jeremy refused to let him leave.

As soon as he had returned, Jeremy had called him into his office. Neither of them had said a word. Jeremy took a seat behind his desk, leaving Graham standing near the door, and finally broke the silence.

"I think you and I need to have words, Graham," he said, making a pyramid with his fingers beneath his nose. "Talk me through what's happened this evening."

Graham explained exactly what had happened since he left the Gherkin earlier that night. He explained how Sally had pursued the kidnapper and the Pope, whilst he had decided to establish who the gunman was. Before he could continue, Jeremy interrupted him.

"That really wasn't your best decision, was it, Graham? You let the office girl go after the Pope, arguably the most important person on the face of the planet, whilst you went off on a wild goose chase that led nowhere."

Graham was silent. He really did not have a response to this.

"And remind me, how did you get on with your little mission?"

Graham didn't reply.

"I asked you a question, Graham."

"As you know, Jeremy, unfortunately the gunman's driver torched the car, and escaped into the woods. I was unable to apprehend him."

"I thought you shot him?"

"I did."

"So – did he explain who he was?"

"No."

"Did you establish who he was?"

"No."

"And you shot him?"

"He was shooting at me. I was defending myself. I was shooting blind and accidentally got him."

"You were shooting blind. You think that's a good idea do you, Graham?"

Graham had no answer.

"Look, Graham. You're having these little accidents with alarming regularity, and I'm getting a little fed up with it. I know your colleagues are too. One more of these little mistakes and I'm going to have to ask you to leave the Hunter Group."

"I didn't want to be in your gang, anyway, Jeremy."

"Look, we'll put this behind us for the time being, Graham. We've got work to be getting on with. Let's change the subject. Have you heard from Sally since she left the abbey?"

"No. Have you?"

"No."

"That was over two hours ago now, though," Graham responded.

"I know. I've tried ringing her, but she's not answering her phone. It's not like her to go off the grid. I'm rather concerned about her, because she has next to no experience in the field, and really shouldn't have taken matters into her own hands. I hope that she's okay, and that she's managed to locate the Pope."

There were a few moments of silence whilst the old friends thought through possible explanations for Sally's disappearance.

"Let me bring you up to date on what we know," Jeremy said. "Hopefully you can make sense of it all rather better than me."

Jeremy started at the beginning, reiterating how a missile had taken out CARN, and then an identical missile had been used to blow up a van that had been reported to belong to CARN. The same gunman had then been driven down to Surrey where he had attempted to kill the Pope, but been killed himself.

Meanwhile, Philip Brown, a pro-Catholic lawyer, had hired a car and driven it to Surrey, where he had kidnapped the Pope. He was last seen driving into the distance, presumably heading back towards London.

Paul Fish, who had been a member of the CARN executive, had been absent from their meeting, and hence had survived. He had met with Philip Brown and then promptly disappeared.

"So what's going on?"

Graham, now feeling in his element, ripped a large sheet of paper from the flipchart in Jeremy's office, and placed into onto the desk in front of him.

"We need to think more deeply about this. It seems to me that there are several organisations out there, and we don't have the faintest idea who is doing what. Let's draw this out," he said, picking up a pen. "We know that New Reformation issued a death threat against the Pope, so we can assume that they mean ill. For the sake of a better term, let's label them the baddies in all of this." Graham headed a column 'Baddies' and wrote NR underneath. "We also know that CARN have, in the past, campaigned against the Catholic Church, and against religion in general. They were found to have a van full of explosives outside their meeting. We have assumed that these explosives were theirs, yet they disappeared after they had all been wiped out. What if we switch the assumption, and say that the van was nothing to do with them, that it was planted outside the flat where they were meeting."

"But why would someone park a van full of explosives where CARN were meeting?" asked Jeremy.

"Let's assume that someone was trying to frame CARN, to make us think that they were planning to kill the Pope. CARN have never shown any inclination to kill, and I don't know how such a bunch of rank amateurs would manage to secure quite so many explosives. They don't seem to have had any dealings with the criminal fraternity before, so to suddenly secure a van full of explosives seems rather unlikely. So, let's assume for a moment that CARN were being framed. Who would do that, and why?"

"Someone who was trying to set them up as potential Pope-killers, to mask their own involvement and shift the blame."

"Who best fits that description?" Graham asked.

"New Reformation, I guess."

Graham underlined NR on the flip chart. At the bottom of the page he wrote a new heading, 'Irrelevant distractions'. Beneath that, he wrote CARN.

"I'm not following this. I still don't get why someone would want to blow up CARN."

Graham refrained from telling Jeremy how dim he was being. He didn't think that this was a good time.

"There are two possibilities, Jeremy. Either, it's someone who believed that CARN were plotting to kill the Pope and wanted to prevent them from doing so because they don't want the Pope dead. Alternatively, it could be an organisation that wants to kill the Pope and take the responsibility for themselves."

"So what you're saying is that someone has taken the defence of the Pope into their own hands through criminal means, or that we're witnessing some kind of inter-gang rivalry."

"Almost, but not quite. I think inter-gang rivalry is too strong. As I said, I think that someone was trying to make CARN the scapegoats for all of this."

"This still doesn't seem to make any sense," Jeremy said.

"No, I agree, it doesn't," Graham agreed. "There's still a lot to unravel. But there's no doubt in my mind who blew up CARN."

"Who?"

"I think CARN were taken out by NR," Graham responded. "I don't know why, though. That's the vital element that we're missing at the moment. If they were trying to set up CARN, why would they then blow them up? Unless perhaps they changed their minds. That still needs some exploration."

"Okay. So we've got New Reformation as the baddies, and CARN as being largely irrelevant. How about Philip Brown? How does he fit in? Is he a member of NR?"

"Brown is a very committed Catholic. That doesn't rule out membership of NR, by any stretch of the imagination. I don't think he fits their profile, though. He tried, somewhat unsuccessfully, to start this 'Infinitum' organisation to portray the church in a positive light. One key aspect of the representation of the church that he sought to challenge was the idea that Catholic priests are all a bunch of paedophiles. Now, it could be that by killing the Pope and replacing him, he could achieve that. After all, the current Pope is thought by many to have tried to sweep the allegations of child abuse under the carpet, which can't be considered too helpful. If Brown wanted the Pope dead, though, why would he not have killed him this evening? He got to the Pope's bedroom before anyone else, and was alone with him. If he had wanted him dead, he could have shot him in the head and then legged it before anyone else was anywhere near him. Instead, he chose to risk his life and remove the Pope from the abbey. What if he knew that the Pope was under threat, and wanted to take him to safety?"

"It seems a little far fetched to me," Jeremy said. "After all, how did he know that the Pope was staying at the abbey? Practically no one knew that. And he shot several people on the way to the Pope's bedroom. I find it hard to reconcile that with the Brown that you have portrayed."

"The guards were tranquilised, they were not shot, and they will be fine," Graham said. "That exactly fits Brown's profile. As for how he knew that the Pope was going to be in Surrey, I have no idea at all, but presumably someone had told him."

"He met with Fish earlier tonight," Jeremy reminded him. "Fish seems to be at the centre of this whole situation. He was a member of CARN. He knew about NR. He knew about Philip Brown and Infinitum. Perhaps he told Brown about the Pope's whereabouts when they met at Liverpool Street."

"Maybe," Graham responded. "We have previously regarded him as a baddie, but there's very little evidence to support this idea. What if he was feeding information about the planned assassination to Brown? I agree, though, that there's also very little to support the idea that he's a goodie. I think we have to keep an open mind on Fish."

"I agree. We can't understate the importance of finding Fish. We need to bring him in, and we need to speak to him. Helena's in Stratford at the moment. Get yourself down there and work with Helena to find him as soon as possible."

Graham got up to leave.

"Oh, and Graham?"

"Yeah?"

"Don't shoot him, for Christ's sake."

By the time Tom and the Brown family – with the exception of Philip – had been safely removed from their burning home, three fire engines, two police cars and two ambulances had turned up, plus a paramedic on a motorbike. Tom had flashed his police warrant card about and quickly taken control of the scene. He had arranged for the family to be taken to a nearby hotel where they would stay at least one night until there had been an opportunity to contact their insurance company and make long-term arrangements. They would not be moving back into the house in Hampstead Lane anytime soon, that was for certain. The whole of the inside of the house had been completely gutted, and the roof had suffered extensive damage. It looked very likely that it would have to be pulled down and a fresh start made.

Tom accompanied the family to the hotel, and sat in the bar whilst he waited for Tessa to try and calm down the two girls and get them to bed. The hotel was operating on a skeleton staff and the bar had long closed for the night, but the night manager, a South African by the name of Trevor, had managed to rustle up some coffee and sandwiches. Tom began tucking in almost immediately. He suddenly became aware of just how ravenous he was.

After about half an hour, he was joined by Tessa, who had changed into a pair of jogging bottoms and a sweat top that Trevor had plundered from the hotel's gymnasium. For a woman who had just been pulled out of a burning building, she looked good.

Tessa sat next to Tom on the leather sofa, and crossed her legs beneath her.

"Where's my husband?" she asked.

"Thank you for rescuing my family and me from certain death in a burning building, Tom. No problem, Tessa. All in a day's work."

"I'm sorry, I'm sorry." Tessa placed a hand on Tom's arm. "I really am very grateful to you. You saved our lives and we're all very grateful. I'm sorry. I guess I'm not thinking straight."

"Don't mention it."

"I am worried about Phil, though. Are you absolutely certain he wasn't in the house?"

"I'm afraid I can't be absolutely certain, but I can be about 99 per cent sure. He definitely wasn't in his office."

"So where is he?"

"I have no idea. I was going to ask you that," Tom replied.

Tessa poured herself a cup of black coffee, and took a sip.

"Why were you at the house tonight?" Tessa asked. "I mean, I'm very glad that you were. You weren't just passing though, were you? It's to do with Phil, isn't it?"

Tom didn't quite know how to approach this. He knew that Tessa would ask questions at some stage, but he hadn't come up with a suitable line yet. As he was trying to think of an answer that would allay Tessa's fears, his phone rang. It was Jeremy.

"Sorry, Tessa, I'm going to have to take this. It's my boss. Don't move, though."

Tom walked to the other side of the bar, taking the call as he went.

"Jeremy, what's up?"

"I gather there's been a situation at Brown's house."

"You could say that. It was on fire when I arrived. I rescued Brown's wife and kids, plus the nanny, but there was no sign of Brown."

"No, I didn't think there would be. We've found Brown. Or at least, we had found him. I'm afraid that he hired a car this evening, drove to Surrey and kidnapped the Pope."

There was quiet whilst Tom took in this latest development.

"I found some stuff in Brown's office," Tom said. "There was a large map with Lambeth Palace, Buckingham Palace, Westminster Abbey, Westminster Cathedral and Hyde Park marked on it. He'd marked out the routes that the Pope might take between them all, too. There were some other bits and pieces, photos and bits. You don't think he's with NR do you? You don't think he's the Pope killer?"

"Graham and I have been thrashing ideas around. We think that Brown is a good guy. Misguided, idiotic and downright stupid, yes, but we think he's trying to keep the Pope safe."

"Sounds crazy, all right," Tom agreed. "Listen, I'm with Brown's wife. What do you want me to do?"

"You can see if she knows where Brown might have taken the Pope. We need to find them both, and soon. As it stands, they're both at risk. Someone clearly has it in for Brown, and I'm sure that his house burning to the ground is no coincidence. It looks to me like someone is trying to warn him off, or possibly even kill him. Can you make sure his family are safe?"

"Okay, I'll see what I can find out from Tessa, although she seems completely oblivious to all of this. I'll arrange a guard at the hotel for them too. You're right, Jeremy. The fire was no accident. Someone was trying to destroy Brown, and I don't want to leave his family on their own under the present circumstances."

"Okay. Do what you have to do but get back here as soon as you can please."

Tom hung up, and returned to Tessa. She really was stunning. Philip Brown was a very lucky man.

"Tessa, I've found Philip. Or rather, my team have."

Tessa's eyes lit up, and she looked longingly at Tom.

"Where is he? Is he okay?"

"This sounds totally incredible, but earlier tonight, Philip hired a car. He drove down to an abbey in Surrey and kidnapped the Pope. We currently don't know where Philip or the Pope are."

Tessa went white, and put her coffee cup back on the table.

"I knew he was up to something," she said. "He's been plotting this for weeks. The maps, the secret meetings, the late nights. I knew it. Is he okay? I guess he's in a lot of trouble?"

"He is in rather a lot of trouble, yes. It goes without saying that you can't just head out and kidnap the Pope. We're concerned about the Pope, but we're also concerned about Philip too. They're both in grave danger, and we need to find them as soon as possible. Have you any idea where they might have gone?"

"Reigate. He'll have gone to Reigate," Tessa replied without any hesitation.

"Reigate? How can you be so sure?"

"His parents have got a house on Reigate Hill. It's a large house on the hill that is isolated from everything around it. His parents only visit periodically these days. They spend most of their time at their villa in Spain. It's empty at the moment. We're supposed to be going down for the weekend next week."

"Fantastic. Write the address down for me, will you? I've got to dash."

"Will he be okay?" Tessa asked as she wrote the address down.

"If he's not silly, he'll be fine. We just need to get him and the Pope to a safe place as quickly as we can. Leave this to us, Tessa, we'll sort it out."

Chapter 14

Philip Brown was rather impressed with his driving. In his youth, he had spent many evenings messing around with his friends in supermarket car parks. They had whiled away many an hour drag racing their cars and practising handbrake turns whilst their parents had assumed they were at football training, or helping out at their local Church youth group. That was until he had been caught by his father, who happened to pop into the church to meet the minister one evening when Philip was supposed to be at youth group, only to discover that his son was nowhere to be seen. By that time, though, Philip was eighteen and about to sit his A Levels. The truth had come out and his father had attempted to reprimand him but Philip was taller - and probably smarter - than he was. He did, however, promise that he would not lie to his parents again, and would certainly not engage in what his parents referred to as "such ridiculous activities" again.

That was all quite a long time ago now, though. Somehow, against all the odds, Philip had become a highly respectable pillar of the community. If any of his friends or colleagues knew of his misspent youth they would be deeply shocked. Philip, they imagined, was the studious, hardworking one who was never parted from his books. That could not have been further from the truth. Philip had not worked particularly hard at school, and it was a miracle that he had found a university willing to allow him to read law. He had well and truly flunked his exams, but luckily the University of Essex was willing to give him a place through clearing. He had bucked his ideas up considerably at university, and had thrown himself into his studies, gaining a very respectable degree by the end of his three years. He had also rediscovered his faith at Essex whilst serving on the committee of the student Gregorian Society, and helping out at the Catholic Chaplaincy. Those three years had been a very formative time for the young Philip, and he had moulded himself into the mature, sensible and intelligent person that he was recognised as today.

Nevertheless, the crazy driving skills that he had picked up as a teenager had come in very useful tonight. He had been rather worried that carrying out a handbrake turn at such high speed would result in disaster. He was rather scared when the car spun quite so fast and quite so much, but somehow he had managed to pull it out of the spin, and get it pointing in the direction he wanted – away from his pursuer.

Philip was shocked when he saw the impact of his actions on the car behind. He had no idea who it was that was chasing him, but he meant them no harm. When he saw the car plough into the road sign he was worried that he might have inadvertently killed someone. He had called for an ambulance anonymously, and said a prayer as he drove, hoping against hope that he had not been responsible for someone else's death. It was bad enough that he had had to shoot the Pope's guards, even if it had only been with a tranquiliser. Needs must though, and what he had done was for the greater good.

Fish had been absolutely right; the Pope had not been safe at Charlwood, and he felt vindicated in his decision to recover the Pope from the abbey.

He had been shocked and horrified by the events of the night. It was a blessed miracle that he and the Pope had survived the attempts to shoot and knife them that night. It was a miracle too that he had managed to shake off whoever it was who had tried to follow him.

Philip had left the motorway several miles ago now. They had driven along the A217 for a short distance, heading away from Reigate. Brown had then turned off onto a narrow road that led deep into a wood at the top of the North Downs. The road got progressively narrower the further they drove down it. After a little while, it became little more than a dirt track. The car bumped its way over the rough surface until it reached the gates to his parents' house.

Brown pressed the remote control and the gates swung open. He drove the car up to the front door, and jumped out, before opening one of the rear doors. The Pope looked absolutely petrified, and was frozen with fear. He was completely white, and had not uttered a single word since Brown had broken into his room.

Philip lent across the Pontiff and unbuckled his seatbelt. He took both the Pope's hands in his, and gently led him out of the car. He opened the large front door, and led the Holy Father up a sweeping staircase to a bedroom on the first floor. He laid the Pope down onto a large double bed and covered him over with a thick duvet.

"Father, I hope you can forgive me but there are people out there who want to kill you," Philip told him. "You'll be safe here with me, though."

The Pope just looked at him, a confused expression on his tired face.

"Sleep well, Holy Father."

Brown left the Pope alone and headed back to the sitting room.

The Holy Father was safe now. No one would find him here. He would return the Pope safely to Lambeth Palace in the morning.

Giuseppe Campanaro had tracked down the Pope with relative ease. A little forward planning was all it had taken. He had wanted to ensure that he knew where the Pope was at any given time whilst he was on the abbey site, and so had made a small gift to the Holy Father of a signet ring with the abbey crest displayed prominently in blue and gold. Before making the gift, however, he had arranged for a friend with technical expertise to insert a tiny GPS tracking chip between the enamel crest and the metal of the ring itself. It was simply a matter of running a small piece of software on his computer, and he could pinpoint the exact location of the Pope to within about thirty metres.

After leaving his office in the main building of the abbey, Campanaro made his way back to his house. He entered quietly via the back exit, because two cars were still hanging around at the entrance gates. Whilst he waited for them to disappear, he booted up his laptop and loaded up the GPS software. There he was, Campanaro thought. The Pope was still wearing the ring, and he had just turned onto the M23 heading towards London.

A few minutes later and both cars had disappeared from the front of the gates. Campanaro picked up his laptop and headed out to his Ford Mondeo. He placed the computer, which was still indicating that the Pope was on the M23, onto the passenger seat, and headed off in pursuit.

Campanaro watched the screen closely to see where the kidnapper was taking the Pope. When he reached the M25 interchange, the driver, turned off to the east, but then suddenly changed his mind, spun the car around, and headed for the west. Five minutes later, Campanaro also reached the M25 junction, and turned onto the westbound carriageway towards Heathrow.

The car only travelled a short distance along the M25, before it turned off at the Reigate interchange. Campanaro looked closely at the dot on the screen as it turned onto the A217 heading north towards London, but just a few yards down the road turned off onto a smaller road, which Google Maps suggested was a dead end.

Campanaro also turned off the M25 onto the A217, and found a lay-by as he watched the kidnapper's movements on the screen. The car had driven about a hundred yards up the road, and had then come to an abrupt stop. He watched for five minutes or so as the dot stayed still, and then, much more slowly and following a more erratic path, moved further north. It moved a matter of feet, and then came to a stop again.

There must be a building there. That's where the Pope is being hidden.

Campanaro started the car and followed the path that the kidnapper's vehicle had taken. He turned off the A217 onto a wooded lane. He was at the top of Reigate Hill, and he knew that this particular area was rather isolated. He drove his Mondeo down the track, checking out his surroundings as he went. The left hand side of the road was completely wild, just woodland, with no buildings whatsoever. The right had side was rather different, lined with substantial properties, each behind gates.

Campanaro looked at the screen. He was practically on top of the dot now. Then he saw it.

Parked in a driveway to his right, in front of an enormous house, was the black Mercedes MPV that had been parked outside the abbey earlier that night.

He continued driving past, and a hundred yards further on came to the end of the road. He turned the Mondeo round, and parked up.

Sally's head hurt like hell. She couldn't remember what had happened. She was just aware of the darkness. And the pain.

Slowly, she became aware of a male voice next to her.

"Can you hear me? I'm Alan from the ambulance. Can you hear me?"

There were flashing blue lights.

She could hear traffic.

She opened her eyes. She could see nothing other than a white cloud.

She tried to move her head, and managed to raise it slightly.

She noticed that her face had been pressed into her car's air bag. She could see more clearly now.

"Hello, love, can you hear me?" That voice again.

"I can hear you. Where am I?"

"You've had an accident, but you're going to be okay. Just sit still and we'll get you out of there. What's your name, dear?"

"Sally. Sally Whittaker."

"Okay, well just sit tight, Sally, and we'll get you freed."

Sally lifted her head back against the headrest. She was on the motorway, and the front of her car had caved in. Her car was wrapped around a road sign. Gradually, it all started to come back to her. She had been chasing a car. It had spun. She had turned round to look at it, and hit the sign.

Why was she chasing the car?

Shit, the Pope!

Sally snapped back to full consciousness.

"How long have I been here?"

"About fifteen minutes, Sally. You've been very lucky. If you'd been driving a different car, you might have been killed."

"Get me out of here now!"

Sally struggled to free herself, but the front of the car had folded in around her legs. If she could just pull herself up, she could get herself free.

"Give me a hand here, will you?" she said to the ambulance man.

"Just sit tight, Sally, the fireman's going to cut you out."

"Don't worry about that! If you just give me a hand, I can pull myself out of here!"

"I don't think that's a good idea until we've seen your legs, Sally. There might be permanent damage."

"My legs are fine, and so am I! Just give me a hand, will you?"

"Okay, let's see what we can do!"

The ambulance man grabbed Sally under the arms and began trying to pull her up. As he did, Sally kicked herself up off the bottom of the car, and pulled herself up using the back of the seat. A few seconds later, and she was standing on the seat. She scrambled round into the back of the car, and let herself out of one of the back doors. She was a little shaky and she had a seriously bad headache, but she was okay.

"Where are the police?" Sally asked. A young PC walked over.

"We're here, madam, there's nothing for you to worry about."

"Look, I work for the Hunter Group, a private security company. You won't have heard of us, but it's absolutely imperative that I get back into central London immediately. Will you give me a lift?"

"We should get you to hospital to get you checked over, first, Sally. You've been in a very bad accident," the ambulance man said.

"I'm fine," she said, turning back to the PC. "Will you take me to London?"

"Are you sure you're okay?" the officer asked.

"I'm fine. Please, take me to London!"

The officer looked at the ambulance man, who just shrugged his shoulders.

"Okay, I guess. Let's go."

Chapter 15

Anthony had emailed Helena Paul Fish's address in Stratford. She had picked up a pool Jaguar and driven out to the address. By now it was approaching 1am, and, apart from the hardened party animals spilling out of pubs and clubs along her route, she had a clear drive and arrived within twenty minutes.

She pulled up alongside the address Anthony had given her. She was in a street of 1930s semi-detached houses, most of which seemed to have been converted into flats. The area, which at one time had been rather upmarket, was now looking rather tired and sorry for itself. The small front gardens had been converted almost without exception into parking spaces to accommodate the cars of the multiple occupants of the houses. Old Fords, Vauxhalls and Japanese cars were in abundance; Helena's Jaguar stood out like a sore thumb in the midst of the older, cheaper models. The now customary wheelie bins appeared to be breeding, and took up every bit of space that did not have a car in it. Most of the properties could do with at the very least a lick of paint, if not a complete refurbishment.

Helena was brought back to reality by a tapping on her window. She jumped up from where she was sitting, shocked by the disturbance. An elderly man in pyjamas and a dressing gown was tapping on her window. She wound it down.

"Can I help you?" she inquired.

"You can't park there, love," the man replied. "It's residents' parking only round here, love."

Who was this old duffer?

"It's quarter past one in the morning! What do you mean I can't park here?"

"Well it's my son, you see, love. He's coming to visit us in the morning, and that's where he usually parks."

"Oh, piss off, you silly old fool."

Helena had no intention of listening to this crank, and began to wind up her window.

"There's no need for that, love. I was only saying. You see the traffic wardens come round here quite regular, like, and they start ticketing at eight. If you're still here then, you'll get a ticket, love."

"Thank you for your concern, but I'm only going to be here a short while. Now why don't you piss off back to bed, you silly old man."

"Don't say I didn't warn you, love."

Helena watched as the local resident shuffled off in his slippers, and then reflected that perhaps she hadn't handled the situation as well as she could have done. Perhaps this crackpot could give her some useful information about Fish. He was clearly a nosy busybody who saw all the comings and goings in the street.

She got out of the car, locking it behind her.

"Look, I'm sorry, sir," she called after the man, who was opening his front gate. He paused and turned round. "It's just been a long and tiring day, and I'm a little bit stressed. I could do with your help, actually."

"Oh yes?"

Helena ran after him.

"Yes. Look, you probably won't understand, but I'm with the Hunter Group, a private security contractor." She held out her ID card, which the old man carefully inspected.

"Oh yes? And how can I help you?"

"I need to know something about one of your neighbours."

"Really? Who's that then?"

"Someone by the name of Paul Fish."

The man's facial expression changed. He looked rather worried.

"Oh dear. You'd better come in, love."

The man shuffled up to his front door, which he unlocked and kicked gently to open. He led Helena into a small, stuffy hallway with brown carpet, brown striped wallpaper, and about a thousand photographs, most of which were of a man, presumably the much-loved son.

"Come through to the kitchen, love."

If he calls me love once more, I'm going to shoot him, Helena thought.

They passed two doors on their left. The first was open, and led into a decent sized sitting room, the walls lined once more with rows and rows of photographs, but also a fairly substantial collection of plates. A large bay window overlooked the street. The second door, presumably into a bedroom, was firmly closed.

The kitchen was immediately opposite the front door, and the décor was just as tasteless as that in the other rooms of the flat. The kitchen units were of a rather old style, painted in cream. The floor was lined with an ageing wood effect lino. It was foul. Up against the wall was a table with three chairs.

"Sit down, love," the old man said, indicating a chair at the table. Helena went for her gun, but gritted her teeth. Perhaps it might not be a good move to shoot this elderly gentleman in his own home, she thought, even if it was very tempting.

The old man put the kettle on and dropped tea bags into two chipped mugs.

"Would you like a cup of tea, love?"

Helena once again went for her gun, but again thought better of it.

"That would be lovely. Milk but no sugar, please."

This had better be worth it, Helena thought. I hope he's not just going to tell me that Fish is an inconsiderate parker.

The old man made the tea, humming away to himself whilst Helena looked around. It didn't look like the kitchen had been updated since the house was built. It really was hideous - old, tatty, and dirty. The floor was covered with dust, fluff and what looked like dog hair. There were no other signs of a dog, so Helena wondered just how long it had been since the floor had been swept.

She looked up to see the old man bringing her the tea. He carefully placed the two mugs down on the table, and pulled up a chair next to Helena. You smell, Helena thought. He had that old cabbage smell so common in old people.

"So you want to know about Paul, do you?"

"I do."

"Why's that, then?"

"We think he might be linked to a major crime that was committed earlier tonight."

"I can't say I'm surprised, love. You should see the kind of people he hangs around with."

Helena took a sip of her tea. It was extremely strong and tasted foul.

"Really? What sort of people?"

"Oh all kinds, love. Darkies, Pakis, the lot."

Great, here we go, Helena thought. Casual racism. Not helpful.

"I see. Does that worry you?"

"Well it's those Islamic terrorists that worry me. It wouldn't surprise me in the least if he was harbouring them in his flat."

"What makes you think they might be terrorists?"

"Oh, you know, you can tell the kind that are likely to blow themselves up on a crowded train, love. You don't get to my age without recognising the type. I'm 87, you know, nearly 88."

Get me out of here, Helena thought. This isn't getting me anywhere. The man's clearly deranged.

"Then there was the whole Popemobile thing."

Helena looked up, her attention piqued by the mention of the Popemobile.

"The Popemobile thing?"

"Yes. He bought one of them big foreign cars the Pope uses. They're German, you know. I fought against those Germans, you know. And for what? So English people could drive around in German cars. We had a perfectly good car industry in this country, you know, and it would still be going today if people hadn't started buying German cars. And Japanese. They're just as…"

"What happened with the German car?" Helena interrupted, sensing that he would go off into a racist rant if she didn't stop him.

"Well he bought one of them Mercedes things and parked it where you parked this evening. I told him he couldn't park it there, 'cos my son parks there when he comes to visit, you see. He didn't move it though, just left it there. Then he started hacking bits off the car with one of them torch things. I asked him what he was doing, and he told me he was making a Popemobile."

Deranged, Helena thought.

"So where is it, this Popemobile?"

"Well I told him again that he couldn't park it there, but he said there was nowhere else to park it, and he had every right to park it there. In the end, I said he could park it in my lock-up. I used to store things for my job in my lock-up, you see, but that was years ago now. It's only got a bit of old junk in it now. So he keeps his car in there, and works on it in there. He made it look just like a Popemobile, you know. Not a bad job at all."

What the hell's going on here, Helena thought.

"Where is this lock-up?"

"Oh, it's just down the end of the road, love."

"Can you show me it?"

"Of course, if you think it would be helpful. You'll have to drive, though; my legs are not what they once were. I used to walk for miles and miles, but then I got old and my legs seized up. All day, I used to walk…"

"Sorry to interrupt, but can we go to the lock-up?"

"Of course we can, love."

Helena didn't know what to make of all this talk of Mercedes cars and Popemobiles. Had Fish really been creating a fake Popemobile? And for what possible purpose? Why would he construct a Popemobile?"

Eventually the old man made it out to the car and they drove the few hundred yards to a block of ancient, crumbling garages at the end of the street. The man showed Helena which was his, and she parked the car right in front of it.

"Now, let's take a look."

The old man got out of the car and tried to unlock the garage. The lock was well past its best, as was the rest of the garage, but eventually he managed to get it open.

Inside, the walls were lined with rotting cardboard boxes. Aside from that, it was empty.

"That's very strange. It was here the other day."

Chapter 16

"I know where he is!" Tom shouted into the hands-free microphone.

"Where who is?" asked Jeremy.

"The Pope! Brown's parents have a house in Reigate. That's only about a twenty minute drive from the abbey. He must have taken him there!"

"Brown's wife told you?"

"Yes. Brown's parents live in Spain most of the time, and Brown and his family use the house as a bolthole for weekends and holidays. I asked Tessa Brown if she had any idea where her husband might be hiding out, and there was no doubt in her mind whatsoever that he would have gone there."

"Did you warn her that Brown was in grave danger?"

"I did, and she's going to phone him and warn him, and tell him that I'm on my way."

"How soon can you be there?"

"It's going to take me forty minutes to reach Reigate."

"I can be there in about the same."

Jeremy started pulling his jacket on and made for the door.

"Anthony, come on, you're driving!" he shouted through to where Anthony was hard at work in his own office.

"Listen, Tom, this is what we're going to do," Jeremy said, turning his attention back to the phone. "It's too risky moving the Pope again unless we absolutely have to. The chances are he's relatively safe in Reigate, so let's leave him there. Instead, I want to get the team reassembled down there. You get there as soon as you can, and Anthony and I will drive down now too. The chances are that we'll get there about the same time that you do. Helena and Graham are over in Stratford dealing with Fish at the moment, but I'll get them down to Reigate as soon as they've finished. Helena can interrogate Fish at the Gherkin whilst Graham joins us down there. We've momentarily lost Sally, but the chances are that she's already there."

"So we're going to leave the Pope where he is?"

"For the time being, I think that's our best option. Just get yourself there as quickly as you possibly can, and tool up when you get there."

"Of course. I'll get there as soon as I possibly can."

"Okay. Well great work, Tom. We'll see you as soon as we get there."

Jeremy hung up.

Tom put his foot down and pushed the Jaguar up to 150 mph, and prayed that he didn't encounter any police vehicles. He could talk his way out of any difficulties, but it would waste time that he didn't have.

As he drove, Tom tried to make sense of what he'd seen that evening. Brown had clearly been aware of the Pope's precise movements - even his secret trip to Surrey - for some time. How had he found out? And if his trip to Surrey had been intended as a rescue mission, why on earth did he attempt it on his own? It seemed like a pretty ridiculous thing to do. Not only was he risking his own life, but he was also risking that of the Pope too. Tom was inclined to agree with Graham and Jeremy that Brown was not a Pope-killer; he had had plenty of opportunities to top the Holy Father if that was what he really wanted to do. He seemed completely oblivious to the risky nature of his actions.

There was still one major development that had yet to be addressed, however. Why had Brown's house been destroyed? Tom did not think for one minute that it was an accident; not only were house fires of that kind very rare, but the coincidences were too striking. Brown had been involved in an attempt to kidnap the Pope, and the same evening his house had been burnt down. Who had done it? And for what reason? If it was a warning, it was rather late. Was it an attempt to kill Brown and prevent him from carrying out his own plan? Was that because his plan risked jeopardising someone else's? Or was it revenge against Brown's family because of what he had done? At that stage, there was little to suggest what the cause of the fire was, or who was responsible for it.

Tom just hoped that Brown and his family would make it through the night alive.

For the first time that night, Jeremy was starting to feel that the Hunter Group were on top of the case. They had located the Pope, and would soon have him secured where they could see him. They had pretty much established that Brown meant no harm to the Pope, and was little more than a highly misguided do-gooder. They would soon have Fish in their custody, and with his cooperation, they would be able to unravel the whole story. It was obvious that Fish was playing a central role in the plans that were unfolding before their eyes that night, and hopefully they could make him talk. There were ways and means of extracting information, and Jeremy had little doubt that they could make Fish cough all he knew. He had every confidence that Helena and Graham would be able to apprehend him and bring him in for questioning.

They still had someway to go to work out the whys and wherefores of what was going on, but they would get there. Their priority at the moment was ensuring the total safety of the Pope.

There was still the issue of the gunman. They had no idea who he was, or why he had obliterated CARN in the Lollard Street incident. It didn't look like they were going to be able to explain that any time soon.

Jeremy's mind turned to the team member that they seemed to have lost contact with. He still had no idea where Sally was, or what she was doing. It was most unlike her to just vanish.

"Listen, I'm going to try ringing Sally again," he told Anthony. "She can't have disappeared completely off the planet."

Jeremy took out his phone and punched in Sally's number. He'd lost count of the number of times he'd tried to ring her that night, but each time her phone had gone to voicemail. He was quite surprised when this time Sally answered within three rings.

"Jeremy!"

"Sally! Where the hell have you been?"

"I had a few issues. I was chasing the Pope's kidnapper, and wrapped my car around a road sign on the M25 and blacked out. I'm okay though, and I've cadged a lift off a policeman back to London."

"Where are you?"

"Just entering Croydon on the A23. I should be with you in about twenty minutes or so."

"Get the driver to turn around, I want you in Reigate."

Jeremy listened as Sally explained to her police driver that there had been a change in plan.

"We know who the kidnapper is – he's a man called Philip Brown – and, what's more, we've managed to locate him. He's in a house on Reigate Hill. Write this down carefully."

Jeremy read the address out to Sally, who programmed it into her iPhone.

"How soon can you be there?" Jeremy asked.

"Fifteen minutes at the speed this guy is driving I should think!"

"Right, get there as quickly as you can. Tom, Anthony and I are all heading in your direction, and Helena and Graham will follow shortly. I suspect that you'll be there first, though, so take care. Have you got a weapon?"

"I haven't, but this police guy's got all the usual kit."

"Not great. Just take care, okay? Get into the house and keep a close eye on Brown and the Pope. We think that Brown is trying to protect the Pope, but just make sure he doesn't do anything stupid. Give me a ring if anything happens. I'll be there shortly after you though. Oh, and Sally?"

"Yes?"

"I'm glad you're okay."

Philip Brown was undoubtedly being paranoid. He had checked on the Pope every ten minutes since they had arrived at his parents' house in Reigate. He did have good reason to be paranoid, however. Somehow, against all the odds, he had succeeded in removing the Pope from Charlwood Abbey, and had got him to safety without being observed by anyone.

There had been several times in the run up to the "kidnap" that Brown had doubted his mission, but he had been thoroughly vindicated by the events he had witnessed that night. Had it not been for his actions, there could be little doubt that the Pope would have been killed. It was a miracle that they had both survived the gunfight that had broken out in the Holy Father's bedroom, and had he not been there, the Pope would now be dead.

God was clearly looking out for Brown that night.

This realisation did not stop him taking precautions, however. Although he was confident that no one could know where they were, he still feared that one of those who wanted the Pope dead would succeed in locating them.

He only had a few more hours to get through, however, and then a drive to Lambeth Palace. By 9am, his duty would be complete, and he could rest once more.

Not for the first time that night, he wondered how his family were. Had Tessa noticed that he had snuck out of his office? Had she noticed that he had not climbed into bed beside her? He hoped not. He often worked late in his office, and Tessa never normally noticed him coming to bed.

He was tempted to phone home to make sure that all was okay, but he had his mobile switched off, and wanted to stay out of communication until the Pope had been returned to safety.

Tessa would understand.

Philip checked his watch. It was ten minutes since he had last looked in on the Pope, and time for another check.

He climbed the stairs, and peered round the door of the master bedroom. The Holy Father was still in the bed, and still sleeping soundly, snoring gently.

Philip was amazed that the Pope had not uttered a single word all night. He was old, though, and probably not really aware of what was happening. He looked happy enough, sleeping in Brown's parents' bed.

Brown headed downstairs once more, and walked through to the large sitting room that stretched across the whole length of the right hand side of the house. He peered round the curtains across the back garden, which stretched across the ridge of the hill. All seemed in order.

Just as Brown dropped the curtain back into place, he thought he saw movement at the far end of the garden. Just out of the corner of his eye. He could not be certain if he had seen anything at all, but he pulled the edge of the curtain back once more.

There it was again. When the curtain moved, whatever it was at the end of the garden froze.

There was definitely something down there.

Brown stared round the curtain, waiting for whatever it was to move again.

No movement.

He closed the curtain up almost as much as he could without completely obscuring his view. As he did so, he caught movement again. Right at the end of the garden, amongst the hedgerows. Almost impossible to see.

Whatever it was was still moving, hidden amongst the plants, moving from left to right.

When it reached the corner of the garden it stopped. Everything was still for a while. Whatever – or whoever – it was was obviously considering their options

A few seconds later, a short, fat man wearing glasses appeared on the lawn.

Brown recognised him instantly. He had studied the faces of those he might bump into at Charlwood Abbey. This was Giuseppe Campanaro, the Headmaster.

How the hell had Campanaro known that he was here in Reigate? And more to the point, what the hell did he want?

Brown had anticipated Adam Michaels' actions. He had known that he was a member of New Reformation, and thought that Michaels was the greatest threat to the Pope whilst he was at the abbey. Was Campanaro also a member of New Reformation? Had he overlooked Campanaro's name on the membership list? No, he didn't see how he could have done.

That made at least two high profile members of the abbey staff who were hoping to kill the Pope. The very idea of the Holy Father visiting Charlwood Abbey looked more and more misguided as time went by.

This was not the time for contemplation, however. The Pope was once again at risk, and Brown was now the only person who could defend him. He checked all the downstairs doors and windows once more; they were all securely locked. He looked through a gap in the curtains again. He couldn't see Campanaro. Where on earth had he gone?

Between the back hedge and the house was about a hundred yards of immaculately maintained lawn. There was nothing on the lawn save for a few trees. The trees were of a reasonable size, but there was no way that someone of Campanaro's bulk could hide behind them. Philip studied the trees more closely. Was there someone hiding in the shadows behind the trees? He didn't think so.

Philip scanned the back hedge again. There was just a faint hint of moonlight in the sky that ensured that visibility was poor. There was no sign of any movement. He studied the hedges at the sides of the garden. No trace of any life.

So where the hell had Campanaro gone? He couldn't just disappear into thin air.

Philip was on edge now. He was absolutely convinced that Campanaro was out there somewhere, and that he would kill the Pope given half the chance, but he simply could not see him.

Brown walked across the hall, through the kitchen, and out into his father's boot room. In the cupboard beneath the sink was a solid steel safe. Philip knew the combination, and opened the safe. Inside it he found his father's hunting rifle. He didn't like his father's hunting habit; it was mainly confined to shooting a few rabbits, but from time to time he did go out on the occasional pheasant shoot. He had been a keen foxhunter, but he felt that he was now too old for this more active pursuit. Tonight, though, he may be grateful for his father's rifle.

Philip took the rifle from the safe, and grabbed a couple of packs of cartridges. He had no idea how many he might need. He hoped he would not need any, but with Campanaro lurking in the grounds, who knew what might happen.

Philip closed the safe and walked back into the sitting room. He looked across the lawn again, but could see no signs of life at all.

He was now in a real quandary. Should he wait in the house, knowing that Campanaro was somewhere out there, but not knowing where? Or should he take the rifle outside and hunt Campanaro down.

He weighed the options in his mind for a moment, and then made a decision. If he went outside he would be fair game for Campanaro if he was armed. Campanaro was hidden, and

211

probably watching for him to make a move. No, that was not an option. He had to wait in the house. Sooner or later Campanaro had to show himself.

Then he heard it. Someone was knocking on the front door.

Chapter 17

Helena was completely flummoxed by the latest developments in Stratford. She was sitting in her car trying to make sense of it. Why had Fish made himself a replica Popemobile? And why on earth did he begin construction out in the road, where everyone could see what he was up to? Surely if he was hatching a plot he would have done it away from the public gaze? The Popemobile was a distinctive vehicle, and no one would be in any doubt what it was that he was trying to build.

Unless his crazy old neighbour was mistaken.

She had just phoned through her discovery – or lack of discovery – to Jeremy, and he had not been able to make any sense of it either. They agreed that Fish was a central character in what was unfolding, but they could not work out what exactly he was up to. They couldn't even agree if he was a goodie or a baddie. Bizarre.

Jeremy had told her that Graham was heading out to Stratford, and she had been given strict instructions to wait until he arrived before bringing Fish in for questioning. Anthony had checked Fish's iPhone again, and it was indicating that he was still at home. They could not risk letting him escape again.

Personally, Helena thought that she would have more chance of bringing Fish in if Graham was nowhere near. Graham had already let Fish

213

escape once that day, and she was loath to let him get away a second time.

Whilst she was thinking about her highly esteemed colleague, she saw his Jaguar approaching. He pulled up into a space just down the road from her, and got out of his car. He locked it, then attempted to open the boot. The car alarm went off, ringing loudly through the quiet of the night.

Unbelievable, Helena thought. Just unbelievable. She looked around and saw several sets of curtains twitching whilst Graham struggled to turn the alarm off. Nothing like a quiet approach, and with Graham there really was nothing like a quiet approach.

Eventually he managed to turn the alarm off, and headed towards Helena's car, jumping into the passenger seat.

"Hello, Gorgeous!" he said. "Are you having a fun night?"

"I was until you turned up. Are you incapable of going anywhere without making a fool of yourself?"

"It's the key to my success, Helena."

"Of course it is, you retard. Now, are we going to get this Fish guy or what?"

"Let's do it!"

"Okay, well this is the plan. We're not just going to ring the bell and hope he doesn't run. It's vital that we apprehend him. We're going to break the door down and grab him. If we have to drag him out kicking and screaming, we'll do that. He cannot be allowed to get away this time. Is that clear?"

"Perfectly, boss."

"Grab the ram from the back, then, and let's do this."

They jumped out of the car, and Graham opened the boot – this time without setting the alarm off. He put on a pair of gloves, and picked up the enforcer, a 58 centimetre steel tube used to batter down doors. He attempted to close the boot, and dropped the enforcer on his foot.

"Shit!" he exclaimed, hopping in pain. The enforcer weighed sixteen kilos, and when dropped onto a foot, even one wearing steel toe-capped boots like Graham's, it hurt like hell.

"You moron!" Helena said. "Give me that!"

She picked up the ram, and headed for Fish's door. Graham eventually limped up the path, moaning under his breath about how much his foot hurt.

Helena prepared to swing the enforcer against the door. It was a flimsy, ageing wooden affair and would not take a great deal to break down.

"Ready?" asked Helena.

Graham drew his gun.

"Ready," he replied.

"Here goes." Helena swung the ram into the door and it instantly splintered as the force of the metal crashed into it. Helena immediately dropped the ram, managing to avoid her feet, and went for her own gun.

They entered the house. It had a very similar layout to the one Helena had entered opposite, although at some point the upper and lower flats had been reunited to form one large house. Interestingly, this had been done so that it still appeared to be two flats from outside.

"Wait here," Helena told Graham when he got to the bottom of the stairs. Helena opened the downstairs doors and checked for any signs of life. There were none.

"Right, upstairs," Helena ordered.

The two agents headed up the stairs cautiously. They did not think that this was an ambush, but it was worth being careful just in case

At the top of the landing, there were five doors. One, directly in front of them, had vents set into it, and so they assumed it was an airing cupboard. That left four doors. Two each.

Helena signalled to Graham to take the two doors on the right hand side of the property. He opened the first. It was an office, fitted with a large desk that was barely visible under a huge stack of paper. A shiny new iMac was visible beyond the paper mountain, its screensaver tracing colourful shapes across the large screen. No sign of Fish, however.

Graham tried the second door. A large double bed was arranged in the centre of the wall. There were two people sleeping soundly in it.

Graham gesticulated wildly at Helena as he entered.

"Cover me," he whispered.

He approached the sleeping man. It was Fish - the same man that he had chased out of the bar at Liverpool Street earlier that evening. He was sound asleep, lying on his front. Graham peeled back the duvet, and poked the barrel of his gun into Fish's neck.

"Don't move," he ordered.

Fish woke up with a start but tried to remain still, aware of the gun pressed into his flesh.

"What the fuck?"

The woman came to and began screaming. Fish tried to calm her down.

"Tracy, Tracy, it's okay, calm down." Fish's voice was muffled by the pillow.

"Get up and put some clothes on," Graham ordered. "We've got the building covered. You can't escape."

He withdrew his gun to enable Fish to climb out of bed, his hands in the air. He was naked. The woman was still screaming.

Fish pulled on a pair of boxers and a pair of jeans that were lying on the floor. He walked towards a chair next to the window, on which a chequered shirt was hanging. As he got to the window, he quickly pulled back the curtains, revealing that it was open. Before Graham or Helena were even aware of what was happening, Fish leapt out of the window onto a flat roof.

"For Christ's sake, follow him!" Helena shouted.

Graham dashed over to the window and jumped out. Fish had already reached the edge, and was preparing to jump down into the back garden.

You're not going to escape this time, Graham thought. He aimed his gun at Fish's left leg and shot. Fish cried out in pain and toppled over the roof, landing face down on the patio below. He landed with a bang and a scream.

"You idiot!" Helena shouted. "Get after him!"

Graham walked to the edge of the roof, and very gingerly let himself down onto the patio, holding onto the edge of the roof as long as he could. Fish was bleeding from his left buttock. Graham had never been particularly good at aiming a weapon, and once again he had missed his intended target. Of more concern, however, was the fact that Fish was out cold, and bleeding from a wound on his head.

Helena had followed Graham onto the roof, warning the woman in the house to stay in the bedroom.

"You've fucking killed him, you moron!" she told Graham.

He put his head up to Fish's mouth to establish whether he was breathing and checked for a pulse.

"He's not breathing and there's no pulse. He might still be okay. I think we'd better get an ambulance."

"No breathing and no pulse means he's dead, you cock. He's just landed on his head and is lying in a pool of his own blood. You've just killed him. He was the key to the whole operation!"

"Sorry, but he sort of brought this on himself. Cuff the woman and we'll take her in. Maybe we'll get something out of her. Have a look in the office, too, and see what you can find. There might be something of use. I'll wait here for the ambulance."

Jeremy and Anthony were well on their way to Reigate when Jeremy thought he'd better give Helena and Graham a ring to see what progress they were making. Helena had now had a good hour and a half or so to make contact with Fish, but had yet to report back. Graham should have arrived at least twenty minutes ago and rendezvoused with Helena. Jeremy had yet to hear from either of them.

He dialled Helena's number, and waited for her to answer.

"Yes!" she shouted as she picked up the call. She sounded unbelievably stressed.

"How are you getting on, Helena?" Jeremy could hear sirens in the background.

"Your moronic friend Chicken Shite Man has just killed Fish, that's how we're getting on!"

There was a moment of silence as Jeremy tried to take in Helena's revelation.

"Killed him? How did that happen?"

"We had him. He was in bed, asleep. We told him to get dressed, and whilst he was doing so he escaped out of the window onto a flat roof. Graham followed, and shot him in the backside. He toppled off the roof and fell onto the patio below."

"Is he definitely dead?"

"There are no vital signs and he's not conscious. His head's bashed in. He looks pretty dead to me."

Jeremy could feel his blood pressure rise. If Fish was dead, it would be a major setback to their investigation. Fish seemed to be the one person who knew exactly what was going on. He seemed to have connections with each of the groups that were at work. Without him, the chances were that they would never truly get to the bottom of what had happened, and there was a very real case that, should the would-be Pope killers strike again, they would not be able to prevent them from achieving their goal.

"What's the situation down there at the moment?" Jeremy asked, trying to stay calm.

"I've cuffed Fish's girlfriend and I'm going through his paperwork. Graham is waiting for the ambulance in the garden."

"Okay. Bring Ms. Fish in and question her. See if she knew anything at all about what Fish was up to. Just bag all the paperwork and we'll go through it later. Meanwhile, I want you to get Graham to follow me down to Reigate. We've found the Pope, and we need all hands to the pump."

"You sure that's a good idea? He's not proven himself a great asset to the team so far tonight. Why doesn't he take Fish's girlfriend in, and I'll come and find you in Surrey."

"Because I trust you to do a good job with the interview. Fish's girlfriend might give us vital information, and I know I can rely on you to handle her well. I can keep a close eye on Graham when he gets here, and I'll have a word with him later."

"Okay, but don't blame me when Graham cocks up again."

Sally was not far away from Reigate when she had taken the call from Jeremy. She had asked her driver, P.C. Trevor Bates, to turn the car round at the first available opportunity, and had briefly explained what the situation was. Bates turned the blue lights on and put his foot down. They arrived in the quiet country road that Jeremy had directed them to within seven minutes.

At Sally's insistence, Bates had turned off the blue lights as they approached the lane, and parked up a couple of hundred yards away from where they believed the house was. They would walk the rest of the way.

The lane was lined with trees, and consequently, was very dark indeed. They could barely make out the track beneath their feet. They could see up ahead of them a large house with lights on. Sally suspected that this would be the house that Brown was hiding out in; who else would have their lights on at this time on a Saturday morning?

Bates was still struggling to get his head round what Sally had told him.

"So the Pope is here, in this lane?" he whispered to Sally.

"Yes. I suspect in that house with the lights on."

"And he's been kidnapped?"

"It seems that way, yes."

"But the kidnapper may have, either intentionally or inadvertently, saved the Pope's life this evening?"

"Yes. We need to get to the house to ensure that he remains safe, though."

"And you're some kind of special agent?" Bates asked in disbelief.

"I suppose you could put it that way. I work for the Hunter Group, which is a private security contractor. We undertake grunt work for the intelligence services. You know, privatisation and all that."

"Right." Bates still could not quite believe how his duty was panning out. He had fully expected tonight to be another dull night shift, driving around the M25, booking the occasional late night driver for speeding, and breathalysing the usual late night revellers who were trying their luck. Instead, he'd pulled a beautiful young lady out of a wrecked Golf, discovered she was a secret agent, and was now tracking down the Pope.

"You realise I'm a traffic cop, don't you? I don't do heroics, just driving round in flash motors for hour after hour."

"Well we're not expecting anything too exciting." Sally didn't divulge that she was the Hunter Group's administrator, and tended to spend her day shuffling papers. She suspected that Bates' typical day was considerably more exciting than hers. "All we need to do is persuade Brown, the kidnapper, that we're not going to harm him and that we want to protect the Pope. We just need to get into the house and act as guards."

"Okay, if you're sure."

Sally had tried to suggest to Bates that he wasn't needed, and that he could return to his duties. He was not going to turn down this opportunity to do something more exciting, however. And Sally was hot.

When they reached the house, Sally recognised the Mercedes in the driveway.

"This is the one," she told Bates.

"What do we do?" he whispered back at her.

"Ring on the bell, I guess, and take it from there."

"Are you armed?"

"No. You?"

"I'm a traffic cop."

"Let's hope things don't get too exciting, then."

"Maybe I should call for backup?"

"Don't worry about that. The rest of my team will be here soon."

Sally led the way through the side gate, and up to the large double front door. She knocked several times on the heavy wooden door and waited.

Her heart was racing. She had no idea what was going to happen next.

Chapter 18

Philip Brown had been on edge all night. Spotting Campanaro in the back garden had almost sent him off the chart. He was petrified. This was supposed to be the easy bit. He'd already gone through more than he had expected at the abbey, and now, somehow, he had been found.

When he heard someone knocking on the door, he had no idea what to do. It had to be Campanaro. But why would he be knocking? Perhaps it was some kind of elaborate game.

If it was Campanaro, how had he managed to get from the back garden to the front without being observed, or heard?

Philip contemplated ignoring the door, but then the knocking started again. He would have to see who it was.

He picked up the rifle, loaded it, and made his way through to the hallway. He edged up to the front door, and peered through the spyglass.

A young, blonde woman was standing on the doorstep. Behind her was a police officer.

Shit, shit, shit, he thought. The police. He looked more closely. The police officer was wearing a flat cap, and the woman was in a suit. Plain clothes.

He dropped the gun into the umbrella stand next to the door, and pulled the chain across the door.

Then he opened it.

"Can I help you, officers?"

"Philip Brown?" the woman asked.

"That's right. Who are you?"

"I'm Sally Whittaker, and this is P.C. Trevor Bates. Can we come in?"

"Can I see some I.D.?"

Sally and Bates pulled out their ID cards and passed them through the crack in the door.

"Okay, Bates, I believe you are who you say you are. But Whittaker? 'The Hunter Group'? Sounds like a secretarial services company if you ask me. Who are you?"

Bates took a step forward.

"Miss Whittaker is working with me this evening. Now, can we come in please, Mr. Brown? We'd like to have a quick word."

"It's not really very convenient. You're aware of what the time is?"

"Please, Mr. Brown. Don't make things difficult for yourself. Are you going to let us in or not?"

Brown closed the door, took the chain off, and reopened it.

"I suppose you'd better come in then."

Sally and Trevor entered the house, and Brown closed the door behind them.

"Expecting trouble?" Sally asked, nodding towards the rifle in the umbrella stand.

"Oh, ignore that. That's my father's. He's getting more and more eccentric in his old age."

"I hope he doesn't intend to use it," Trevor said.

"No, no, it's purely for show. It wouldn't work even if he tried to use it. Come through to the kitchen, won't you?"

Brown led the way into a large, country-style kitchen, complete with oak units, a large ceramic sink and an Aga. He indicated a large oak table, and Sally and Trevor took a seat.

"Can I offer you a drink, officers?"

"Maybe later," Sally replied. "We need to talk to you as a matter of some urgency."

Brown pulled out the chair at the head of the table and sat down.

"How can I help?"

"I'm not going to beat about the bush," Sally said. "We know exactly what you've been up to tonight. And we know who you're hiding in this house."

"I don't know what you mean."

"If you want to walk away from here tonight, Brown, I strongly suggest you stop playing games with me," Sally said, surprising even herself with her authoritarian tone. "It was me that you knocked off the road. It was me who pursued you from Charlwood Abbey. It was me who saw you driving away with the Pope in the Mercedes that is now parked in the front drive."

"I see. Can I just say that it is not what it seems?"

"You kidnapped the Pope, Brown. How else can this be seen?"

"I saved the Holy Father's life tonight. If it hadn't been for me, he would have been killed in his bed in that vipers' nest. I have no idea who thought it was a good idea to have him stay at an institution in which several people want him dead. I have no idea who thought it was a good idea to have such minimal security. Had I not, as you put it, 'kidnapped the Pope', he would be dead, and you know it. I'm on the Pope's side, and he is safe here with me – far safer that he was at the abbey."

"I'm sure you're right, but you can't just kidnap the Pope, Mr. Brown, you must understand that, surely?" Sally said.

"Of course I do. But what did you expect me to do? Leave him to be killed at Charlwood, knowing full well that I could have done something to save him? I risked my own life to remove the Pope to safety."

"Yes, yes, I know that's what you think," Sally responded. "But if I have managed to track you down, who else will be able to do so? There are people out there who will clearly stop at nothing to kill the Pope, and I think you might be a little misguided if you think you can guard him on your own here tonight. That's why I'm here. And that's why my colleagues will be arriving shortly. We're here to protect the Pope. At some stage I'm sure we'll have to take action against you, but for now, let's work together. We want the same thing, after all; the Pope to be safe."

There was silence as Brown contemplated all that Sally had said. She seemed to be speaking sense. Perhaps the Pope was not as safe as he thought he would be here. After all, Whittaker and Bates had located him, and it looked like Campanaro had too. He had to tell them about Campanaro, he thought. Before he had the opportunity to, however, he heard a scrabbling from the back door.

"What the hell's that?" Bates asked, jumping up from his chair.

"I have to tell you something," Brown said.

"Go on, what?" Bates replied.

"I've seen Giuseppe Campanaro, the Headmaster of Charlwood Abbey School, skulking about in the garden. I thought you were him when you knocked on the door."

"Giuseppe Campanaro? You're going to have to fill me in here," Sally said.

"I know almost nothing about him. I know that at least one member of staff at the school wanted to kill the Pope, but he was killed this evening. I also know that there's an organisation called New Reformation that wants the Pope dead, and that the dead teacher was a member of their group."

"And Campanaro? Is he a member of New Reformation?"

"Not as far as I know. It seems that either I overlooked him or that he wants to kill the Pope regardless of his relationship with New Reformation."

"And he's outside?" Sally asked.

"Yes."

"Is he armed?" asked Bates.

"I don't know, but I've seen some very highly armed people attempt to kill the Pope tonight. I think we have to assume that Campanaro is armed too."

"I'm not armed," Bates stated. "Do either of you have weapons?"

"None at all," Sally replied.

"There's my father's rifle," Brown commented. "That's all, I think."

"The one in the hall? I thought that didn't work?" Sally said.

"It works alright, and my father has plenty of ammunition for it. I wasn't going to tell you that, though, when I didn't know what you were here for!"

The scrabbling at the door started again, this time with more force.

"What do you suggest we do?" Bates looked to Sally for guidance.

Sally thought about coming clean and telling the two men that she was actually just the administrator of the Hunter Group, a secretary. She decided that would not be the smartest move at this point. Not only would they lose any confidence that they had in her, but they might lose any motivation to stand up to Campanaro. No, she had to keep going.

"Brown, get your rifle, head upstairs to the room above the back door, and let out a warning shot. All we need to do is keep Campanaro at bay until backup comes."

Anthony was parking the car up outside the gates of the house when he and Jeremy heard the rifle shot.

"Shit! What's going on?" Jeremy said. "Let's get a move on."

Anthony abandoned the car, and they both jumped out and grabbed as many weapons from the boot as they could carry. Jeremy slung a Heckler & Koch MP7 over his shoulder, and headed for the door of the house. As he approached, he heard shouting from the back of the property.

"Stay here!" he whispered to Anthony as he headed towards the side of the house.

Jeremy found a side gate, and let himself through it. He found himself in a narrow passageway that ran between the wall of the house and the garage. A light was on in the house, the light shining through a window illuminating the passageway.

Jeremy paused to see if he could hear movement. All he could hear was the steady traffic flow on the nearby M25. He waited, trying to establish what was happening at the rear of the house. The shot and the shouting had definitely come from the back of the property, but he could hear nothing at all.

Then, from the end of the garden, he heard another gunshot. There was definitely someone in the garden, and they were shooting at the house.

Jeremy hoped that they were not too late. Clearly someone was trying to get into the house.

He wondered where Sally was. She must have reached the house by now. Perhaps it was her firing the rifle into the garden.

Keeping one eye on the back garden, he pulled out his phone and sent Sally a quick text. "At side of house. Advise situation."

Almost straight away, he received a response. "In house with Brown and police officer. Someone in rear garden."

He put his phone away, and edged towards the corner of the house, keeping himself pressed against the side of the building. It had been a while since Jeremy had been active in the field, and he hoped he was still up to it. If there was only one intruder, he was confident that he could deal with the situation.

As he reached the end of the wall, he saw a figure dash away from the house into the shrubbery at the edge of the garden. He had been unable to spot who it was, but it looked like someone fairly large.

Jeremy trained his gun on the shrubs and waited for movement. None came. He was convinced that someone was sitting in the undergrowth, waiting to move. He could sense their presence, but he could not see them.

He considered his options. He could attempt to find the intruder in the bushes. That would be too risky, he decided, since whoever was in the shrubbery would surely see him before he saw them. He could head on to the back door, but the person in the shrubs might spot him. The best option was to head back to the front.

He made his way round to the front door. He knocked, and within seconds, Sally appeared, opening the door a crack, and then gesticulating to Anthony and Jeremy to enter.

"Thank goodness you're here!" she exclaimed.

"What's going on?" Jeremy asked, heading straight through the hallway into the back of the house.

"In a nutshell, Brown is here. He believes that he rescued the Pope, and that he is safe here. I've just arrived with a police officer called Trevor Bates who drove me here. We've spotted Giuseppe Campanaro, the Headmaster of Charlwood Abbey School, who is lurking in the undergrowth. We let off a warning shot from upstairs. He responded. We believe that he's armed with a rifle. We keep losing him though."

"Christ, has everyone at Charlwood got it in for the Pope? Whose idea was it to take him there? Campanaro's in the bushes to the left of the garden."

"What do we do next?"

"We wait. There are five of us now against one of him, and we've got plenty of weapons. There's no way he can get in here now. Next time he reveals himself, we'll blast him to kingdom come. Anthony, do you have your laptop?"

"It's in the car."

"You must be Philip Brown," Jeremy said to Brown. "Have you got a computer we can use?"

"Yes, in the study, through there." Brown indicated a room next to the kitchen.

"Anthony, pull up that list of NR members. Check to see if we've missed anyone else at Charlwood. Specifically, see if Campanaro is on it. Then see what else you can find out about him. Leave your weapons here."

Anthony dropped a stash of weapons onto the floor of the hallway, and headed into the study. Jeremy added his own weapons, except the Heckler & Koch, to the pile.

"Where's the Pope?"

"He's in the master bedroom upstairs," Brown replied.

"What's the outlook?"

"It's in the centre of the back of the house."

"Right. Sally, grab a gun and head upstairs and get to the left side of the back of the house. You see anything move, you shoot it. We'll ask questions later. We can't afford for this to go wrong. Police guy, what's your name?"

"Trevor, Trevor Bates."

"You had any firearms training?"

"None whatsoever."

"No worries – it's easy. Point the gun at the baddie, pull the trigger." Jeremy grabbed a semi-automatic rifle and threw it at Bates. "I want you on the right side of the rear of the house. See something, shoot it. Is that clear?"

"Perfectly."

Sally and Trevor headed to their posts.

"Right, Brown, I want you at the front of the house. Get yourself as close to the middle as you can. You see anyone, you let me know. Don't fire unless I give the orders. Some more of my team are arriving soon, and I don't want you shooting them."

"Yes, sir."

Brown hurried off to the first floor, and Jeremy went to find Anthony in the study.

"Christ, this is a mess, Anthony. I'm going to have a heart attack in a minute. I can't believe that we've ended up guarding the Pope in an ordinary house in the middle of nowhere."

"At least we've found him," Anthony said. "We're in a much better position than we were earlier on this evening. We've got the Pope, we've got Brown, and both the gunman and Fish are dead."

"True, although I'd really rather that Fish was alive. We might never get to the bottom of this all now. You're right, though. Our priorities in the short term must be to preserve the Pope's life. Any luck on that membership list?"

"None whatsoever. There's no Giuseppe Campanaro on it. The only person I can find on the list from Charlwood Abbey is Adam Michaels, and he's dead."

"What the fuck is Campanaro doing here then?"

"I haven't the faintest idea. We've got the place covered, though. There's no way he'll get in here tonight."

Campanaro was shocked at his failure to get to the Pope. He had understood that Philip Brown was alone in the house, and yet there seemed to be several of them in there now. What's more, they were armed. There was no way he would be able to do what he had to do now.

He needed backup, and he needed it now.

He retreated to rear of the garden, forcing his way through the dense shrubbery at the side of the property. When he got there, he pushed his way right to the back, up against a high wooden fence, and placed a phone call to the 'acquaintance' who had put him up to this.

"I need support."

"Where are you?"

"Brown's place in Reigate. He's got reinforcements and they're armed."

"What do you expect me to do?"

"Are you not listening to me? I need support!"

"And what do you want me to do about it? Mobilise an army or something?"

"That's exactly what I want you to do. Get them up here now! And arm them, for God's sake. We can do this, but I can't do it on my own."

"Bloody Michaels. If he hadn't been such an incompetent moron we wouldn't be here now."

"No, well we are. What you going to do about it?"

"Sit tight, Giuseppe. I'll have people up there in fifteen minutes."

Chapter 19

Graham arrived at the house in Reigate about twenty minutes after Jeremy and Anthony. During those twenty minutes, nothing of any great note had happened. They were beginning to wonder if Campanaro had done a runner, since he had not shown himself for some time. They remained at their posts, however, and Anthony joined the others by taking a ground floor window at the front of the house, from which he could monitor the front door, the driveway, and some of the track leading to the house.

At least once, Jeremy found himself wondering if perhaps he'd gone mad, and was guarding an empty house. What if Brown was simply a decoy, he thought. What if the Pope's not really here at all? He reassured himself by peering into the master bedroom and observing the Pope asleep in his bed. How he was managing to sleep with everything that was happening around him was something of a mystery to Jeremy, but he guessed that this was probably fairly normal for a man who was probably the most famous person in the world.

Jeremy had avoided laying into Graham for his actions at Fish's house. He was still fuming that Graham had succeeded in killing their only real hope of establishing what, exactly, was happening that night, but the time would come for Graham's chastisement. For now, it was all hands on deck to guard the house against any would-be Pope-killers that came along.

It was ten minutes after Graham's arrival that the situation began to heat up once more.

Sally was still on guard at the back of the house. She had been staring out across the rear lawn for some time and was beginning to think that they were wasting their time when she first saw movement. In the centre of the hedgerow at the far end of the garden, she thought she saw movement.

"Did anyone else see that? There's something at the end of the garden," she shouted.

"Nothing yet," Trevor replied.

Jeremy and Graham rushed into the bedroom in which Sally was standing guard.

"It was right in the middle of the hedge," Sally told them as they peered out of the window.

"Are you sure, Sally?" Jeremy asked.

"Yes, definitely. Look – there it goes again, slightly further along this time."

"You're right – there's something there," Jeremy agreed. "Did you see it, Graham?"

"I did."

"Get through to Trevor, and have your weapons ready."

Before Graham had even left the room, the sound of a shot reverberated around the house.

"What was that?" Philip shouted.

"Someone's taking pot shots at us," Jeremy responded. "Brown, move the Pope to the front of the house."

Graham dashed through to join Trevor in one of the other bedrooms. They both looked at each other, and put their guns up to the glass.

"Just to let you know, I've never fired a gun in my life before," Trevor told Graham.

"Don't worry about it. I'll take the lead, you just follow."

A second shot pinged the brickwork just beneath the window that Trevor and Graham were standing at.

"Jesus, that was close!" Trevor remarked.

"Can anyone see where these shots are coming from?" Graham shouted.

"There's at least one person in the hedge at the bottom," Sally replied.

"How many of them are there?" asked Graham.

"No idea," Sally replied.

For a few moments, all was quiet. No more shots were fired, but the tension in the house only increased as the Hunter Group began to wonder what the next move was going to be. Then, they saw them.

From out of the hedges, three men dressed in black robes appeared, dropped to the ground, and began shooting at the house with semi-automatic weapons. They scored direct hits against the first floor windows, which were all blown into the room.

Trevor dropped to his knees screaming.

"What's happened?" asked Jeremy.

"They've got Bates!" Graham replied. He looked down on the floor. Trevor was clasping his arm, which was gushing blood. He was hyperventilating.

"Jesus," Graham remarked, dropping down to try and calm Trevor. As he did so, another burst of gunfire burst through the now glass-less windows, flying over Trevor and Graham's heads. The fire was answered from the other room by Sally and Jeremy.

"They're fucking monks!" Jeremy shouted. "We're being attacked by the fucking monk army! This is mental!"

Graham watched Trevor struggling. He was reacting very badly to the wound.

"We need an ambulance for Bates!" he shouted.

"That'll have to wait!" Jeremy shouted back.

Graham grabbed the sheet from the bed and attempted to bind it tightly around Trevor's arm. It was a nasty wound, but he would be alright. Having bandaged him up as well as he could manage under the circumstances, he cautiously lifted himself up and peered through the window. There was no trace of the gunmen.

"Where did they go?"

"They're regrouping in the hedges!"

This all seemed wrong to Graham.

"Can we just think about what we're doing here?" Graham shouted. "Why are we being besieged by a group of monks? Does that not strike anyone as slightly wrong?"

"They're trying to kill the Pope," Jeremy responded. "We have to defend the Pope!"

Before they could continue the discussion, the three monks appeared on the lawn again.

"Shoot!" ordered Jeremy. He and Sally let off a round of bullets as Graham watched. They got one of the monks who dropped to the ground. The others shot through the glassless windows once more, and then retreated back into the hedges.

"There're three at the front!" shouted Brown from his position at the front of the house.

"Shoot the bastards!" Jeremy said.

Graham was getting a very bad feeling about this. He just could not believe that a group of monks wanted the Pope dead. It didn't seem right. There was a massive warning siren in his head.

"This is wrong!" he shouted again.

"For fuck's sake, Graham!" shouted Jeremy. "Until they stop shooting at my team I'm not even going to think about that! They're coming from the rear again!"

Graham ducked down as bullets sailed in from the back as shots were simultaneously fired at the front of the house.

"We're under siege!" shouted Anthony. They're coming for the door!"

"Get them!" Jeremy ordered.

Anthony looked out of the window as three monks equipped with machine guns walked straight up to the front door and started firing, letting off round after round into the thick wooden door. He should shoot them. Jeremy wanted him to shoot them. But he couldn't help agreeing with Graham that there was something wrong with this whole situation.

Jeremy and Sally were shooting back against the monks in the back garden as well as they could, but it was proving difficult. They could either shoot at the monks and expose themselves, or shelter beneath the safety of the wall. The monks were ruthless and showed no fear whatsoever. Clearly they believed that what they were doing was right, and they were willing to die if necessary. They let off another round of bullets, and Jeremy and Sally ducked down. Sally quickly peered over the wall again as the bullets stopped, and one of the monks started shooting again.

"Just get them, Sal," Jeremy told her. "I'm going to sort out the front."

Jeremy crawled on his hands and knees to the bedroom door, and ran down the stairs. As he reached the hallway bullets blasted through the front door, heading straight across the house. He threw himself to the floor, propped himself up on his shoulders and waited for the door to open.

Sure enough, a split second after the shooting, someone outside put a boot against the now rather tattered door, and it came crashing in. Three black clad figures let off a burst of bullets around the ground floor. Jeremy aimed at the central monk and fired. He fell to the floor. He aimed at the left monk. He fell to the floor. The right monk ducked outside the door, in the direction of Anthony's vantage point.

"Shoot the fucker!" he shouted at Anthony. Jeremy listened as shots were let off. Anthony screamed.

"What's happening?" Jeremy shouted to Anthony.

"He got me!"

"Return fire, for God's sake!"

This was rapidly becoming a nightmare. They'd taken out two monks. God knows how many more there were. And Campanaro was still unaccounted for. Meanwhile, two of their team had been shot.

Jeremy waited for the other monk to show himself through the front door. He waited for what seemed an age, and he didn't appear. He waited longer, listening to the continuing gun battle at the back of the house.

Eventually, he stood up, and, his gun out in front of him, made his way to the front door. He cautiously peered out. And saw nothing.

Where was that bloody monk?

He had to bring an end to this.

He needed the element of surprise.

He checked his gun and made his way to the passageway at the side of the house. He dashed along it, and reached the corner of the house.

Three monks were kneeling on the far end of the lawn, shooting at the house.

Jeremy dived in the bushes at the side of the garden, and began making his way through the undergrowth to the rear of the garden.

When he got there, he could not believe what he was seeing. There were at least twelve monks, all kitted out with state of the art machine guns, preparing to show their faces and shoot at the house. Briefing them from the rear was a short, fat man dressed in a suit.

Campanaro.

He had to be the brains. He had to be in control.

If I can just get Campanaro, I can bring this to an end, he thought.

There was no way he could get a clear line of sight to Campanaro from his current position; he'd have to shoot four monks in the process, and that would draw attention to his presence. If he gave himself away now, there was no way he could get Campanaro.

He continued pressing on to the back of the garden, hoping to get into a position where he could take Campanaro out directly. As he moved, he heard Graham shouting to the monks from the house.

"What do you want?"

What was he up to? He was rapidly becoming a liability. He owed Graham a great deal. He owed Graham his life. But things couldn't go on as they were. People were going to get hurt if Graham couldn't control himself rather better.

One of the monks responded to Graham's shout.

"Just give us the Pope and we'll leave!"

"We're not letting the Pope out of our sight!" Graham responded.

"We just want to get our Holy Father back! We know you want him dead. You'll have to kill all of us before you take him!"

Fools, Jeremy thought. If they had wanted the Pope dead, they could do it now. They had the Pope after all, not the monks.

"We just want to take the Pope to safety!" the monk added.

There was silence from the house.

Before the discussion could continue, before the shooting could restart, a figure dressed in white appeared on the back lawn, his hands in the air.

Bloody hell, thought Jeremy. The Pope! What's he doing out here? Wasn't Brown supposed to be guarding him with his life? What had happened to Brown?

Before Jeremy could consider what to do, he saw four of the monks run out for the Pope.

Jeremy had to get to the Pope before the monks did. He ran out of the undergrowth towards the Pope.

To his left, Jeremy saw Campanaro running out towards the Pope.

Time froze as Jeremy watched the scene play out, waiting to discover which of them would reach the Holy Father first.

The monks were old and slow

Campanaro was fat and slow.

They had an advantage over Jeremy in that they were closer.

Jeremy had to run faster. He sped up, his heart in his mouth.

Campanaro was running flat out. He was going to get there first.

The monks were slowing down.

Jeremy was getting closer, but not fast enough.

Campanaro reached the Pope. He put a big, fat arm around the Pope's neck, holding him out in front of him.

Shit, shit, shit! Jeremy thought.

Campanaro pulled a revolver out of his waistband and held it to the Pope's head.

No, no, no! This shouldn't be happening!

"Take a step closer, any of you, and I'll blow his head off!"

Jeremy stopped running.

The monks stopped running.

There was silence in the garden.

There was silence in the house.

One of the running monks broke the silence.

"What are you doing, Giuseppe?"

"Any of you move and I'll shoot," Campanaro reiterated.

"Giuseppe, put the gun down, please!" one of the other monks pleaded.

"Campanaro, just drop the weapon. There's no way this can end well if you shoot the Pope," Jeremy said.

"You in the house, come out onto the lawn with your hands up where I can see them," Campanaro ordered.

One of the monks, his hands held high, began approaching Campanaro.

"Stop right there, Father Peter!" Campanaro ordered.

"I can't believe what you've done, Giuseppe!" Father Peter said, continuing to slowly approach Campanaro and the Pope with his hands up. "You told us these people wanted to kill the Holy Father, and all along it was you who wanted him dead. What are you doing this for? Please, just drop the weapon."

"You lot, you bloody Catholics, you're all the same with your holier-than-thou, God loves us all bullshit, aren't you? Well, where's your God now? I don't see him rushing to protect his representative on earth! You bloody Catholics have destroyed my life. You've destroyed my family. You've destroyed my school. You and your fucking, senseless abbot, who talks crap all the time. I've had enough! It ends tonight!"

Campanaro pulled the Pope closer to him, and stuck the muzzle of the gun tighter into the Pope's neck.

"I'm going to shoot unless you back off, Father Peter!"

The monk continued to approach slowly. Jeremy watched on as he wondered if Campanaro would really kill the Pope or not.

As Father Peter got closer to the Pope, Campanaro pulled his gun away from the Pope, and shot the monk in the head. He dropped to the ground, dying instantly.

"Any of you others try that and it'll be your Pope that dies, not you!" Campanaro told them.

It was starting to become clear in Jeremy's mind what was going on. Graham had been right all along, as he always was. He should have listened to him. The monks were attacking the house because Campanaro had manipulated them. They believed that Jeremy and his team were going to kill the Pope, and they had thought that they were rescuing him. All the time, it was Campanaro who had wanted him dead.

"Where are your mates from the house?" Campanaro shouted to Jeremy. "Get them out now before I blow this old Nazi's head off!"

"Graham! Get everyone out of the house straight away!" Jeremy ordered.

Sally, Anthony, Bates and Brown slowly walked out of the house, their hands in the air. Both Anthony and Bates were looking very much the worse for wear. Graham was nowhere to be seen.

Trust Graham, he thought. He knew he would have the intelligence to work through a solution to this problem. Campanaro had no means of knowing who Graham was, nor how many of them there were in the house. Or so he thought.

"Where's the other one?" Campanaro yelled. "I know there's one more lurking in the shadows! You're not going to outwit me! Get out here now!"

Graham appeared in the doorway, his hands in the air.

"All of you, come and form a nice little group over here where I can see you all, okay?"

Those who had been in the house moved round and joined the group of monks and Jeremy on the lawn.

Now what, thought Jeremy. How are we going to resolve this situation?

"I'm going to walk out to my car with Popie here, okay, and none of you are going to attempt to follow me, otherwise I'll kill him. Is that clear?"

"Perfectly," Jeremy answered.

Campanaro started slowly edging backwards moving towards the side gate of the garden, keeping the Pope in between him and the others at all times, his gun firmly pressed into the Pope's neck.

This is not going to end well, Jeremy thought.

Then, he thought he saw her. Hidden in the passageway between the house and the garage, lurking in the shadows. Yes, it was Helena. And Campanaro had his back to her.

Milliseconds later, a gun shot echoed around the garden, and Campanaro dropped to the ground.

As did the Pope.

Chapter 20

Everyone in the garden rushed over to where Campanaro and the Pope had fallen, hoping against hope that the Pope was still alive and uninjured.

Helena was the first to arrive. She pushed Campanaro's enormous body off the Pope, and crouched down to check the Holy Father's vital signs.

"He's breathing and there's a pulse!" she shouted as the others gathered around her. "And wait, he's conscious!"

"Was... Helfen Sie Mir!"

"Your holiness, just relax, you're in safe hands now," Helena said to the Pope. "Just try to stay calm and don't speak. We'll get you inside. Sally, give me a hand will you?"

The two women grabbed the Pope under his arms, and gently lifted him to his feet.

"Get him inside," Jeremy said. "Brown, you'd better go and make sure he's comfortable. And Bates, you'd better go inside and get the girls to check you out when they've finished with the Pope. We'll sort out here."

Helena and Sally led the Pope in, followed by Brown and Bates.

"Who's in charge amongst you lot?" Jeremy asked the monks.

"That would be me," one of them said, stepping forward. "I'm Father Andrew, and I'm the Prior of Charlwood Abbey."

"Perhaps you'd like to explain what the hell has been happening here," Jeremy demanded.

This was the end. He was going to die. He could feel himself fading.

There was no pain.

He could hear voices.

With a great deal of effort, Campanaro opened his eyes.

The Pope was nowhere to be seen. He assumed he'd failed. People seemed calm. They wouldn't be calm if the Pope was dead.

He strained his eyes. Gradually, the dark shapes took on human form. He could see the monks. He could see Father Andrew. And he could see someone else. A tall man in a suit. He was talking to Father Andrew.

He tried to move his arms.

It was a struggle to breath. He knew he only had seconds left to live.

He had to act.

His weight was on his left arm. It wouldn't move.

He managed to move his right arm. He found his gun with his fingers. He clasped his hand around it, and dragged it across the ground until it was level with his face.

He could see the man in the suit. He aimed the gun at him. He tried to aim for the middle of his back, but it was a strain to hold the gun up.

He pulled the trigger.

He heard two shots.

He heard a shout.

Tom finally arrived at the house. It looked like he was too late. The windows had all been shot out. The front door was hanging off the frame, attached with only one hinge, and was riddled with bullet holes.

A couple of men in dressing gowns were hesitating around the gates to the house, clearly uncertain what they should do. Probably neighbours, Tom thought.

Tom jumped out of the car, grabbed a rifle from the boot, and walked cautiously towards the house.

"What's happening?" one of the men in dressing gowns asked.

"I have no idea," Tom replied. "I'm a police officer, though, and intend to find out. Do me a favour – go back to your homes, keep everyone inside and away from the windows, and call the police for me. Tell them that Superintendent Tom Sutcliffe of the Met is on scene and requesting backup."

The two men scurried off, and Tom continued to approach the house.

He looked at the front door, and considered whether he should enter the house. He had no idea who was inside, what had happened, and, perhaps most importantly, whether the Pope was still alive.

He had a change of plan, though, when he heard a gunshot from the back garden. A gunshot, followed by the scream of the victim, followed by more general screaming.

Tom saw a gate at the side of the house, and ran up to it. It led into a narrow passageway between the house and a large, brick garage. He cautiously edged his way along to the end, and crouched in the shadows, his gun ready, watching what was happening in the garden.

He saw two figures on the ground. One of them was the Pope. He had no idea who the other figure was. All attention in the garden was on the Pope. He watched as Helena and Sally led him into the house, followed by someone he recognised from the photos he had seen at his house as Philip Brown and a police officer.

He was rather shocked to see a small group of monks also on the back lawn. What were they doing there?

He watched as Jeremy began making conversation with one of them, an elderly looking man.

Then he saw the fat man on the ground.

The others clearly thought he was dead, but had not bothered to check.

He saw the fat man go for his gun, and aim it directly at Jeremy's back.

No one else had noticed. He had to act.

He took aim at the back of the fat man's head and pulled the trigger.

He was a split second too late.

The fat man had got a bullet off before him.

"Jeremy!" he shouted, trying to warn his boss, knowing that it would be too late.

Helena and Sally laid the Pope back into the bed that he had slept in earlier that night. It was nearly six o' clock, and would soon be time to move the Pope again, this time for his breakfast meeting with the Archbishop of Canterbury.

Helena made a quick examination of the old man. He seemed to be uninjured, but, unsurprisingly after what had been a very difficult night for him, was completely exhausted.

"Just rest yourself, Your Holiness," she said.

"You are very good to me," he replied. "And this man," he grabbed Philip's hand, "he saved my life. I am very lucky."

"You are," Helena replied. "Someone up there clearly doesn't think it's your time yet. Now, just rest yourself. We'll take care of everything."

Sally returned with a large glass of water. The Pope drank deeply.

"Is there anything else I can get you?" Sally answered.

"No, you've done too much. I need to sleep."

He passed the glass back to Sally, and turned over, just as they all heard two shots in quick succession from the back garden.

They dashed over to the glass-less windows to see what was happening.

Father Andrew noticed Campanaro go for his gun. It was almost too late. In the split second it took for Campanaro to pull the trigger, Father Andrew considered his options.

This man in the suit was clearly good.

Campanaro was clearly bad.

As Campanaro pulled the trigger, he shoved Jeremy to the ground hard.

Jeremy was caught unaware, and, a surprised look in his eyes, toppled to the ground.

Father Andrew knew it was too late.

He tried to move, but he was too slow.

Jeremy picked himself off the ground and looked around. Campanaro was lying in an ever-expanding pool of his own blood.

Tom was walking across the lawn towards him, his gun in his hand.

Jeremy tried to walk towards Tom, but found himself unable to move.

"What the hell happened there?" he asked, as Tom approached.

"I think you forgot to check that fat bloke was dead," Tom said casually. "He wasn't. I had just arrived, and noticed him going for his gun. I shot him in the back of the head. Sadly, I was too late. He let his bullet off before I did."

"So Father Andrew...?"

"If you're referring to this monk character on the ground, he saved your life. He pushed you out of the path of the bullet, and took it himself."

Jeremy found himself choked. This monk who just a few minutes before had been his enemy, who had been shooting at him, had tried to kill him, had just saved his life.

"I think I need to sit down," Jeremy said, dropping to the grass.

Several of the monks were tending to Father Andrew's body, and were saying prayers. One of them walked over to Jeremy and Tom when he saw them looking at them.

"How are you, my friend?" he asked.

"I... I... I don't understand," Jeremy found tears rolling down his face. He had been in all manner of tricky situations before during his career, but nothing had affected him like the events of tonight.

"Just take some deep breaths," the monk said, placing a hand on Jeremy's shoulder.

"But we were trying to kill each other a moment ago!" Jeremy said, before placing his face in his hands.

"We all make mistakes," the monk said. "It seems that we've been suffering from a case of mistaken identities this evening. You see, we've always had a great deal of respect for Mr.

Campanaro. He lived amongst us, he dined with us, and he prayed with us. He ran our school. We believed him to be a good man. When he told us that you had kidnapped the Pope and were going to torture then execute him, we saw no reason to doubt him. He asked for our support, and told us that we needed to kill you and your friends before you killed the Holy Father, and we believed him. I guess we were wrong. I guess he deceived us."

"We've been trying to save the Pope all night!" Jeremy exclaimed. "We're not the ones who want the Pope dead, we're the ones trying to protect him and keep him safe!"

"So it now seems," the monk said. "When we saw Giuseppe grab the Holy Father and hold a gun to his head, we knew that we'd been lied to. We realised then that we had made a terrible mistake. A mistake that I don't know how our community will ever recover from. A mistake that cost several of our brothers their lives, including our dear friend Father Andrew."

"He died for me."

"'Greater love has no one than this, that he lay down his life for his friends'. The words of our Lord and saviour Jesus Christ in John's gospel. As monks we live our lives to serve the Lord, and we know right from the start that the ultimate sacrifice we make is with our lives. After all, it was Jesus who laid down his life for us, taking our sin upon himself when he died upon the cross, so that we could have eternal life. Jesus rose from the dead three days later. Father Andrew led a good life. He will rise again in heaven, the fulfilment of his life's work."

Jeremy did not know what to say. He was not a religious man, but he found himself genuinely moved by the warm, compassionate words of this kind and loving man who should hate him for what he had done.

"What's your name, friend?" the monk asked, looking directly into Jeremy's eyes.

"It's Jeremy."

"Jeremy, don't worry. We don't hold you responsible for anything that has happened tonight. It's a sad night for the monastery. At least four of our brothers have died here in this garden, but they died thinking that they were fighting for what they believed in. It is Campanaro who will have to defend his actions come judgement day. Your conscience should be clear."

There was a brief moment of silence, as both Jeremy and the monk reflected on what had happened over the last hour or so. The sun was rising, and the darkness was surrendering to the light. In the woods around the house, the birds were gradually waking, their calls seeming to usher in the new day. The garden, torn by gunfire and hatred that night, was suddenly calm and peaceful, the monks praying over the body of their friend and supporting Jeremy in his moment of crisis.

It's nearly over, thought Jeremy. They had stopped several attempts on the Pope's life, and they had all lived to tell the tale. It would soon be time to take the Pope back to London for breakfast, and then on to Hyde Park to celebrate Mass with the faithful. Then they would put him on a plane back to the Vatican, and their worries would end. No one would be any the wiser about that night's events. As far as the general public were concerned, it would seem that the Pope's visit had passed without event.

It was Tom who finally broke the silence.

"Let's get you all inside," he said. "I think we need to put the kettle on."

Chapter 21

Conversation was awkward in the Reigate house that morning. Eight remaining monks, the six members of the Hunter Group, a police officer and a civilian found themselves chatting over coffee in the living room whilst the Pope slept peacefully upstairs.

Philip Brown did much of the talking. He knew a great deal about the plans that had been made to kill the Pope and was happy to explain.

"I first became aware of the plan to kill our Holy Father about three weeks ago. I was contacted out of the blue by a man named Paul Fish, a member of a group calling themselves Campaign Against Religious Nutters, or CARN. They were a rather small group with no more than eight members who had been speaking out against organised religion for several years. They tried to portray themselves as a group with a philosophical problem with religion, but in truth they were closer to being a vigilante group. They liked to make a nuisance of themselves when events took place that were co-ordinated by religious groups. They were particularly concerned about the spread of Islam, but were not afraid to engage in a bit of Catholic bashing when they felt like it."

"What did Paul Fish want from you?" asked Graham. "Correct me if I'm wrong, but you're a very committed Catholic, and your group Infinitum aims to portray the Catholic Church in a more positive light. You seem like unusual acquaintances."

"Yes, Infinitum. That's more of a distraction than anything else. I tried to encourage my fellow Catholics to take action in their own communities to show that we're loving, compassionate, friendly people. The Church has had so much bad publicity in recent years, not least with the paedophile scandal, and we wanted, or perhaps I should say that I wanted, to try to rehabilitate it in the eyes of the public. Sadly, the group never really took off, and has to all intents and purposes been dormant for the last few years."

"So Fish?" Graham asked again.

"Hold on, I'll come to that," Philip responded. "Fish was fine with the activities of CARN all the time they were simply engaging in demonstrations against organised religion. Despite what you might think, he was an intelligent guy. He believed that religious people had been brainwashed, and should be shown that what we believe is stuff and nonsense, and nothing more than fairy tales. Their leader, though, was Dan Johnson, a rather unsavoury character if ever there was one. Johnson was a nasty piece of work, well known to the law. He spent time at Her Majesty's Pleasure for assault, GBH, and armed robbery amongst many other crimes. He believed that CARN were soft, and that they needed to be more forceful. He saw in CARN the opportunity to make a name for himself in the criminal underworld, and determined that the organisation should change direction."

"And this new direction did not go down with the other members of CARN?" Jeremy asked.

"For the most part, it went down very well indeed. Johnson had been a member of the organisation since its inception four years or so ago, but had spent much of that time in jail. When he came out, he seized the leadership, which had been his anyway. He was disgusted with how ineffective the group had become whilst he was in prison, and aimed to return the group to prominence. The other members were for the most part delighted with this. They hoped that they would win notoriety under Johnson's leadership."

"How did they hope to win notoriety?" Graham asked.

"They wanted to strike at the heart of organised religion. When they heard that the Pope was visiting the UK, they saw the perfect opportunity to take action in a very significant way. They planned to target the Pope."

"And that didn't go down well with Fish, I take it," Helena asked.

"Fish found himself in a bit of a dilemma. He wasn't really sure what he should be doing. He genuinely believed that religious groups were evil, and that religious people were deluded and misguided. He thought that the Pope, in particular, was profoundly evil. At the same time, though, he had a real issue with the plan to kill the Pope. He thought that was wrong, and that Johnson was going too far. He also did not want that kind of notoriety. He'd recently set up home with his long-term girlfriend, Tracy, a lovely girl, and she was expecting their first child. He was not a killer, and he certainly did not want to end up in prison, just as things were starting to go so right for him. At first, though, he thought he had to go along with the plan. He was petrified of Johnson, and thought that if he didn't do as he was told, Johnson would string him up."

"That plan involved the construction of a fake Popemobile, I take it?" Helena said.

"I believe so," Philip replied. "I'm not familiar with the intricate details of the plan, but I believe that they intended to construct a dummy Popemobile which they would use as a decoy somehow whilst they captured the real one."

"I would have liked to see them try that one," Jeremy said. "There is absolutely no way that plan could succeed."

"Fish was well aware of that, which is why he went along with it to a certain extent. He was a resourceful guy and was given the task of constructing a new Popemobile. Johnson had access to large amounts of cash, and so money was not an issue when it came to building it."

"So how did you come into contact with Fish?" Graham asked. "I still don't see how someone like Fish could possibly have anything in common with you?"

"Had things continued as they were, I have no doubt that I would never have come into contact with Fish. Things changed somewhat rapidly, however, when Fish made a discovery. He was researching Catholic groups, which is, incidentally, how he found out about me. One day he came across a group called New Reformation. New Reformation is made up of Roman Catholics who hate the Pope. That might sound like a contradiction, but actually, if you study the membership, it kind of makes sense. Most of the people in NR were either abused by Catholic priests as they were growing up, or have close friends and family who were. They hold the current Pope personally responsible for what happened, believing that he instrumented a cover up whilst he served as Prefect of the Sacred Congregation for the Doctrine of the Faith. They believe that had he not led a cover up, many of the cases of child abuse would not have occurred. Members of NR also maintain that whilst the current Pope leads the Church, Catholicism will continue to be the target of abuse from the media, and will suffer acutely from the bad publicity that the Pope's leadership attracts. They want justice for the way that they were treated as children, but also want to remove the Pope and replace him with someone who can portray the Church in a more positive light. In that sense, the views that they hold are not dissimilar to the views that I hold, although I would certainly not take it as far as advocating the murder of the Pope."

"It was New Reformation that we believed were planning an attack on the Pope," Jeremy said. "What is the relationship between NR and CARN?"

"A very poor one. Fish discovered the existence of NR whilst undertaking his research. He was intrigued by their hatred of the Pope, and met with a senior figure within the movement. Fish soon discovered that NR were planning to assassinate the Pope, and let slip that CARN were planning the same thing. Initially, CARN and NR planned to work together; NR would provide the intelligence, whilst CARN would provide the muscle. Fish explained this to Johnson, and he was very happy with the arrangement. It was arranged that CARN would be the ones to strike the Pope, with financial resources and intelligence provided by NR. CARN were effectively acting as guns for hire."

"So what happened?" Graham asked. "Something must have gone wrong somewhere."

"Fish got cold feet. Having discovered NR and chatted to them, he was intrigued with what he read about Infinitum. He saw that we – or should I say I – hold similar views on improving the world's view of the Catholic church, but without the violence. He came and had a chat with me. He wanted to meet twice more after that, and I suppose we struck up a kind of friendship – a rather unlikely bond, perhaps, but a friendship nonetheless. On our third meeting, he revealed the plot to kill the Pope. We spoke about this a great deal, and by the end of the meeting, Fish was convinced that killing the Pope was not the way forward, and was totally wrong. Yesterday, he hid the Popemobile to stop anyone else in NR or CARN using it, thereby thwarting the plan. NR were absolutely furious, and believed that they had been betrayed by CARN. They had given them plenty of cash, and put their whole organisation at risk by liaising with CARN."

"It was you chatting to Fish in the pub at Liverpool Street last night," Graham pointed out. "What were you discussing?"

"Fish asked to meet because he was horrified by what he thought was going to happen. He thought he was going to be killed by NR, because they held him responsible for reneging on their agreement. He was also very concerned because he had acted unilaterally in cancelling CARN's plan, and preventing it from taking place. He had not told Johnson what he was doing, and he was concerned that Johnson might well kill him too.

"During the afternoon, Fish kept a close observation on NR, and learnt that they were still planning to kill the Pope. It turned out that they had a backup plan just in case they were let down by CARN. They also decided to make CARN pay for what Fish had done. It was they who set

CARN up with the van packed with explosives outside the flat. They abandoned it, and tipped the police off that it was there. They also arranged for CARN to be taken out. Fish discovered this and panicked. He asked to speak to me, and I agreed. We met at the pub last night."

"I take it Fish did not let CARN know about NR's plan to blow them to kingdom come?" Tom asked.

"He thought about it, but really did not know what to do. If he didn't tell them, they would surely be killed. If he did tell them, they would escape and he would surely be killed. So it was a tricky position that he found himself in. Things didn't look good for him either way."

"So what was NR's plan that Fish found out about?"

"They had hired a professional assassin to kill the Pope. The plan was that the assassin would first of all kill CARN. Having done his work there, he was tasked with tracking down the van filled with explosives and destroying that, to prevent it being linked back to NR. Then he was to find the Pope and kill him whilst he slept."

"How did he find the Pope, though?" Jeremy asked.

"That was easy – really easy. NR had contacts who worked at Charlwood Abbey. When they discovered that the Pope would be spending the night there, they let the NR leadership know.

They tipped off the assassin, and you know the rest. Of course, the major mistake was moving the Pope to the abbey. The original plan had been for him to spend the night at Lambeth Palace, where it would have been very, very difficult for them to strike. Charlwood Abbey made things really easy for them."

"Adam Michaels presumably decided to take matters into his own hands," Graham said.

"Yes. That was not part of the original plan. He was clearly an idiot, and could have messed everything up for NR."

"As it was, he helped us out, because he was a useful distraction whilst you removed the Pope, and I took care of the assassin," Graham pointed out.

"That is very true," Philip agreed.

"So Fish thought that you may be able to help him bring about an end to the whole episode?" Helena asked.

"I guess so," Philip replied. "He was having a real crisis of conscience. He came to me because we had become friends, and because I was the only person outside the organisations who knew what was going on. He begged me to undertake a rescue mission, to drive down to Surrey and to remove the Pope."

"And you just did it?" Graham said.

"For the good of the Pope, and for the good of the Church, I didn't feel there was any option."

"That was either very brave or very stupid," Sally said.

"Very stupid, I suspect," Philip agreed. "I really had no choice in the matter. A big part of me didn't want to, because I knew that I was putting myself at risk. But if I didn't do it, no one else would. I hired a car, drove down there, and waited until I knew that everyone was in bed. Paul gave me a gun with ketamine tipped bullets that I used on the guards. I didn't want to, because I was concerned that they might not wake up, but I had to take action fast."

"Well, it worked," Jeremy said. "You did a very good job indeed. I'm not sure I would have recommended you do what you did, but under the circumstances, you did well. Without you, the Pope would almost certainly be dead. Well done."

"Where do we go from here?" Graham asked Jeremy.

Jeremy looked at his watch.

"It's nearly seven o' clock," he said. "We need to get the Pope on the road soon. He's going to be late as it is. Before we do, though, there are a couple of things I need to mention to you, Philip. First of all, I'm afraid I have some very bad news indeed. It seems that someone has tried to send you a warning tonight, although - as it turns out - rather too late. Someone set fire to your house in Highgate. Before you worry too much, though, all of your family are safe. You have Tom to thank for that. He drove out to yours earlier on to have a few words with you, but found your house ablaze. He managed to get Tessa and the girls to safety. They're now in a hotel down the road."

Philip went white. He did not know what to say.

"Thank you. Thank you so much, Tom." The two men stood up, and Philip embraced Tom before sitting down again.

"Someone must have seen me meeting with Paul," he said. "I knew this would be risky, but I didn't think for one minute I'd be endangering the lives of my family. I'd never have pursued this if I thought I was putting them at risk. Thank goodness they're safe, though. What was the other point you wanted to mention, Jeremy?"

"I'm afraid that there was an accident earlier on tonight. We tracked Fish down and wanted to ask him some questions. He took flight and fell off his roof. He died instantly."

There was another pause.

"I don't know what to say. I know how it must have looked, but Paul Fish was a good man. He had a conscience and tried to do the right thing. Perhaps he should not have got mixed up with all of this at all, but I know that deep down he was a delightful man. It's tragic that this should have happened to him, but I'm sure he knew the risks."

"Now, I think we'd better start moving this forward," Jeremy announced. "Graham, you and I will drive the Pope up to Lambeth, and the rest of you can surround us. Tom and Anthony, you will need to get onto the police and fill them in with what happened. We need to make sure that all the leaders of NR are rounded up as soon as possible to ensure that nothing else can take place today. Get onto that. Once we've dropped the Pope off at Lambeth Palace, we'll rendezvous back at the Gherkin. Philip, you're coming too. For now, though, our work here is done. Let's go, people!"

Chapter 22

The drive back to London was uneventful. They dropped a rather-tired looking Pope off at Lambeth Palace at half past seven, just half an hour later than planned. The team then headed back to the Gherkin for further briefing.

The first to arrive at the Hunter Group offices were Jeremy and Graham. Jeremy called Graham into his office for a chat.

"Take a seat, Graham," Jeremy said, sitting down on an armchair and indicating his small sofa to Graham.

"Quite a night, I'm sure you'll agree," Jeremy commented.

"Quite a night."

"We've all been under a great deal of pressure tonight, Graham, and I think a significant amount of that pressure has fallen on you. You were involved with the shoot out at Charlwood Abbey, and you saved the Pope's life. For that you deserve the highest praise. You've also made some ridiculously poor decisions this evening, though, as I'm sure you're aware."

"Decisions that, as you rightly point out, were taken under pressure."

"That's right. At the same time, though, I do have grave concerns about two things that you've done tonight. As I've already mentioned, I'm appalled that you told Sally, who is after all simply our administrator, to chase Brown and the Pope whilst you went off on a wild goose chase. Sally should not have been out of the office at all, and I recognise the fact that it was partly my fault, but she certainly should have not been involved in a high-speed car chase. Not only did she lose the Pope, but she was almost killed herself."

"I made a decision that could, with hindsight, seem to be the wrong one. I made a call, and that call was to track down the origin of the gunman who nearly killed the Pope. I hoped to bring in his driver, which could have opened up a rich vein of information for us."

"But which didn't," Jeremy said. "You shot him. You couldn't even manage to bring him in. Okay, perhaps you're right, maybe he could have been a useful lead, but as it was, your whole little exploit was a dead end."

"If he hadn't started taking pot shots at me I could have brought him in and made him talk."

"Maybe, but your attempt to capture a mere pawn in tonight's events almost lost us the Pope. Can you imagine how that would have gone down? If it was discovered that we had the Pope in our sights, that we were at the scene of his kidnapping, but we let him go? There would have been hell to pay."

"Did my admittedly rather stupid decision actually have any lasting impact, though?" Graham asked. "We lost the Pope, but then we found him. Sally could have died, but didn't. In fact, Sally was the closest to the house in Reigate when we located the Pope and was first on the scene, specifically because she had crashed her car. And when she got there, she did a brilliant job. Look, Jeremy, I've not been a great friend of Sally, but she has real potential. She's wasted pushing paper in this office."

"That's something we'll consider another time. For now, though, there's another serious issue that I want to raise with you. I'm sure you know what that is."

"Fish?"

"Exactly Fish. As it turns out, Fish was practically an innocent bystander in all of this. But tonight, you were responsible for his death. That is a very serious position to find yourself in."

"I understand that," Graham said, "but at the same time, I can't accept that I was responsible for his death. Ultimately, he ran. He jumped out of the window. And he fell off his roof."

"You broke into his house in the middle of the night and held a gun to his head. You can't blame him for taking flight."

"Had he obeyed instructions, he would still be alive."

"How did you introduce yourself to him? Did you tell him who you were?"

"As I recall, there was little opportunity for introductions."

"So the poor man had no idea who you were. You should have introduced yourself. As it was, he saw you in the pub and you chased him. Then you broke into his house and threatened him with a gun. It's not surprising that he ran. This could be very, very bad for us if his girlfriend or his family make a complaint."

"He was hardly an innocent man though, was he? I mean let's face it, he had been involved in a plot to kill the Pope. He had been constructing a Popemobile to use in their plan. He was hardly an innocent bystander in all of this. He had greater control over his destiny than you make out."

"You still can't blame the man for running. You still can't get round the fact that you were a contributory factor, if not the cause, of his death."

"So the charge has been reduced from cause to contributory factor now, has it?" Graham was starting to lose his rag. "Look, Jeremy. I'm tired. I haven't slept for over twenty-four hours. I was hard at work all day yesterday and then tonight I've saved the life of the Pope not once, but twice. I've been involved in not one but two shootouts. Do you really think that any blame for tonight's events can be pinned on me?"

"Sadly, I do, Graham. Now, just calm down, will you? We'll try and work this out."

"Calm down, you say? Calm down?" Graham was on his feet and shouting now. Jeremy, in all the years he had known Graham, had never seen him like this. He was usually a calm and placid person. "I never wanted to be a secret agent, you bastard! I never wanted to join your team! I know it might shock you and the rest of your stuck-up colleagues, but I'm quite happy delivering chicken for a living! So I have no ambition? I don't care! I live in a nice house, have a job I enjoy and I have everything I need. You're an idiot, Jeremy Hunter. You're a total bastard. And I want out!"

Graham stopped shouting, and walked to the glass, looking out over London as it sprang into life at the beginning of another day.

"Graham, I'm sorry you feel that way. I thought I was helping you out. I thought I was helping you to recover. I thought I was giving you purpose."

"I don't need purpose, Hunter," Graham said, his anger under control now. "I have all the purpose I need."

"Think back to what you were like when you joined the group, though, Graham. You were a wreck. You were in debt. You were an alcoholic. Hell, you were a druggie. Your life was leading nowhere except to an early grave. You were out of control."

"And you think that working for you has brought me back under control? It was the love of my parents and friends that did that."

"I saved your life, Graham, and you know it."

"It was me that saved your life, Hunter, and don't you forget it."

Jeremy had a flash back to that night in New York. He had been working for Westhaven Military Intelligence. Graham had been bumming around the city trying to find drugs. It had been at City Hall Subway, of all places. Jeremy had found himself confronted by a madman with a machine gun. He had recognised the assassin. He had half expected it, just not in such a public place. He knew at that moment that it was all over, that he was going to die on the platform. There was no way out.

Until Graham, pissed out of his skull and desperate for a line, had found him.

Something had happened in Graham's head. There was a glimmer of recognition in his brain. He hadn't seen Jeremy for years, despite their close friendship at school. Graham could not even have managed to exchange pleasantries with Jeremy, he was so drunk. Despite his inebriation, he tackled the assassin from behind, and neutralised the threat. He put himself at risk to save the life of his old friend.

Jeremy was overcome with gratitude. He was also shocked and horrified at what had become of his old friend. He vowed that night that he would help him to get clean and sort his life out. He paid for him to go into rehab in California and visited him regularly. He paid for Graham's parents to fly out to the US to be with him, and paid for them to stay in a smart hotel in LA. He paid for them all to return to the UK once Graham's treatment had been completed.

It was round about that time that Jeremy was approached to start his private security group. He needed to assemble a team that was smart, intelligent, dynamic and capable of anything. Jeremy knew instantly that he wanted Graham to join his team.

Graham had shown tremendous bravery that night in New York. But he was also one of the smartest people that Jeremy had ever known. Scruffy, awkward and lazy – Graham was all three – but he was also as sharp as a knife, highly intelligent, and could see a solution to any problem.

So it was that Jeremy had recruited Graham to join his team. Partly out of duty, but largely because he knew of no one who could do the job better.

And now, here they were arguing. Shouting at each other for the first time ever.

"Graham, I'm sorry. If you were anyone else, I would have to throw you off the team. You've become a liability. But I don't want to do that to you. We've been through too much together. This team couldn't function without you. I need you. I'm going to have to take you off front line duties for a while, though. If I don't, the rest of the team will be up in arms. They already think that I cut you too much slack, and I must be seen to act on tonight's events."

"Do what you want, Jeremy. I'm going to hang around for the rest of the day, simply because I want to see this through. As soon as the Pope gets on his plane back to Rome this evening, though, I walk, and I want nothing more to do with you or your little team of spies."

"Graham, please don't. I'm serious. I can't do this without you. You're our problem solver. You're the one who can see solutions when no one else can. Please don't leave."

"You've got me for another twelve hours, and then I'm clearing off. I'd rather clean deep fat fryers than spend a single day more with you and your crackpot bunch of wannabe spies."

"If that's the way you feel, then I'm not going to stand in your way. But please reconsider. Anyone can see that we need you. Yes, you've made some mistakes tonight, but as I said, if it wasn't for you, the Pope would be dead. You undoubtedly saved his life tonight, and prevented a huge amount of turmoil that would have inevitably been sparked off by his death. You spared the world from that. The world is a different place tonight – a better place – because of you."

"Sod the world, and sod your poxy little spying game. Six o' clock tonight, I'm off."

Chapter 23

The Pope completed his breakfast with the Archbishop of Canterbury at nine o' clock. The Hunter Group were at Lambeth Palace to meet him and to take him to Hyde Park ready to conduct Mass for the expected eighty thousand Catholics at half past ten. Originally it was intended that the Pope should be driven through the streets of central London in his Popemobile, but after the events of the previous night, this was considered too dangerous. So it was that the Pope was bundled into the back of an unmarked, bullet proof Jaguar, owned by the Hunter Group, and driven by Jeremy Hunter. Jeremy had tried to encourage Graham to accompany him in the car, but he was sulking after their earlier meeting, and so Helena, as Jeremy's deputy, sat in the front of the car alongside her boss.

Expectant crowds had gathered along the route from Lambeth Palace, rather sparsely at the Lambeth end, but getting thicker and thicker as they approached Hyde Park.

When they arrived at Hyde Park, they drove through the gates, and into the secure pen behind the extraordinarily large staging area. Once there, Helena opened the car door for the Pope, and he climbed out and headed straight into a specially constructed Papal dressing room. Two armed police officers were guarding the door.

Helena had the privilege of accompanying the Pope into his dressing room, where the Abbot of Charlwood Abbey was waiting for them.

"Your Holiness, I'm so glad to see that you're okay," the Abbot said, bending down on one knee and kissing the Pope's ring. "I am so very sorry indeed about last night's excitement at the abbey. Had I known that two of my staff meant you ill, I would not have invited you. I gather that we all owe a gratitude of thanks to these people for protecting you, however." The Abbot turned to Helena. "Thank you, thank you from the bottom of my heart for all that you and your team went through last night. I know it was truly terrible what happened last night, and if there's anything that I can do to help, please just let me know. We, of course, also suffered last night. I believe that four of our brothers lost their lives defending the Pope."

"You are forgiven, Timothy. It was not your fault," the Pope said. Helena was surprised. After everything that had happened, she realised that she barely heard the Pope speak.

"I take it my appointment will still go ahead this morning?" the Abbot asked.

"Timothy, I want you in my College of Cardinals, and will be confirming the appointment at Mass this morning. You have been a good friend to me, and a loyal servant of the Church."

"Thank you, Holy Father."

At that moment, Graham appeared in the dressing room. Helena glowered at him as he entered.

"I've been sent to offer the Holy Father additional protection," he said half-heartedly.

"Ah! Graham! We meet again!" the Abbot said. "This man, your holiness, was instrumental in saving your life last night. Had it not been for him, I fear we would not be sitting here this morning. Thank you, Mr. Chapman, for all you did for the church last night. Your actions will not be forgotten."

"All in a day's work," Graham responded.

"I must say, I am deeply shocked at what did happen last night. I can't believe that there are people out there who would wish the Holy Father ill. He is a kind and loving man, aren't you, your holiness?"

The Pope remained silent. Three altar boys and a papal official entered the room and started preparing the Pope for Mass.

"To think that two of my staff would have been involved horrifies me. I always viewed Giuseppe Campanaro as a good Catholic man, an honest and faithful servant of the church. It just shows how we can all be wrong. And as for Michaels – well, I knew he was an idiot, but I really didn't think he was enough of an idiot to attempt to kill the Pope, certainly not with a kitchen knife. I mean, a kitchen knife! What an imbecile! If it hadn't been for you, Graham, we could have found an even worse scenario developing!"

Graham blanked the abbot out. He couldn't bear to listen to the constant ramblings of this self-important man. He had bigger issues of his own. He was looking forward to returning to the comfort of his own home and his parents. He had been out for over twelve hours now. He had only set out to deliver a few boxes of chicken. Then his car had developed a puncture. Then he was picked up by Jeremy and Helena. And then the nightmare had begun.

He was so tired, and he ached all over from lack of sleep and from the running he had done on several occasions that night. The more he thought about it, the more he believed that he had made the right decision. He was not cut out to be a member of the Hunter Group. He was flattered that Jeremy viewed him as such an important part of the team, but he knew that he wasn't being entirely truthful. They would cope perfectly well without him, and, if they so wished, could recruit someone to fill his shoes with no difficulty at all.

All he wanted to do was to disappear into the sunset. To work at his parents' fried chicken takeaway, and return home at the end of the day to a good book or an episode of EastEnders. He had never enjoyed being a secret agent, not least because he hated having to lie to those he was closest to. He could do without looking death in the face every day. He could do without being shot at. And he could do very well without the nagging and hassling of Jeremy and the rest of his team. Right then, he despised them all, and would be perfectly happy never to see them again.

Not long to go now.

Sure enough, at that moment, the Pope was led onto the stage area to conduct Mass. Graham followed, and stood in the wings. The Pope was greeted with rapturous applause from the eighty thousand gathered Catholics. Little did they know how close they had come to losing this man, their leader.

Graham watched as the event unfolded. The Archbishop of Westminster, the leader of Catholics in the UK, opened proceedings by praying, and then passed over to the Pope himself. The Pope began by saying how delighted he was to be in London, and how grateful he was for the love of his people. He then began the canonisation of the Abbot, a short but distinguished affair. Finally, it was on to the Mass itself, a celebration of the death of Jesus Christ. The Pope broke the bread and blessed the wine, and for the next twenty minutes or so the crowd lined up at one of the dozens of small altars erected around the park specifically for the event.

After an hour, the event was over. Graham breathed a sigh of relief. All they needed to do now was get the Pope to Buckingham Palace for a lunch with the Queen, and then to Heathrow to catch his flight back to Rome.

Things were coming to an end.

The Pope was led back into the dressing room, and Graham and Helena followed, as did the church's newest Canon. The Abbot immediately started waffling on, and Graham immediately zoned out once more.

The Abbot was keen to travel to the Palace with the Pope, and so together they walked to Helena's Jaguar. It had been decided that she would drive the Pope to meet the Queen, with Graham as back up. Graham let the Pope and the Abbot into the back, whilst Helena jumped into the driving seat.

Within minutes of the Mass finishing, they were on the move again. They left the park and headed for Buckingham Palace.

Whilst Jeremy, Helena, Graham and Tom were at the Hyde Park mass, Anthony and Sally remained at the Hunter Group offices with Philip Brown. Before tackling any other task, Sally released Tracy, Paul Fish's girlfriend, apologising profusely and saying that they would be in touch in due course to discuss matters further. She did not leave quietly and promised that she would be suing the Hunter Group for every penny that they had.

Once Fish's girlfriend had left the premises, Sally joined Anthony and Brown, who were huddled over a computer in Anthony's office. They had emailed a list of the known leaders of

New Reformation through to one of Tom's contacts at the Metropolitan Police. Now they faced the task of trying to work out who was the mastermind behind the organisation.

"So you really don't have the faintest idea who is behind this group?" Anthony asked Philip.

"None whatsoever. I managed to build a profile around the names of all of the leaders that are shown on that list with the exception of the person described as the 'Chairman' of the group."

"I did much the same," Anthony reported. "I've got a list of five key figures, all of whom are clearly real people. I've found their National Insurance numbers, their home addresses, their office addresses and more. Everything that we could possibly need. According to the profiles that I've constructed, though, none of them look like they're the kind of figures who might instigate bombings across London, which could, and did, lead to the deaths of ordinary people."

"I don't think you should underestimate the anger that these people feel towards the Pope, Anthony," Philip responded. "I have spoken to three of those five figures myself, and have researched a great deal into the backgrounds of all of them. Each of these five men was sexually abused by Catholic Priests whilst they were young boys. Each of these men had their childhood stolen from them by people that they had grown to trust. That leaves an indelible mark on a person's soul that lasts for the rest of their life. And I should know."

Philip put his head in his hands, and slumped over the desk.

"You mean, you..." Anthony asked.

"Yes. Yes, I was." Philip sat up, tears running down his face.

"I was thirteen years old, and was serving as an altar boy in my local church. Our priest was called Father David. I had known him my entire life, and trusted him implicitly. My parents regarded him as a firm friend. Then one day, out of the blue, he started touching me inappropriately. At first, I didn't see anything wrong with it. We'd always had a fairly tactile relationship. He would place his hand onto my head when he prayed with me, and touch my shoulder to comfort me. It just seemed like a continuation of that. But over the next few months, it got, shall we say, more intimate."

Philip stopped talking and started sobbing. Anthony and Sally looked at each other with disbelief. Here was a strong man, who had accomplished so much, in tears before them. They didn't know what to do.

Sally was the first to take action. She touched his shoulder, but he immediately pulled away.

"I'm sorry," she said, realising that perhaps her comforting action was not entirely appropriate after what he had said to her. "You don't need to say any more, though, Philip. We understand."

She and Anthony looked at each other. Neither of them knew what to do next. They could see the same thought was running through each of their heads, though.

"Why don't you go and wash your face and have a drink of water," Anthony suggested. "We'll wait for you before we do anything else."

Philip stood up without speaking, wiped his face with a white handkerchief, and left the room.

"You don't think?" Sally asked.

"No. There's no way," Anthony responded.

"You were thinking it though, weren't you?"

"That Brown is involved with NR? I was, but no, he can't be. He knows a lot, but he's not a bad man, is he?"

"I'm sure that none of the others are bad men," Sally said. "As Philip said, being abused as a child can have a profound influence on someone's life. It surely has the potential to impact on the behaviour and actions of people later in life, and perhaps make them do things that they otherwise would not do."

"But he's had ample opportunity to kill the Pope. There's no way that he wants him dead," Anthony commented.

The two of them sat in silence for a little while as they reflected on the possibilities.

"No, you're right," Sally said, breaking the silence. "That little outburst came rather out of the blue though."

They looked up, and saw Philip enter the room.

"Are you okay, now, Philip?" Sally asked.

"I am." He had regained his composure, and it was as if the last couple of minutes had not happened.

"I'm really sorry about that. It might surprise you to know that I haven't ever told anyone about that. Not even my parents knew what was going on. And many of the people in New Reformation are in exactly the same position as me. They never mentioned their abuse growing up, and it wasn't until this group began to come together when the current Pope was made that they discussed it at all. But that's exactly what I mean. That hatred inside them, inside us, left to fester, can become a very, very dangerous thing. Ordinary, decent people who would never normally hurt a fly can turn into ogres when they think about how they were treated, and, confronted with a chance for revenge, they can find themselves in a position where they will stop at nothing to get it. These five senior members of NR, I've studied them all, and they're not bad people. I've met and spoken to three of them, and they are some of the loveliest people you could ever hope to meet, all of them still good Catholics who go to Mass every Sunday, and seek to serve the Lord. But that festering hatred boiled up to the surface when the current Pope was made, and they decided they wanted him punished. Punished because he allowed their abuse to happen. But also punished to try and bring an end to this dark history of the Church, and to move on, to return to the purity of Christ's teachings, which is what Catholicism should be about."

"Do you think that anger is strong enough that they can contemplate the death of ordinary people, though? Quite a number of innocent bystanders have been killed during the course of tonight. Hiring the Russian assassin pretty much guaranteed that that would happen," Anthony said.

"That's difficult, and I've been pondering that a while. I don't think that the three leaders I know would be entirely happy with that. I don't even think that the other two who I haven't met would tolerate the deaths of others. That's not to say that I think they wouldn't countenance it under any circumstances, but I don't think that they would be likely to devise a plan that has quite so many casualties."

"So we think that this chairman that we can't trace is responsible for bringing this darker streak to NR?" Anthony suggested.

"That's what I believe," Philip agreed. "I've tried for over a year now, though, and I can find very little about this figure. None of the other people in NR know very much about him either."

"What's his name?" Sally asked.

"Gavin Whitehead," Anthony replied, reading it off his computer screen. "I have done some serious searching, but I can't find any trace of him after 1988."

"Where's he gone, then?" Sally asked. "Assuming he's still alive?"

"I have no doubt that he's still with us," Philip said. "He's certainly the brains behind tonight's events. It's just a case of finding out who the hell he is."

"Well let me tell you what I've got," Anthony suggested. "Born 1952 in Melbourne, Australia. Spent his childhood in Australia, but came to England in 1970 to study French at Cambridge University. He graduated with a second-class degree in 1973, and then spent five years in France, working as an accountant. In late 1978 he returned to the UK, and got a job in London with a large auditing company where he worked until 1988. Then he vanishes off the radar completely. How does that compare with what you've got, Philip?"

"Practically the same. I contacted his last known employers, though, and discovered that he had some kind of burn out and went off to do some voluntary work, but no one seemed entirely sure what it was. There were very few people who remembered him, but those that did said that he was a very quiet, thoughtful character who kept himself to himself."

"So we've reached a dead end," Anthony said.

"It seems that way," Philip replied.

"Come on guys, let's not be defeated over this," Sally said. "Let's think of all the possible reasons for his disappearance. The obvious one is he died, but you don't think that's what happened in this case, so we can probably rule that out. Second, he moved overseas again, perhaps returning to his native Australia. You've checked that out, Philip?"

"I have as far as I could. His father died when he was a kid, and his mother died in 1984, and he was an only child, so the obvious reason for returning, to be closer to his family, does not seem to stand. I tried to locate a Gavin Whitehead in Australia, but couldn't find anyone that seemed to tie in with our man."

"Why else might someone seemingly disappear, then?" Anthony asked. "There'd be plenty of records if he went to prison. What if he changed his name? He wouldn't completely disappear, but it would certainly make it harder to track him down."

"Under what circumstances might people change their name?" Sally asked. "Maybe when they get married, but that's more usual in the case of women than men."

The three of them were baffled at how someone who was supposed to be the leader of a large and powerful organisation in the present day could also have disappeared years before. They sat in silence as they tried to figure it out. After a while, Brown spoke out.

"Oh my goodness!" Philip exclaimed. "I know who he is!"

"How? Who is he?" Anthony asked.

"Men change their names when they become monks. He's a bloody monk, isn't he?" Philip replied.

The revelation hit all three of them hard.

"Oh shit!" Anthony said. "He's not at Charlwood, is he?"

"I have a very, very nasty feeling about this," Philip said. "I don't know this for a fact, but how many Australian monks can there be in England? Abbot Timothy has a very slight Australian twang when he speaks. I only noticed it because my sister developed a similar trace of an Australian accent after she lived there for five years."

"Not the abbot, please, not the abbot," Anthony said. "I've got to get Jeremy."

He picked up his phone and hit Jeremy's speed dial number. Jeremy picked up almost straight away.

"Jeremy, listen, we think we know who's masterminding this whole operation! It's the abbot from Charlwood, Timothy!"

Jeremy could not believe what he was hearing. This just could not be true.

"Oh shit!" He replied. "He's just got into the back of a car with the Pope! Get over here now, all of you!"

Chapter 24

Graham had zoned out. Helena was pissed off and not talking to him yet again, the abbot was yabbering away in the back, and the Pope had fallen asleep. Graham had started to drop off himself when Helena poked him hard in the thigh.

"What?" he asked her.

She said nothing, but gestured to the back of the car with her eyes.

Oh shit, Graham thought.

The abbot had a gun, and its muzzle was against the back of Helena's neck.

Graham immediately went for his.

"Do that and I'll blow your friend's head off," the abbot said.

It was a tempting offer, but one that Graham decided he should decline.

"What do you want, you bastard?" he asked.

"I want you to do exactly as I say. If you do, then no one will get hurt. Well, you won't. The Pope will die whatever."

Graham glanced over to the Holy Father on the back seat next to the abbot. He was still asleep.

"Just drive the car, bitch, and follow the precise directions I give you."

"You realise we're in a convoy, don't you?" Helena asked. "There's no way we can just disappear. Plus the car has a tracker installed. They'll find us, whatever."

"Just drive, bitch."

Within minutes, if not seconds, they would be at Buckingham Palace. There just wouldn't be time for the abbot to try anything, Graham thought.

"Turn left now!" the abbot ordered.

Helena turned the car into a very narrow street lined with mews cottages on either side. It was a one-way street, going in the other direction.

Helena looked behind her. Jeremy's Jaguar had gone straight past the junction. Tom was nowhere to be seen. They were on their own.

A large four by four was heading directly for them. The irate driver was sounding her horn. The abbot wound down the window and pointed the gun at the oncoming car. The driver reversed as quickly as she could, but hit a parked car in the process, obstructing the road.

"Just drive!" the abbot shouted.

"There's no room!"

"Drive!"

Helena put her foot on the gas, and smashed her way between the now stationary four by four and a parked taxi. The car made a loud screeching noise as the bullet proof panelling of the Jaguar stood firm against the flimsier bodywork of the other cars. They made it through the gap.

"Turn left at the end, and put your foot down!" the abbot ordered.

Helena turned left onto another one-way street, but this time they found themselves going with the traffic flow. Or they would have done if the traffic had been flowing. It was stationary.

"Mount the pavement!" the abbot ordered.

"I can't, there are pedestrians!" Helena replied, the fear evident in her eyes.

"Do I look like I care, woman? Just do it!" The abbot pressed the gun tighter into Helena's neck.

Helena jumped the car up the kerb, and onto the pavement. It was not particularly wide, and there was still not enough width for the car.

Helena put her foot down, and the car scraped its way through the gap between the stationary vehicles and the buildings. Irate drivers jumped out to protest. A mother and a pushchair froze when she saw the car heading straight for her, but managed to pull the buggy into a shop just as the car passed.

"Now turn right!"

"I can't turn right, you moron! I'm on the left hand pavement with a line of stationary traffic between me and the turning!"

"I don't care! Just do it!"

Helena found a small gap, and pushed the car through it, damaging two more parked cars and taking yet more paint off the side of the Jaguar. She found herself on a clear road, and put her foot down.

"Take a left at the end."

Helena turned left.

"There's an abandoned office block on the left with an underground car park. Pull into there."

The road was lined with office blocks built in the 1970s, most of which now seemed to be abandoned. She drove slowly down the road.

"This one, turn left here!" the abbot ordered as they approached one of the shabbier offices. Helena began turning into the road leading down to the car park. The entrance was closed, a latticed metal gate sealing it off.

"I can't get in."

"Take a run-up and smash your way through," the abbot ordered.

Helena backed up the short drive as far as she could, put her foot down, and smashed through the gate. She hit fifty as they entered, and burst through the gate with a loud smash. Helena immediately applied the brakes and slowed the car down. The wheels screeched loudly as it came to a halt.

"Drive to the far end. There's a container over there."

The car park was in semi-darkness, but with the headlights on Helena could see an abandoned shipping container on the far side of the car park. She drove up to it and pulled up alongside it.

The abbot went for the door but found that he was locked in; the child lock was activated. He got suddenly angrier.

"Let me out of here!" the abbot ordered.

Helena started to move.

"Not you, you bitch! You do it, Graham!"

Graham jumped out and ran round to the rear door of the Jaguar. The abbot climbed out and switched the gun onto Graham.

"Let our friend out, now."

Graham walked round the back of the car and opened the Pope's door, wondering what the abbot had planned next. The Holy Father was now awake, and looked shocked, confused and very tired. He did not move.

"Get him into the container!"

Graham helped the Pope out of the car, and led him into the dirty shipping container, followed by the abbot, who still had a tight grip of the gun.

"There's a chair at the far end. Put him on it, and tie his feet and hands together."

Graham led the Pope into the dark recesses of the container, and the abbot flicked a switch, a bright light momentarily disorientating Graham. Graham saw the seat, and carefully sat the Pope down. Underneath the chair were some coarse ropes.

"I'm sorry, your Holiness," Graham said, as he began binding the Pope's hands behind his back. Hands bound, he moved onto his feet.

"Put the bag over his head."

Graham looked around him but couldn't see a bag.

"It's over there, moron!" the abbot yelled.

On the bottom of the container a few feet away from the abbot was an old potato sack.

Graham went to pick it up. As he bent over, the abbot kicked his backside. Graham was taken by surprise and fell forward, bashing his nose against the metal side of the container. He picked himself up. His nose was bleeding and hurt like hell. He thought it was broken.

Graham walked back to the Pope, and dropped the sack over the old man's head.

"Now, sit at his feet!"

Graham sat down. The abbot turned away, and spoke to Helena.

"You, bitch. Stay outside. Shut the container door, and don't open it again until I give the order. If you disobey, your friend here will die. If you even think of contacting anyone else, your friend will die. If you run off, your friend will die. Do I make myself clear?"

"Perfectly," Helena replied.

"Seal us in, then, bitch."

Helena began closing the door to the container, thinking that the abbot was clearly completely mental. In all her years in the field, she had never known anyone ask to be sealed in a container. Still, if that's what he wanted...

The door closed with a clunk, and Helena pulled the locking mechanism into place.

Jeremy and Tom had pursued Graham and Helena's car as well as they could, but had nevertheless managed to lose them rather quickly.

After hitting traffic and losing sight of them, they both pulled over. Tom abandoned his car, ran over to Jeremy's car and jumped in.

"We're going to have to try this a slightly different way," Jeremy said. He turned on the car's satnav, and pulled up Helena's Jaguar in the POI list. As soon as the GPS had settled down, they saw their own car displayed on the screen, and a couple of seconds later, a red dot signifying Helena's car. The satnav started giving directions to where Helena now was.

"It's directing us straight through the middle of this traffic jam," Tom said.

"Don't worry about that," Jeremy replied. He backed the car up, and turned down a narrow side road, which fed onto a busy but free flowing road.

"Did you have any idea?" Tom asked.

"None whatsoever."

"Did Graham have any inkling about the abbot? He's normally good with this sort of thing."

"Not that he mentioned to me. He's spent more time than any of us with the abbot, and yet he's said very little about him."

"I suppose it makes sense. I mean, two of his senior members of staff tried to kill the Pope tonight. It makes sense that the abbot would have known something about what was going on. He probably put them up to it."

Jeremy returned his concentration to the satnav. The dot had slowed down in a side street not far from where they were. It came to a stop.

"Right, let's get them," Jeremy said as he put his foot down.

"It's gone," Tom said.

"Bugger."

Sure enough, the red dot on the screen had disappeared.

"What could have caused that?" Tom asked. "It should still show up even if they've turned the engine off, shouldn't it?"

"It should. It must have gone out of view of the satellites. There must be a garage or warehouse there. If they've stopped, we can get to them easily. Phone Anthony, will you, and tell him where they are."

Tom placed the call whilst Jeremy continued to drive the car to its last known spot. He pulled into a narrow street that was clearly a service road of some description. Office blocks lined the street, but these were not the expensive front facades of the buildings. These were the back entrances.

"They must have pulled into one of these buildings," Jeremy said. "Keep your eyes peeled for any tell-tale signs."

"They're all sealed with roller doors," Anthony pointed out. "They could be in any one of these."

"The satnav thought that they were further down."

They continued slowly along the street, looking for any indication that Helena and Graham might have driven into one of the buildings.

"There. Look." Anthony pointed down a ramp towards a smashed up set of doors. "Do you think that's an armour-plated Jaguar shaped hole?"

"Could be, could be. Let's get out and take a closer look."

For the first time in a very long while, Graham felt scared. He'd been through all manner of risky situations in his time with the Hunter Group, but this had to be the worst. He was beginning to feel very claustrophobic, and was struggling to breathe. He really hoped that this container was not airtight, otherwise all three of them would be in trouble.

He felt that he was on his own. It was him against the abbot.

I have to win, Graham thought. If I don't, the Pope dies, and it will all be down to me.

Without warning, he felt himself overcome with claustrophobia and fear. He slumped to the floor, clasping his throat.

Come on, sort yourself out, he thought. You can be a hero.

Not without oxygen.

There's plenty of oxygen. You're panicking. Pull yourself together.

Graham became aware of a voice. He looked up and saw the abbot towering over him. He was fit and healthy. There was clearly plenty of air. He was panicking.

"Do you know why we're here?" the abbot asked.

Graham remained silent, trying to pull himself together.

Everything would be all right.

How could it be?

You've still got your gun, you moron.

The abbot lurched towards Graham and put his gun against his head.

"I said, do you know why we're here?"

"Because you're insane and are going to kill us both," Graham gasped.

"No. No, I'm not," the abbot replied. "Do you have any idea how bad it would look if I was to kill the Pope? I mean, I'm the abbot of Charlwood Abbey. I'm a Cardinal of the Catholic Church. I'm not a murderer. But you, well, that's another matter. I've already witnessed you murder people. You're a murdering scumbag. You need to be locked up to prevent you killing anyone else."

"I'm not going to kill the Pope."

The abbot stepped away from Graham and dropped the gun down to his side.

"To be honest, Graham, even if I do kill the Pope, you're the only witness. It will be your word against mine. Did you kill the Pope? Or did

I kill the Pope? I'm a man of God. You're a druggie, an alcoholic, a chronic gambler and a professional deliverer of fried chicken."

Graham looked up, shocked that the abbot knew so much about him.

"Oh yes, Graham, I know all about you. I've been watching you for some time. And I've done a little research. There's no way that anyone would believe that I killed the Pope. You, on the other hand, well. People will wonder why Jeremy ever trusted you. They'll look at your track record and think that Mr. Hunter was mad to take you on. The Hunter Group will be exposed, people will question the judgement of its leader, and it will be forced to shut up shop."

He had a good point, Graham thought. He was more convinced than ever that should he survive this, he would quit the Hunter Group. It was for the best – both for him personally but also for his colleagues.

"I know all about your secret little organisation too. Can you imagine what it will do for the intelligence community as a whole, and even the government, if they discover that a murdering, drugged-up chicken delivery boy like you was entrusted to maintain the security of the nation? Well, that could bring the government down."

Once again, he was probably right. He might be a madman, but on this point he seemed to have a better grasp of reality even than Jeremy.

"I gather that you've met my own secret little organisation this evening too?"

Graham didn't say anything, but the abbot clearly recognised the confusion in his eyes.

"Oh yes, my little monk army. I'm rather proud of them, 'The Boys' as I call them. I've been drilling them for years waiting for this moment. I knew there would come a point when I needed them for a mission such as this. It makes a change for them. Normally they just murder people who speak ill of the Lord."

This man was clearly completely off his rocker.

"You see, Graham, it's rather easy to condition people so that they can no longer tell the difference between right and wrong. It's especially easy if they live together in a big house in the country, and have little or no contact with the outside world. All it needs is a little work, and you can confuse anyone into thinking that what is right is wrong, and what is wrong is right. It can come in quite handy, you know. If you've got a persuasive personality, it's quite remarkable what you can do. I've even managed to do the same to that idiot little man Campanaro. He's only been at the school five minutes, but I can already control everything he thinks and everything he does. He doesn't even realise it half the time!"

Campanaro. So he was working for the abbot. Things were starting to fall into place. This crazy, deluded man had been behind everything that had happened that night.

"I wonder if that's what Mr. Hunter is doing to you? After all, he insists on absolute secrecy. You're not allowed to tell anyone what you do. You listen only to him. Are you sure that your grip on reality is all there? What if I'm right and you're wrong?"

How did this man know all this? The Hunter Group was a top secret organisation and barely anyone knew they even existed. It was impossible that the abbot could know so much about them.

Graham had to pull himself together and stop this evil man. He was beginning to feel a little better. He had managed to convince himself that there was no way that he was going to suffocate in this container. He could see light from the car park outside seeping through holes and gaps all over the container. There was no need to panic. The box was not airtight.

Graham very carefully started reaching for his gun.

The abbot noticed, and landed a heavy black boot in Graham's ribs. He winced with pain. That was not what he expected from a man of God.

"Give me the gun, Graham," the abbot ordered.

Graham did not move.

The abbot pushed his own gun deep into Graham's neck.

"I said, give me the gun," he whispered into Graham's ear.

Graham passed the gun across.

"Any more weapons I should know about?"

Graham did not move.

"I can see I'm going to have to be careful with you."

Graham suddenly felt stupid. He'd thought this man, the abbot, was warped from the start. Ever since that first meeting where he had chatted relentlessly, he had been wary of him. He just spoke too much. He suffered from severe reality distortion. This was not a man who lived in the real world. Why had he not thought before that something was wrong here? Graham thought he had simply been unable to see beyond the fact that this man, Abbot Timothy, was a monk.

"I know what you're thinking, Graham, 'but he's a monk'. How can I be acting like this?"

Graham began to panic that perhaps the abbot could read his mind.

"You don't think I'm a monk because I accept the quiet, living-for-God bullshit, do you? I'm not that naïve. I became a monk because I knew where it would lead; to me becoming the Pope! Since I became a monk, and particularly since I became the abbot of the abbey, I've had the media world flocking to me. Newspapers come to me when they need a different perspective on the world. Magazines from across the globe have run profiles on me. Radio stations fall over themselves to get me on their shows. I've been on breakfast TV more than most of the presenters. The BBC even ran a documentary about me! See, I'm famous! I've achieved fame beyond your wildest dreams! Whilst you're slaving away over a deep fat fryer, I'm dining with the rich and famous and being paid thousands to address their meetings and dinner parties! Who'd have thought that it would be so easy! It doesn't stop there, though, Graham, oh no! You're about to witness my masterstroke, my final transformation. I'm going to be Pope!"

"Yes, of course you are. Moron."

Resorting to childish insults when he was under stress was a very bad habit that Graham had found impossible to shake off. He should have been able to find something a little more eloquent to say, but calling the abbot a moron just seemed appropriate.

"Do you not see? If I wanted the Pope dead, I could have done it before now. I could have done it months, if not years ago! But no, I wasn't ready for him to die. I knew that if I waited, if I built up a sufficiently high profile, the Pope would make me a cardinal, and that would be the time to strike. Well, I'm a cardinal now, and the time is right! When he goes, I'll be one of the front-runners to succeed him!"

"Go on, then, do it," Graham said.

"Be my guest," the abbot said, handing Graham his gun back. Graham accepted the gun and put it back into his belt."

"Are you mad?" Graham asked. "A minute ago you took my gun off me, now you've given it back to me."

"Do you know what, Graham? I think there is a hint of madness running through me. But, you know what?"

The abbot dropped his voice, and gestured to Graham to approach him. Graham stood up and walked over.

"It really doesn't matter, because I'm about to become the most powerful man on planet earth. There are over a billion Catholics in the world, all of whom do exactly what the Pope tells them. Who wants to run a country when you can lead the Catholic Church!"

"I thought your God taught that the last shall be first, and the first shall be last," Graham, commented.

"Ah, bollocks to all that. Who believes in that drivel anyway?"

"Well, your monks do for a start. Several of them died this evening, believing that they were fighting for what was right. And I would guess this gentle man here does too. You know what? There have been times in my life too when I've thought that perhaps there is a God, and perhaps he is good, and loving, and cares for his people. And if there is a God, if what you purport to believe in really is true, then you're going to be burning in the fires of hell when you go."

"Who gives a damn," the abbot replied. "There's fame, prestige and wealth beyond your wildest dreams ahead of me. Presidents and monarchs will ask me to dine with them. Celebrities will want to be seen with me. I'll have millions of people all around the world wanting to support me. Graham, even if there is a heaven and a hell, I would gladly swap eternity in heaven for the life that I'm about to begin."

"You're a cock," Graham said, again descending to ridiculously immature insults.

"Maybe, Graham, maybe. But I'm going to be a rich and powerful cock. I'm also a very intelligent cock. After all, you had no idea about my plans at all, did you? You, supposedly one of the most intelligent figures in the intelligence community, couldn't even see what was before your eyes, could you! Who's the imbecile, Graham, you or me?"

Graham remained silent. He was waiting for the appropriate moment to strike. Any minute now this idiot would leave himself exposed, and when he did, Graham would blow his brains out.

"Come on, Graham, tell me. Did you know when you met me earlier that it was me who wanted to kill the Pope?"

"You're an opportunist, nothing more than that."

"Of course I'm not. This whole plan has been carefully concocted from beginning to end. And you've fallen right into it. All my little side shows and diversions have distracted you from what was really going on here – that I'm going to kill the Pope and be Pope in his place."

"Of course."

"Don't you see? CARN were incompetent morons. I thought about using them, but they couldn't organise a piss up in a brewery. They were a useful distraction though, weren't they? How much time have you spent wondering what was happening there? How much time have you spent pondering who killed them and why? Quite a lot I should imagine. Well, Graham, I'll let you into a little secret."

The abbot knelt back down to Graham again and whispered in his ear.

"It was me, Graham, it was me."

Graham listened in disbelief as the abbot stood up once more.

"Oh yes. I arranged the van, and I even arranged the assassin. He was rather good, wasn't he? In some ways it was a shame that he died, but there you go. He fulfilled his purpose. Or sort of, anyway. That little trip down to Charlwood was just something we tacked on. If that busy body Brown hadn't tried to save the Pope, it wouldn't have been necessary. I tried to sort him out by ordering his house to be torched, but it seems that I got what I paid for on that front. The idiot evidently turned up too late, after Brown had left."

Graham looked confused. He had always assumed that the gunman was at Charlwood to kill the Pope. Was he not? The abbot evidently picked up on Graham's confusion.

"Oh yes, he was there to kill Brown, not the Pope. I didn't want his Holiness disappearing, did I? As it was, he saved him from that bastard Michaels anyway. I knew that he was NR, of course, but he wasn't supposed to try and kill the Pope. The poor fool. His own hatred clearly got the better of him."

Graham was getting more and more fed up with the ramblings of this delusional man.

"For goodness' sake, will you button it?" he asked.

"Oh no, certainly not! I've seen spy films. This is where the baddy spills his guts."

"Shortly before being killed by the goody," Graham added.

"You reckon you're the goody, do you? That's interesting. You see, my friends at New Reformation thought they were the goodies too. They thought that if they killed the Pope, the Church would be cleansed and the world would be a better place. Idealistic wankers. You probably know that I joined them and led them for a while, as their secretive, elusive leader. They seemed to enjoy that. I had hoped that they would be more instrumental in my plan, but they just couldn't get their act together. Never mind, they were another distraction that proved to be very useful. Whilst you lot thought they were going to kill the Pope it took all the attention away from the real killer. Me! See, I'm a criminal mastermind!"

"You're a cretin, that's what you are," Graham said. He couldn't believe that the abbot had planned tonight's events. If anything, he had been following events. They seemed to have run out of control.

"The Organisation will reward me richly for this!"

Graham froze with terror. He had hoped he would never hear that name again. He hadn't heard their name mentioned since he saved Jeremy's life in New York, when the gunman had uttered it. Surely they couldn't be back? Surely the abbot couldn't be an Acquaintance, a member of The Organisation?

"The Organisation?" Graham asked. "Which Organisation?"

"You know what I mean, Graham! Anyway, enough of all this idle banter. It's time for my favourite bit, the bit we've all been waiting for! The execution! Now, if you would be so kind as to shoot the Pope for me before I shoot you both."

"You're mad, quite, quite mad. You want the Pope dead. Do it yourself."

"Fair enough, if that's how you want to play it."

Graham was shocked at how quickly the abbot moved. Before he could do anything, the abbot had his gun in his hand, and had it aimed directly at the Pope.

Enough is enough, Graham thought, as he hurled himself at the abbot. He was aware that he was putting himself into the firing line, but it had to be done.

The abbot dropped to the floor, Graham on top of him. Graham tried to wrestle the gun out of his hand, and as he did so, the gun went off. The bullet ricocheted around the container.

Graham jabbed his elbow into the abbot's face, breaking his nose with a single stroke. Blood started pouring from the broken appendage, and the abbot screamed. He kept a firm hold on the gun, though, and attempted to get up.

Graham landed a punch firmly on the abbot's broken nose. He screamed as the sound of ripping cartilage echoed around the metal container.

Suddenly and unexpectedly, the abbot flipped over and was now on top of Graham, and he was angry. Graham looked into his eyes. He had never before seen eyes so full of anger. Before he had chance to fight back, the abbot had him firmly pinned to the floor. He swung his elbow into Graham's stomach. Once. Twice. And a third time.

Graham got that claustrophobic feeling again. He struggled for air. He could not believe that this supposed man of God was fighting back so hard.

As quickly as he had flipped Graham, the abbot jumped to his feet and turned to the Pope. He could not believe what he was seeing. How had this happened?

No time for wondering, though. Now was the time for action.

He pulled his gun out, aimed it squarely at the Pope's head, and pulled the trigger.

Chapter 25

This is just weird, Helena thought. She had no idea what to do at this point. Never before had she found herself in a situation that was anything like this.

She considered her options. She could very easily just open the container the same way that she had shut it. That would be no problem at all. There was one big problem with this idea, however. The fact that a seemingly insane gunman was inside the container, along with her esteemed colleague, Graham, and the Pope. If she opened the container, she had no doubt at all that the abbot would simply kill the Pope and Graham before she could even draw her weapon.

If she left them to it, though, there was also every possibility that this would turn out badly, and that the Pope would be shot.

What exactly have we got here, she thought. Is this a hostage scenario? Is the abbot going to pass out a list of demands, no doubt including a helicopter and a million pounds in cash? If this wasn't a hostage-taking, then what was it? An execution? That didn't bear thinking about, but sadly seemed to be the most likely scenario.

What was to be done?

Helena pulled out her mobile phone and called up Jeremy's number. Whatever was going on here, she needed to let him know.

Damn, no signal.

Two choices – head out of the car park to place the call and walk away from the Pope, or wait and see what happened.

Helena decided to follow the latter course of action. She had no doubt that Jeremy and the rest of the team would be here soon. Jeremy and Tom had been following her, and should be able to locate her without too much difficulty. Plus there was the GPS chip in the car. They would have been able to track her journey to the entrance to the basement car park with no difficulty. The fact that she had rammed her way through the doors to the car park would also provide an easy way to spot where she had gone.

No, they'd find her. She should stay here.

The car park was an eerie place to be holed up. It had clearly been abandoned some months before. Most of the lights were out, and it was littered with junk. In the half darkness Helena spotted several abandoned containers. It struck her as rather strange that there were so many of these large shipping containers lying around. It must have been rather difficult to get them into the car park. She assumed that they were the remnants of an office move, presumably not required when the companies that had vacated the building had moved on.

She considered investigating further, to see what was in some of the other containers, but decided against it. That would be a distraction.

She had to remain focused on the task in hand – whatever that might be.

Helena thought again about what she should do. It was up to the Hunter Group to protect the Pope, and she decided that there was no way that she would leave that to Graham. He had proven time and again that he was useless, completely incompetent.

No, she might be stuck outside the box, but she had to take action.

Helena stepped back from the container and looked at it more closely. It was a standard shipping container of the sort seen travelling around the UK on the backs of lorries every day. It was painted red, with no discernable markings. There was evidence of rust around the edges and in patches over the skin of the container. In some places, the metal had rusted through, and small holes had formed through the steel.

Helena found a hole and peered through. The light inside was dim, even dimmer than the half-light outside, and it took a second or two for her eyes to adjust. The scene was much as it had been when she had shut the crate. The Pope was sat at the far end on a chair, a sack over his head. His hands and legs were bound. The abbot was pacing backwards and forwards, a gun in his hand. Graham, meanwhile, was slumped in a heap on the bottom of the crate.

Oh, for heaven's sake, she thought.

She looked more closely at Graham. She had not heard any gunfire so clearly he hadn't been shot. So what was wrong with him? There was nothing visibly wrong. He was being pathetic.

Come on, Graham! You're the one person who can resolve this situation, she thought.

She wandered round the crate, heading to the end where the Pope was sat. Right behind his back was a hole where the steel was rusting away. From this vantage point, Helena could see little more than the Pope's back, and his hands tied together firmly behind him. The hole was sufficiently large that she could get her gun through into the crate with relative ease, but it was simply too dangerous to let off a shot. The Pope was a significant obstacle, sat as he was directly in front of the hole. Even if she had managed to manoeuvre the gun into a position where it wasn't pointing directly at the Pope's head, the hole was not large enough to enable her to see into the container and to poke the gun through.

About half a metre up from this hole, Helena found another, rather smaller one. If she stood on her tiptoes, she could just about see into the container. She could clearly see all the action in front of her. The Pope remained seated, the abbot was still pacing, and Graham was still slumped on the floor.

Someone had to take decisive action here, she decided, and if it wasn't going to be Graham, then it would have to be her.

If she was to get a clear shot of the abbot, she had to shoot through the upper hole. It was simply too dangerous, though, unless she could also see into the container.

She had to make the hole large enough that she could get the muzzle of her gun into the container and also be able to see what she was doing.

Helena inserted her fingers into the hole in the steel, and carefully tried to curl the metal back. It was completely useless; the steel was tough, and the edges were sharp.

She tried the same tactic with the lower hole. Whilst the metal had rusted away to form the hole, the metal was still too hard to manipulate with just her fingers.

Any action that Helena took would have to rely on the existing holes.

Whilst she was trying to work out whether she could shoot into the container, she saw the abbot press a gun into Graham's neck.

Come on, Graham, she thought. Sort yourself out!

For the first time in her life, she found herself willing Graham to do the right thing. Never before had she wanted Graham to make the smart move and she was struck by the change. She was always hoping that he would make a mess of every situation he found himself in. She was more concerned with looking competent than necessarily bringing about the right result. Graham messing everything up made her look better. Graham's incompetence was good for her, because it convinced her of her own abilities. Maybe, she thought, she should put her own selfishness behind her and learn to work as a part of a team.

Maybe that was her problem. Make she simply did not know how to work in a team.

Perhaps she was learning. Maybe, if she and Graham could come out of this alive, she should make more of an effort to get on with him, to work with him. Whilst he had his inadequacies – he was clumsy, unreliable, and a bit of an idiot – he was also extremely switched on, and very, very bright. Jeremy could see Graham for what he was. Maybe she should too.

Enough of this, she thought. I need to sort this out.

Helena decided that the only way she was going to be able to reliably shoot the abbot would be if she was in the container. That was clearly not an option. She had to find another solution.

Then it hit her.

She could use the Pope.

He was in the container.

He could act for her.

But how? He was tied up.

Helena dashed back to the Jaguar and opened the boot. In amongst the other weapons and tools, she found what she was looking for.

A knife.

If she could only get the knife through the hole and cut the ropes that bound the Pope's hands. She would need a little extra help reaching the ropes, though. The knife was not long enough to reach on its own.

She put the knife on the ground, and continued rummaging through the boot.

If only we had a Q, like in the Bond movies, she thought. He always seemed to conveniently equip Bond with whatever piece of equipment he needed for his mission.

No such luck in the real world.

Helena gave up on the car, and decided to see if she could muster anything from within the car park. She needed some kind of pole. It didn't need to be very long, because the Pope was seated only about two feet from the side of the container.

Then, propped up against one of the other containers, she found exactly what she was after.

A broom.

Just as Helena began to prepare to execute her plan, she heard people running down the ramp of the car park. She looked up to see Jeremy and Tom running into the underground car park. Helena gestured to them to remain quiet, and gesticulated to them to come and join her.

"What's going on?" Jeremy asked.

"The abbot has the Pope and Graham in that container," she replied, pointing at the closed red shipping crate.

"Are they locked in?"

"The abbot asked me to seal them in. I didn't have a choice. He's armed, and completely off his rocker."

"He's the missing link," Jeremy said. "Abbot Timothy is the leader of New Reformation. He's also brutal. Whilst the others have rational reasons for wanting the Pope dead, he is completely irrational, and probably certifiable."

"With respect, Jeremy, we can talk about your views on the rationalism behind tonight's activities later," Helena commented. "We have more pressing affairs at the moment."

"Fair enough, fair enough," Jeremy conceded. "Let's think through what we have here."

"Look, Jeremy," Helena replied. "I'm really sorry, but this is a time for action, not for sitting down working out nice little plans. I know what needs to be done, and I'm going to do it."

"Right," said Jeremy, slightly taken aback by the attitude of his second in command.

"The most useful thing for you lot to do is to stand by at the front of the container, just in case anything should happen."

"Why don't we just storm the container?" Tom asked. "There's more of us, and we can overpower him easily."

"Good in theory, but as soon as we open that door, we've lost," Helena replied. "All he needs is a split second, and he can shoot the Pope dead, and we have failed. He has nothing to lose whatsoever. It's going to take us twenty seconds to open that container at least, and as soon as we start sliding the bolts, he'll know what we're up to. That gives the abbot a twenty second head start, when he needs less than one."

"So what do we do?" Tom asked.

"You leave this to me, and do as I say – stand by at the front of the container ready to go in just in case."

"Helena's right. Let's just do as she says," Jeremy said.

Jeremy and Tom each grabbed a semi automatic from the boot of Helena's car, and stood waiting at the front of the container, whilst Helena continued with her plan.

She grabbed the broom handle, and bound the knife tightly to it using a bungee from the boot of the Jaguar, and returned to the container.

She slowly pushed the knife through the lower hole into the container, the width of the handle just about allowing enough space for her to see through.

Luckily, the Pope was sat near enough the hole that she wouldn't lose too much control of the knife due to the distance between her and the blade. The proximity of the Pope also meant that unless the abbot happened to be directly watching, he would not notice Helena's little operation.

The knife through the hole, she began sawing through the ropes, being careful not to accidentally cut the Pope. The rope was new and firm, but luckily was not too thick. It took her a good five minutes or so of sawing the blade back and forth, but eventually she saw the rope fall away.

The Pope's hands were free. They dropped to his side.

Either the Pope was unwilling to move, asleep or dead, because he did not seem to react at all to Helena's actions. She was quite surprised.

Helena pulled the broomstick back out of the container, and removed the knife. Next she inserted just the pole into the container, and raised it up to the Pope's head. She began trying to nudge the back of the sack that was covering the Pope's head. It was not as easy as she thought it would be, and she was not at all successful at removing the sack. She did, however, accidentally jab the Pope in the back of the head, causing him to wake with a start.

Realising straight away that his hands were no longer bound, he went to remove the sack from his head. Helena realised that perhaps this was not the correct next move, and so gently placed the broom handle on the top of the Pope's head, to prevent him from removing it. Sensing that someone was trying to help him, he dropped his hands back behind his back.

Excellent, Helena thought. We're getting there.

She next wanted to get her gun into the container to pass to the Pope. This was not going to be easy, since, if she just dropped it in, it would hit the metal floor with a loud clang.

Helena pulled the broom handle out of the container, and reattached the bungee, leaving the hook on one end clear. She carefully placed the gun onto the bungee using the finger guard, and tested that it would not fall off. It seemed secure enough.

She very carefully pushed the gun through the hole, trying to make sure that it didn't fall off. When the gun was through, she pushed the bungee, and then the end of the broom handle through, and guided it towards the Pope's chair. She managed to get it right to the front of the seat, and then, very carefully, she lowered the gun to the floor, and attempted to unhook the bungee. It was quite a fiddly operation, but after a few seconds she had managed to release the gun. She nudged the Pope's legs with the pole to try and indicate to him that there was something waiting for him under the seat, and then she pulled the handle up to the back of the sack, and indicated to the Pope that he should now remove it by lifting it up as much as she could.

The Pope got the idea, and carefully pulled the sack over his head.

Helena quickly pulled the handle out, and nodded to Jeremy and Tom to indicate that things were about to happen. She jumped up to the upper hole as quickly as she could to watch what was going on. The abbot hadn't noticed that the

Pope was now hood-less, and was wrestling Graham on the bottom of the container. At last, she thought. Graham was trying to take action.

Whilst the abbot was distracted with fighting Graham, she saw the Pope feel beneath his seat. He found the gun, and prepared to shoot. He knew he had to get the abbot. He seemed to realise that after all he had been through over the course of the last night, he had to take action to bring the night's activities to a close. He tried to aim at the abbot, but he could not get a clear line of sight that would enable him to shoot the abbot and not Graham.

Don't shoot, don't shoot, Helena thought. Knowing Graham's luck, you'll just get him.

Then, much to both the Pope and Helena's shock, the abbot leapt up off the floor and aimed his gun at the Pope. He hesitated.

The Pope was unbound, the sack had been removed from his head, and he was aiming a gun at him. There was a look of confusion in the abbot's eyes.

The Pope's hand was shaking as he held the weapon. He knew what had to be done, but he also felt reluctant to go through with it. It was not in his nature to kill someone, even in self-defence. If the time had come for him to die, he would take the bullet. He calmly dropped the gun to the ground and raised his hands in the air.

"May God bless you, my child. May God save your soul," the Pope said calmly to the abbot.

The abbot froze. His mind was racing. He had waited months for this. He had thought about this moment for years. This was his time. But he had not expected to be the one to go through with the shooting. That had never been the plan. He realised he had to do it.

He approached the Pope, aimed his gun at his head, and prepared to pull the trigger.

Not taking his eyes off the scene in front of him, Graham quickly pulled his own gun out of its holster. He did not want to shoot the abbot. This man clearly needed help.

Graham did not understand why the abbot was hesitating. He had clearly planned to execute the Pope in this container, so why was he having second thoughts?

Do I shoot him? Graham wondered.

He watched as the abbot moved closer to the Pope. Was he going to shoot? He couldn't be sure.

He could not risk the Pope dying.

He pointed his gun at the back of the abbot's head, and slowly pulled the trigger.

As he did so, he heard the abbot fire.

Shit, Graham thought. Too late.

His bullet flew through the air in slow motion. He watched as it edged towards the abbot's head. He watched as it made contact. He watched as it entered the man's skull, blowing the back of his head apart.

The abbot fell to the ground.

Graham looked at the Pope. Had he been shot?

He was sat calmly on his chair, looking at the body of the abbot at his feet.

The abbot's bullet had sailed clean through a neat, new hole in the top of the container.

The Pope was safe.

It was over.

Chapter 26

As soon as he had been released from the container, Graham had walked away from the underground car park as quickly as he possibly could. The others were too busy fussing around the Pope and the abbot's body, and did not notice Graham wander off.

His ears still ringing from the shots in the confined space of the container, feeling dazed after all he had gone through, and exhausted from lack of sleep, he wandered the back streets of London until he found a tube station. He took the tube to Victoria, and then caught the first train back to Redhill. As soon as he sat down, he dozed off, not waking until the train passed through Merstham station.

Graham got off the train, and walked into the town centre. He needed some time to get his thoughts together, and bring himself back to reality before he ventured back to his parents' chicken restaurant. He had made a decision, and a decision that he intended to stick to. He hated working for Jeremy. He had never wanted to be a secret agent, and had had just about enough of the Hunter Group. There was no way he would return to working with them. He earned peanuts delivering chicken, and it was a boring job, but it was a safe job. Graham had never been ambitious; he wanted to earn enough money to survive, and had no desire to earn more than he needed for the simple life that he desired. He had come through a period in his life when he had literally stared death in the face, and he had no intention of returning there. When he had come out of rehab, he had a far better understanding of what was important in life; a roof over his head, enough food to eat, money to pay the bills, and above all, family and friends. The trappings of modern life – the mortgage, the fancy car, the expensive holidays and ridiculous gadgets – held no attraction for him. No, as far as he was concerned, it was family and friends all the way.

It was because of his long-standing friendship with Jeremy that he had joined the Hunter Group in the first place. He and Jeremy had always got on well, and when Graham needed a friend, when he was a pathetic druggie roaming the streets of New York looking for his next fix, it was Jeremy who had rescued him. Jeremy had, quite literally, saved his life. Had they not had that sudden and surprising encounter at the subway station in New York, there was no doubt in Graham's mind that he would be dead by now.

But then, he had saved Jeremy's life too. His bumbling ineptness had ensured that Jeremy was able to escape from the assassin. Had Graham not turned up at exactly the right moment, Jeremy would be dead.

One good turn deserved another, but surely Jeremy and Graham had repaid any debt that they had to one another? Their mutual life saving surely cancelled out any obligation that one of them had to the other.

So why did Graham still feel in Jeremy's debt?

There was no reason he should feel that way.

He had gone into the Hunter Group because he felt indebted to Jeremy, and he still felt that way today. If that was the only reason he continued working for Jeremy, then it was a bloody stupid reason.

No, the time had come for him to part company with the Hunter Group. Jeremy would be far from happy with Graham's decision, but if Graham's departure meant the end of his friendship with Jeremy, then so be it.

He could not sustain this lifestyle. He hated lying to his family and friends about where he was, but the rules of the Hunter Group necessitated that. They had initially viewed Graham's frequent disappearances as evidence of his rather nonchalant approach to life. At that stage, they had humoured him. Now, however, they viewed his behaviour as unreasonable and worrying. Time and time again, he had to reassure those that loved him that he was not back on the drugs. They often worried that Graham disappeared to go on an all night bender, but that was far from the truth. Graham had been clean for years. He never even touched a drop of alcohol and never smoked so much as a cigarette. He had seen what drugs could do. He also recognised that he had a character prone to addiction.

Graham hated having to burn the candle at both ends. Frequently, after a day at work cleaning the kitchens, he would spend his evenings delivering chicken, and would then be called in to a job with the Hunter Group. That was exactly what had happened last night. Sometimes he would have to go days on end without sleep. There was a time when he could cope with that kind of behaviour, but his body found it increasingly hard to cope with the abuse that Graham handed out to it.

He hated chasing after bad guys. He'd never been fit, and, since he had returned to the UK and starting working for his parents, his sedentary lifestyle and poor diet had ensured that he was just about as unfit as it was possible to be without dropping dead. And yet, he regularly found himself chasing after criminals or terrorists. That was never going to end well for him. Pretty much everyone on the face of the planet was faster than he was. And yet he kept doing it. He kept finding himself in the position where either he ran, or the world as everyone knew it would come to an end. Surely that was not a sensible situation to be in? Surely Jeremy, the Hunter Group, and the wider world would be much better off if he packed it all in, and he allowed someone much fitter to replace him.

As for the shooting – well, that was something he truly hated. He had killed last night. He had shot three men. Just three of many. It was not in

Graham's nature to even injure anyone, let alone kill them. Yet he had become an unwilling killer. He hated himself for it. Just thinking about it made him deeply unhappy. He also would rather not find himself at the wrong end of a gun, and yet that was something that seemed to happen with alarming regularity. Having almost killed himself through drug abuse, he now valued his own life far more than at any previous time. He knew that he did not want to die yet. His life expectancy as a member of the Hunter Group was surely not very good. He couldn't go on like this.

Some people longed for the excitement of Graham's life, he knew that. Well, let them have it. He did not.

Graham was also completely fed up with the attitude of the other members of the Hunter Group. They all seemed to regard him as a joke, and he was fed up with it. What gave them the right to treat him as an idiot? True, he had probably made his fair share of mistakes, but then who hadn't? He might not be the best field agent in the team, but on many occasions he had been able to establish facts that no one else had been able to see. Had he not been a member of the group then several of the cases on which they had worked would still be unsolved. Jeremy clearly recognised that, but none of the others seemed to notice, preferring to use him as a butt of all their jokes.

The events of that night were a case in point. Perhaps he had been stupid to get Sally to chase after Brown and the Pope, but he thought that it had been the right decision at the time. He personally thought that Sally was much more competent than any of the others seemed to give her credit for. He would like to see her as a fully-fledged field agent. She could probably even show Helena, with all her experience, a thing or two.

He also felt sorry for Paul Fish's death, but at the same time there was no way that he was going to accept responsibility for it. Fish had made the decision to run. If he had not done so, he would still be alive now.

The night hadn't been a complete failure as far as Graham was concerned, though. It was he, after all, who had ultimately brought the operation to a close, shooting the abbot and saving the life of the Pope.

And yet Jeremy still wanted to suspend him.

There was no justice.

Fair enough he did not want to be a member of the Hunter Group any more, but he also felt that Jeremy was being extremely unfair to him.

Should he stay with the team?

No, his mind was made up. He would quit the Hunter Group, and never return.

During the afternoon, after facing his parents and their questions as to where he had been, Graham managed to get a few hours sleep. His parents insisted, however, that he turned up to work that evening. So it was that, at nine o' clock, Graham found himself driving round the streets of Redhill, in a car borrowed from his sister, delivering boxes of fried chicken.

He had just made a delivery of a family box of wings with fries, coleslaw and baked beans to a flat in a block next to the railway station when, sitting in the driving seat, he noticed the familiar car pull up behind him.

It was a silver Jaguar.

Jeremy was driving and Helena was in the passenger seat.

Graham made no attempt to hide, but sat, watching the two senior figures of the Hunter Group in his rear view mirror.

After a good couple of minutes or so, Jeremy got out of the Jaguar and approached Graham's car. He climbed into the passenger seat beside Graham.

"Evening," he said, that slight American twang noticeable once again.

"What do you want?" Graham asked, looking dead ahead.

"You weren't at the debrief."

"Funny that. You made it clear to me that you didn't want me on the team, so I thought I'd make things easier for both of us."

"You did a good job last night," Jeremy commented.

"So good that you want to punish me for the death of a man who killed himself."

"You saved the Pope, Graham. You finished it off. You showed great bravery when effectively held as a hostage, and you ensured that the Pope survived. That was the result that we all wanted to bring about, but you were the one who was responsible for it."

There was silence in the car, both men avoiding looking at each other. Graham was the first to break the silence.

"What do you want, Jeremy?"

"I want to say sorry, Graham. I'm sorry that I was so harsh on you earlier on. You know that we were all under pressure, and I reacted badly. That's no excuse I know, but I am nevertheless very sorry. I'm sorry also if I implied I want you off the team. Nothing could be further from the truth. You're my best agent, Graham. And you're also my best friend."

"What's friendship got to do with any of this, Jeremy? You've always been the first to maintain that when we're working, business comes first. And you know that most of the rest of the others believe that I'm only on the team because we're old friends. That's not good, Jeremy, and you know it. The others all think I'm useless. And you know what? Maybe they're right."

"I think you'd be surprised," Jeremy commented, turning to look at Graham for the first time. "The others all spoke very highly of you at the debrief this afternoon. Even Helena was saying how much she respected you because of your actions in that container. They realise that perhaps they are a little unfair on you, and that perhaps you should be shown greater respect."

"That's never going to happen, though, is it? Once you've lost your credibility, it's impossible to get it back."

"Look, Graham, I'm going to come to the point. I want you on the team. The Hunter Group can't function without you. I'm sorry I was unfair on you, and I want you to come back. We all do."

"I can't do that, Jeremy."

"What do you mean, you can't do that?

"I can't come back. I don't want to work for the Hunter Group any more. I'm fed up with the lies and deceit. I don't want to constantly put myself in danger. I don't want to be responsible for the safety of our country. I want a quiet life. I just want to get on with my life as a chicken delivery driver. I'm not cut out for this lifestyle, Jeremy. You must see that."

"We need you, though, Graham. Take some time out, a few weeks or so. We'll cope. But come back, please. The safety of our country depends on you."

"That's just the kind of pressure I don't need, though, Jeremy. Look, you're a smart bloke. You're ambitious. You want to get on. You want to earn good money, own a big house, and drive a flash car. But that's not me. The most important things in life are happiness, family and friends. Working with the Hunter Group means that I'm not happy, and it's also putting a great strain on my relationships with my family and friends. If I go on as I am, I'll lose those I love the most. My unhappiness will deepen. It's not worth it."

"I'll double your salary."

"Do you really think this is about the money, Jeremy? After everything I've just said? I wouldn't work for the Hunter Group if you paid me a million pounds a year."

"Please, Graham, I'm begging you. You have to come back. We need you."

"You don't need me, Jeremy. If I don't come back, you'll just replace me with someone even better. I'm not that good."

"What can I do to make you return?"

"There's nothing you can do, nothing you can offer me. My mind's made up, and my decision is final."

"Is this the end of the so-called Chicken Shak Spy, then, Graham?"

"I guess it is. Now, if you don't mind, I have chicken to deliver."

Jeremy opened the car door and got out. He turned back to Graham.

"Thank you, Graham, for all that you've done. For the Group, and for me. If you change your mind, you know where we are. There'll always be a place for you in the Hunter Group."

As Jeremy was about to slam the door shut, Graham spoke up.

"You know it was The Organisation, don't you?"

Jeremy froze. He turned back to look at Graham, his face ashen. He climbed back into the car and closed the door.

"I told you never to speak of them again," Jeremy said.

"Well, tonight, it was them. I think you knew it. I don't think you bought this CARN and NR stuff at all."

The two men were silent. Jeremy looked deep in thought. Suddenly he opened the door and sprang out of the car.

"Goodbye, Graham."

He slammed the door, climbed back into the Jaguar, and drove off.

Graham had known Jeremy would react in that way. He knew that he could not face the truth. And he knew it would always be thus.

Still, Graham was determined to put all that behind him.

Watching the Jaguar drive away, Graham was hit by a sense of freedom. It was as if a massive weight had been lifted off his shoulders. For the first time since he had come off the drugs, he felt free. He could do what he wanted. Provided he kept the fryers clean at his parents' restaurant and showed up to deliver chicken, he could do what he wanted, go where he wanted and see whom he wanted. No one had any expectations of him.

It didn't matter what security situations developed, he was no longer involved. Gone were the days of staring death in the face and saving the world.

The pressure was off.

Graham felt happy.

It was better than leaving rehab. He felt like a child again. Nothing he did or didn't do mattered anymore. He'd finally got his life back. No drugs. No gambling. And no secret exploits.

It felt good.

He got out of the car, grabbed a box of chicken from the boot, and set about what he should have been doing all along.

Delivering chicken.

AUTHOR'S NOTE:

I hope that you enjoyed reading The Chicken Shak Spy! This book is intended to be the first of a series of books following the adventures of The Hunter Group, and more particularly Graham Chapman, the Chicken Shak Spy.

Should you have any feedback at all about this book, please get in touch with me using the following details:

Website: http://www.simonlucas.co.uk
Email: simon@slucas.co.uk
Twitter: @simonlucas
Facebook:
http://www.facebook.com/thechickenshakspy

Acknowledgements:

Thanks must go to the following people who have supported me during the creation of this book: to Stephen Wigner for his meticulous proof reading; to Ian Davis for reading early drafts and providing feedback; to Alex Walters for his feedback on an early draft; to my parents, Peter and Kay Lucas for their constant encouragement; and last but by no means least to my beautiful wife, Claire Lucas, for supporting me whilst I write, for putting up with me when I talk constantly about the book, and for being generally wonderful.